Staying In
The Game

Staying In
The Game

Nann Dunne

QuestBooks
a Division of
RENAISSANCE ALLIANCE PUBLISHING, INC.
Nederland, Texas

ISBN 1-930928-60-2

First Printing 2001

9 8 7 6 5 4 3 2 1

Cover art and design by Linda A. Callaghan

Published by:

Renaissance Alliance Publishing, Inc.
PMB 238, 8691 9th Avenue
Port Arthur, Texas 77642-8025

Find us on the World Wide Web at
http://www.rapbooks.com

Printed in the United States of America

ACKNOWLEDGMENTS

My thanks go to Kas for her critical eye; to Sue Cole for her generous advice; to Cathy, Linda, Barb, and all the staff at RAP for their personal touch; to Kath T., for sending delicious pastries to "feed the bard"; to Pitipup/Morrig for finding some loose ends that needed tied up; and to Linda Callaghan, for her exquisite cover illustration. I am also grateful to all the people who sent me words of appreciation and encouragement. Your support means a great deal to me.

This book is dedicated to my family, my friends, and especially to Dad and Toots for their constant support; and to Karen Surtees, whose friendship and encouragement continue to reach across the barriers of time and distance to urge me onward.

Staying in the Game

The cast of one takes center stage
But does she know her part?
She needs to say the proper words;
The play's about to start.
Which actor wields the slashing blade
And wants to steal her fame?
You think she can survive the cuts
And still stay in the game?
Will Comedy or Tragedy
Come stepping to the plate?
The first mask laughs; the second weeps;
Which one foretells her fate?

—Nann Dunne

Prologue

As she toyed with the knife, she mused that she was both producer and director of the play about to unfold—a play that took center stage each time she finished selecting her next leading lady. The tall, dark-haired girl stroked the knife's edge with her fingers, aroused by the very real danger of slicing them open on the razor-sharp steel. *Surgical steel,* she snickered. *How appropriate.* This caress was a familiar one to the young woman; it touched a chord deep within her, and she repeated it over and over as she pondered the next move in her self-made drama.

Her face, suffused with passion, could have belonged to a woman embracing her lover. Indeed she did love the weapon. She loved its heft and balance, its smooth, shiny surface, the *snick* it made as it popped open, and its graceful, yet utilitarian shape. She loved the ultimate power over life and death with which it endowed her.

But most of all, she loved the delicious facial contortions of agony and horror that she could summon at will from her lead actress, just by means of the artistry with which she wielded the blade. Like now. *Let the play begin.* Her breath quickened as the sharp point pierced the cheek of the bound girl she faced. Slowly, with fanatical precision, she carved a wandering groove from the base of her eye to her jawline, shaking her head as the woman screamed.

"Just speak the lines I want to hear, and this act will be finished," her silky voice purred as perfect teeth gleamed in a grotesque grin. "I promise."

Chapter
1

The sky above the softball field sported tufts of snowy clouds dotted across a blanket of robin's-egg blue. Women moved around various parts of the field, warming up their muscles in anticipation of practice. Balls flew back and forth or skittered across the ground between fielders.

Angela Wedgeway listened to the dull *whap* as leather struck leather. She took a deep breath, smelling the light aroma of lilac on the early spring air. Finished with her warm-up calisthenics and anxious for practice to start, she welcomed the familiar chalk, dust, and oiled-leather scents that originated from the field and its environs. *Even my sweat smells good,* she kidded herself. *It feels great to do something physical once in a while.*

Tryouts had been held a few weeks ago, and the girls who survived the cuts had gelled into a decent team. Except for first and second base and catcher, most of last year's starters had graduated, and Coach Palmer was faced with another year of rebuilding. Over the past few weeks, the team had undergone a series of intense fielding practices, and today the coach wanted to concentrate more on batting, to sharpen the eyes of her known hitters and to see what other unknown talent might be brought to light.

Waiting to start the batting, Angela picked three bats out of the rack and slung them over her shoulder. A couple inches above average height, with a square, muscular, well-shaped body, Angela was one of the team's best hitters. Shoulder-length auburn hair, sun-streaked into red, brushed her collar. She turned hazel eyes flecked with green and yellow toward a new movement on the infield and watched the slim back of a tall, dark-haired girl who walked across the ball field toward the coach. She wore the same clothes some of the others did—jeans and a T-shirt—but somehow managed to draw the attention of nearly everyone on the field. *Wonder who that is? Different looking walk; she's practically swaggering. Wide shoulders, narrow hips, tight jeans...Gotta admit they look better than sweatpants.*

"First dibs on the new player." Marva Derby had sneaked up behind Angela to murmur in her ear.

Startled, Angela jumped then poked an elbow back, bringing an "oof" from Marva's chest. "You're welcome to her, Marv, she's not my type."

Marva's eyebrows lifted. Large brown eyes feigned surprise and a wide smile graced a dark face topped with hair fashioned into intricate cornrows. "Hmmm, I don't know about that. Tall, boyish figure, short black hair, blue eyes to die for—sounds to me like just your type. Matter of fact, soon as I saw her I said to myself, 'Self, leave this one alone, she is perfect for Angie.'"

Angela snorted a laugh. "Sure you did. She must look like a dog for you to back off." Angela enjoyed teasing Marva. The woman made a pass at almost any female she thought might be gay, but seldom hooked up with anyone, even willing ones. "Just testing the waters," she called it. "Looking for my soulmate."

I hoped I had found mine. Angela's heart wrenched at the unbidden thought. Memories surfaced of the elegantly sophisticated Vicki, who had only pretended to love her. *Cut it out, Angela; don't even go there.*

Marva laid her hand against her chest and looked aggrieved. "Girl, stop making me sound like a predator. You know I just like to flirt."

"Right. And I just like to look at food," Angela replied.

Marva bumped her shoulder against Angela's. "Hey, good one, Ange. I'll have to remember it." Her eyes swung back to the girl in question just as the coach's eyes moved toward them. "Oh, Palmer's looking this way. I think she's...here they come." She brought her eyes back to Angela's face, curious to see her reaction when she caught a good look at the newcomer. Marva had seen her from the front as she approached the field, and the black girl had done a double take. Raven hair, cut very short in back and longer on top, capped a triangular face. Long-lashed, pale blue eyes, a slender, high-bridged nose, and chiseled lips, coupled with a slightly arrogant expression, gave the girl a haunting beauty. *Angie likes those tall, reedy, boyish types, and this one's gorgeous. They'd make a perfect match.*

Angela wasn't stunning, but she attracted her share of attention. A small, slightly blunt nose and full, softly formed lips rested on a broad face. High cheekbones caused an attractive tilt to hazel eyes that used to sparkle with her love of life. That sparkle had dimmed when the lover Angela had fallen hard for had dumped her eight months ago, trampling big-time on her self-esteem. Marva would be ecstatic if her friend could find someone who would appreciate her love and loyalty. But Angela had pulled herself into a shell, and nothing had been able to dent it. She wouldn't even discuss it with anyone, though several friends had tried to get her to open up about it. Even Angela's best friend, Merrill, hadn't had any success, so Marva knew she didn't stand a chance.

Marva saw something flicker across Angela's face, but it died as swiftly as it was born. *Yes!* She smirked, willing to clutch at straws. *This just might be an interesting season.*

Coach Ann Palmer walked straight to them. Her companion was half a foot taller. "Marva, Angela, I'd like you to meet a new candidate for our team...Shelley Brinton." As they shook hands, Palmer continued the introduction. "Angie is one of our pitchers and our first baseman, and Marva is our catcher." Shelley nodded to each of them as she lifted a hand to push some stray locks off of her forehead.

"Shelley just transferred here from another college. She tells me she was a starter on her last softball team. She missed the tryouts, so we're going to take a look at her skills today."

"What position do you play?" Marva asked.

The low, throaty voice was icing on the cake as far as Marva was concerned. "I pitch," Shelley answered, then looked straight into Angela's eyes, "and play first base."

Marva's head jerked toward Angela, and her heart sank as she saw the tight smile. *Damn, she's given up already. Sure wish the old Angie would come back.* "Looks like you two will have to fight it out, huh?" Marva rushed to say, hoping to get a rise out of Angela. But her friend just kept the smile and didn't say anything.

"That's the idea," Palmer threw in as she looked from Angela to Shelley. "Competition should be good for both of you. And for the team."

"I sure hope so," Shelley remarked smoothly. When Marva glanced back up at the tall newcomer, she realized that she had locked her remarkable eyes on Angela's and hadn't let go.

Coach Palmer got a little uncomfortable as the look stretched on. The last thing she needed was territory trouble between two of her players. "Well, let's get started. Shelley, you go on out to first base. Angie's starting today's batting practice." She looked toward the pitcher's mound where one of the girls was warming up. "Bobby Sue will begin the pitching."

First to turn away, Angela headed toward a spot where she could swing the three bats to loosen up her shoulders. "Good luck," Shelley smirked and jogged off to first base.

Marva already had her shin guards on. She went to the bench to snap on her chest protector and pick up her mitt and face mask. She ducked past the backstop and squatted behind the plate just as Angela stepped up to it. "Come on, babeee! No batter, no batter. Show me some heat!"

❖ ❖ ❖ ❖ ❖ ❖ ❖

After practice, Marva and Angela walked to their car. As luck would have it, the school parking lot was a long walk from the softball field, making tired legs even more tired. Both women had apartments in the same off-campus complex and always came to practice together. Their roommates, also on the team, had been excused from today's workout.

As the girls tossed their sports bags in the back seat, Marva noticed Shelley coming toward them and hollered, "Can we drop you somewhere?"

"No, thanks," the rangy girl answered, pointing to the bike racks. "I have a bike."

Marva waved and entered the driver's side of the car, where Angela had already established herself in the passenger seat. "Too bad, might have given you a chance to get to know her," she said, smiling at Angela.

"You can take off your Cupid mask, Marv. I'm not interested," Angela stated emphatically.

"Damn, Angie, you'd have to be dead not to be interested in someone that beautiful. She looked impressed with you."

Angela gave Marva a disparaging look and neglected to answer. But memories of Vicki pushed their way into her consciousness again. *What the heck is this, "kick your own heart" day?*

Vicki hadn't been beautiful. She was what Angela would call handsome with her oblong face and cool brown eyes framed by shoulder-length champagne-blonde hair always perfectly in place. That the good-looking senior had even glanced twice at a sophomore thrilled the younger Angela, and she entered the relationship full of love mixed with gratitude. Even Vicki's lovemaking had been cool and detached but that just made Angela try harder, believing she could warm the woman with her own ardor. *But that was a losing battle. I should have recognized her detachment for what it was—not love at all. I was just someone for her to play with—and torment.*

With the passage of time, Angela could look at their disastrous relationship with clearer eyes. She and Vicki had spent many wonderful moments together, but Angela now recognized that Vicki had practically owned her. Angela had thrown herself into loving her and would do anything she asked. *That wasn't a two-way street; I was like a damn puppy dog, or worse, a slave. No wonder she wanted me around all the time—it had to be great for her overblown ego. She was queen of her own little world, and I was her admiring servant. Everything was fine as long as it ran the way she demanded.* Angela remembered various taunts when she thought Vicki was just teasing her. Now she realized that Vicki was trying to show her domination by tormenting her. At the time, Angela loved her too much to recognize it—until Vicki visited her home.

Frustrated by her memories, Angela shook her thoughts back to the present as Marva pulled into the parking lot. Their off-campus home was in A building, one of four large brick edifices housing mostly students. They had just climbed the three steps to the entrance when Merrill Lakins pulled into the same lot.

"You need any help?" Angela called, but Merrill shook her head, jostling her chestnut ringlets. Grabbing a canvas overnight bag from the back seat, she exited the car, threw the bag's carrying strap over her shoulder, and joined them.

"You okay?" Angela asked, giving her shorter friend a one-armed hug. Merrill was just returning from a few days away to attend her grandmother's funeral. Angela and Merrill had grown up together in Chester County in the southeastern corner of Pennsylvania. They had been best friends since first grade, when a rowdy boy had pestered the tiny Merrill. Angela had pushed him into a ditch and warned him against ever messing with a friend of hers. Not only had he not tormented Merrill again, but he became Angela's first admirer. Now, to everyone's great satisfaction, Jim Dursik was Merrill's fiancé.

On her last trip home, Angela had accompanied Merrill to her grandmother's house and was grateful that she had a chance to visit with her before her death.

"Yeah, I'm fine, Ange. I'll miss Gram, but she suffered for a long time and now she's at rest."

As Angela let go of the hug, she patted Merrill on her back. "How's your mom doing?" Merrill and Angela had been showered with so much attention from each mother that they felt beloved by both. When she learned of the grandmother's passing, Angela had called Mrs. Lakins and been assured that she was fine, but the redhead wanted to hear firsthand how her "second mother" was coping.

"She's actually taking it pretty hard and that's to be expected, but you know Mom, she likes to put on a good face for the rest of us."

"Sort of like her daughter, huh?" Angela gave her friend another pat and received a sweet smile in return.

Marva followed the two into their apartment and sat on the edge of the bed where Merrill flopped her bag. "We got a new player today, Merry. Looks like she's going to give Ange a run for her money."

Merrill glanced up from her unpacking. "How so?"

Marva lifted a hand high over her head. "She's about ten feet tall and plays a really mean first base. She went up in the air nearly three feet for an overthrow that nobody else would have come close to and pulled it in. And stretch! She does a split on her stretches, clean down to the ground. It hurts just to watch her."

Merrill picked up a pile of clothes to put in the hamper and cocked an eyebrow at Angela, who was leaning back against the wall, arms folded. "Can she hit?"

Angela couldn't keep from looking and sounding disappointed. "She needs some work on her hitting, Merry, but there's no doubt she's a helluva lot better first baseman than I am. Looks like I'm about to get bumped."

Merrill walked to the hamper. As she expected, it was empty, and she dumped her dirty clothes into it. One reason she and Angela got along so well as roommates, besides being best friends, was that they both were neatniks. They willingly picked up after each other, too. In a small apartment with a tiny living room, kitchenette, bathroom, and a bedroom with two beds, two bureaus, two desks, and one closet, that feature became increasingly important.

Continuing to her taller friend's side, Merrill reached up and patted her shoulder. "You're too good a hitter to get bumped. Coach Palmer will have to put you somewhere."

"But where?" Angela's self-deprecating grin crawled up one side of her cheek. "I haven't the arm to play anywhere else except maybe second base, and I wouldn't want to bump you, Merry, even if I could. Besides, I'd never make a strong relay throw."

Merrill chewed her bottom lip as she walked back to the bed to finish unpacking. It was frustrating to think of Angela getting bumped from her position. Softball was Angela's favorite sport and during the season she lived and breathed it, throwing herself into it with a passion. A consummate fielder and strong batter, Angela missed Olympic status only because of her weak throwing arm. Years of effort hadn't improved this one outstanding gap in her skills, and she had reluctantly accepted it.

"Maybe Coach will put you in right field," Merrill suggested.

"Whoa!" Marva bounced on the bed. "Hurtz wouldn't like that one bit...but that probably is where you'll go. You're a lot better than she is. Just be careful, Angie, she could get pretty nasty if you push her out."

"We don't even know where I'm going, yet, Marv. Or if I am."

Merrill turned her large brown eyes from one to the other. "So what's this fantastic first baseman like? Something that crawled out from under a rock? Can I hate her?"

"She's gorgeous," Angela answered, drawing a surprised reaction from Merrill. Angela hadn't paid any attention to anyone's looks for months.

She switched her inquiring eyes to Marva, who smirked and winked. "That she is: tall, skinny, and gorgeous. Just right for Angie."

"Will you cut it out? She probably just knocked me out of a

job. Stands to reason I would notice what she looks like. Besides, we don't even know if she's gay."

Merrill slid another glance toward Marva and they both grinned. *Sounds like a tiny bit of interest to me.*

Shelley cycled her way back to the apartment complex, found her room, and chucked her sports bag into a corner. The practice was an eye-opener. She had been impressed with the talent on the team, especially her rival for first base. The girl could lay a bat on just about anything, and when she took her turn at playing first, she fielded everything near her with effortless confidence. *But I think I've got you beat out for first base, Angela.* Her lips twisted upward in a self-satisfied smile. *Sometimes it pays to be tall.*

She checked her watch and groaned. Peeling off her clothes, she dropped them on the floor as she headed for the shower. Fifteen minutes later she threw on a clean white shirt and belted dress slacks over fresh underwear, kicked the dirty clothes into a pile next to the hamper, and loped out the door, combing her damp hair into place with long fingers.

She unlocked the chain from her bike, climbed on, and hurried away, grimacing at the painful tugs she felt in the leg muscles she had overused today at softball practice. *Show off! Should have taken it easy on those splits.* Shelley loved the game, thriving on the intimidation she generated when she pitched and the aggressiveness she demonstrated when she batted. After some youthful problems stemming from her hot temper, she had tried to cultivate a laid-back attitude around other people, but her actions on the field belied it.

One of the few places I can really be myself. Or almost myself.

Chapter
2

Angela had pulled the couch cushions onto the floor and lay stretched on her stomach across them, reading a textbook that she had propped against a wall. Merrill threw a down comforter and pillow on top of the couch's barely covered springs and spread herself along it to do her studying. Forty-five minutes later, a familiar knock sounded at the door and Angela jumped up to answer it.

As expected, Marva stood there with her roommate, Kathy O'Brien. Kath was of average build and as Irish-looking as her name. Sandy-brown, curly hair fell softly around a cute, lightly freckled face before cascading to her waist. Her cinnamon eyes gleamed at Marva's moments of mischief, while her cautious nature helped contain her friend's more boisterous urges. They had been assigned as roommates from their first day of college and they had roomed together ever since.

At first, Kath had been uneasy to be paired with a black girl, let alone one who was gay. Her parents had taught her to be tolerant of differences in people but the small town she grew up in had no black residents or any obvious gays, and she was nervous about how Marva might act toward her. *Maybe she won't be happy with me, either.*

She needn't have worried. Marva amazed her with her forthrightness about being gay, obviously comfortable with herself. Within a few hours it was apparent that this gay black girl from

New York City had a heart as big as the Empire State Building and a sense of humor to match. She won over the straight white kid from the sticks and they had been inseparable friends ever since.

"You guys want to go over to the Steak House and get a beer? Maybe grab a sandwich?" Marva mimed eating a sandwich while Kath tipped a drink from an imaginary bottle.

Merrill sat up, swung her feet to the floor, and closed her book. "Anything to stop that act," she taunted with a twinkle in her honey-brown eyes. She stood up and stretched. "What do you say, Ange?"

"Hey, I'm game. Just give us a few minutes to straighten up and get our shoes on." Five minutes later they were on their way to the Steak House, a favorite watering hole of many of the college crowd. As they walked in, two girls from the softball team who were seated at an otherwise empty table waved them over, and they sat down.

Allie Monroe, the husky brunette, played in the outfield, and Amber Zorno, shorter and blonde, was a second-string infielder. Allie had transferred from a private girls' school in Florence, Italy, where she had studied art. But she wasn't happy out of the States and, after a couple of months, had persuaded her parents to allow her to return. Obviously well-to-do, she had come home with expensively tailored clothes which tended toward somber colors. She seemed a quiet, reflective person, so the colors suited her. But she was pleased to be back playing softball. The Italian school didn't have a team, and Allie was an outstanding player.

Amber, on the other hand, was bouncy and friendly. She had come to Spofford on a partial art scholarship and knew she wouldn't have been able to attend college without it. She usually had a sketchbook with her and had numerous drawings of the girls on the team in action on the field.

The two weren't especially close friends. They tended to hang out with each other because they had the same major and both played softball, but everyone was used to seeing them together.

Allie's eyes flicked over Angela admiringly. *There's just something about redheads...*

"Thanks. I never thought we'd get a seat at a table," Angela said, smiling at the two. It struck Angela as odd that the girls didn't resemble each other at all except for their almost identical cornflower-blue eyes. *I wonder if they're related somewhere along their genealogical trees?*

"Marva asked us to hold one for you all," the shorter girl answered.

"I knew I liked you for a reason, Marv," Angela kidded her as the waitress approached.

The woman pulled an order pad, with a pencil attached, away from her belt. "What'll you have?"

The words yanked Angela's head around and up. "Hi," she said after a momentary pause, "I didn't know you worked here."

Cool ice-blue eyes touched hers, immediately displacing any thoughts of cornflower-blue ones. Shelley stood a little straighter. "I just started tonight."

"Oh, yeah," Marva chimed in, "you just transferred here, didn't you? What college were you at before?"

"Penlyville."

"Penlyville?" Amber echoed. "Did you know two girls from there were murdered not too long ago?"

Shelley ignored the question, her eyes darting nervously toward the area where the owner usually sat. "Come on, guys, I need to take your order."

"Pizza and beer okay with everybody?" Merrill asked. When they all nodded, Merrill ordered two large pepperoni pizzas and two pitchers of beer. Shelley took the orders and left.

"She sure is a looker. Bet she has guys fighting over her all the time," Allie remarked.

"Or girls," Marva said and waggled her eyebrows at Angela, who tried not to encourage her by laughing.

Merrill gave Marva a warning frown, then turned her attention to Amber. "Tell us about the murders at Penlyville. What the hell happened?"

"A guy I grew up with is a police officer here in town. He called me just before we came out this evening to warn me. Said some loony is murdering coeds in this area—four so far. He cuts up their faces and chests then stabs them in the stomach and drops them by the river." Amber screwed up her face in disgust. "Two of the victims were from Penlyville College, one from Scatsboro University, and one from Boliss Women's College. You know, all of them are right around us here at Spofford. The one from Boliss they just found this morning. She was murdered last night."

A combined gasp escaped from the girls, and they looked at

each other with worried frowns.

"We ought to check into this," Angela exclaimed. "Someone should be warning the whole school."

Amber nodded. "Joe said the department was sending a bulletin to Dean Lohman, and the newspapers would probably be picking up on it. Apparently the cops connected the first three murders as soon as a second girl was killed at Penlyville. They hushed it up for a while, hoping the murderer would get careless, but this fourth one made them decide to release the information."

Shelley came back with their order and set it on the table. "Pay her, honey, will you?" Merrill asked Angela, who reached into her back pocket for her wallet and paid the tab.

While she waited for the money, Shelley glanced surreptitiously at Merrill. *Honey? Who's this character? Angela's girlfriend?* Shelley berated herself for finding that possibility unpleasant. *What the heck do you care?* Shelley wasn't even looking for a date, let alone a girlfriend, and she wasn't thrilled that Angela had made an impression on her. *Like you have time for a love connection. Keep your distance, girl. It could be dangerous for you to get too close to someone. Or vice versa.*

"Do you know anything about the girls who were murdered at Penlyville?" The girlfriend looked up at her with huge honey-brown eyes that seemed to hold a hint of accusation.

Stop imagining things! Shelley jutted her chin out but tried to keep her tone from sounding too cold. "Only what I read in the paper. They were on the junior varsity basketball team, one a sophomore, one a freshman." She counted out Angela's change and dropped it into her palm. Hazel eyes glanced up at her, then darted away, as Angela grabbed the pitcher and poured everyone a beer.

"You live in the Brickhouse?" Marva asked.

"Bricker Apartments. You call it the Brickhouse?"

"Yeah, we're on the first floor. Kath and I live in 110A and Angie and Merry are next to us in 112A. Why don't you stop by after work and fill us in on these attacks? We'd like to hear more about them."

"Sorry, I can't. I have a previous appointment. Maybe some other time." Shelley shrugged. "I don't know much more about them, anyway. Just that they're dead." Her voice flattened on the last statement, and Angela caught sight of a strange expression on her face as she turned and walked away to wait on another table.

"I have a previous appointment," Marva mimicked the low, velvety voice almost perfectly. "Where the hell could she be going at midnight in this town?"

"Maybe she has a boyfriend, Marv. Some people do, you know. Or a girlfriend." Angela's voice sounded wistful even to herself. She lifted her mug and took a long drink of beer, then wiped the suds from her upper lip with a sharp flick of her hand.

Merrill's eyes had followed Shelley after she left their table, and now she turned to Angela, watching the play of emotions across her face. She hadn't missed the wistful note and guessed that maybe Angela's insecurity was at the root of it. *That damn Vicki knocked her for a loop.*

She touched Angela's arm. "I don't think there's any boyfriend waiting in the wings, Ange. Or girlfriend either. Shelley has trouble keeping her eyes off of you."

"Right," Angela hooted. "Marva been prompting you to say that? I'm not even interested in the girl."

"Right," Merrill and Marv echoed in unison.

"Okay, girls, eat and drink up. We have a practice tomorrow at nine," Angela reminded them, adroitly changing the subject.

"Nine," Kath groaned. "Saturday morning practices should be banned."

"Your dental appointment already got you excused today. If we're gonna win, we have to practice. You want everything your way?" Marva teased.

"Yes, yes, yes," Kath stated emphatically, thrusting a bread stick through the air.

"Then you better marry a wimp," Marva advised. "A rich wimp."

"Nah," Kath said with a serious look, "I'd rather marry a guy just like you, honey. A male Marva."

"What?" Marva looked startled. "I don't always let you have your way." She looked around the circle of the table for support. "Do I?"

Five grins were her only answer.

Everyone managed to get to the field on time Saturday morning, but it took an intensive round of calisthenics to wake everyone up.

Finishing up, Angela had unwrapped her leg from around

her neck and was jogging in place to cool down when Coach
Palmer came over to her. "Ange..." Palmer looked down at her
clipboard then back. "This is really hard, Angie. You've played
first base for us for two years now, and you've done a masterful
job. But everyone has to fight for their position each year,
and..."

Angela took pity on Coach Palmer. Her choice wasn't anything personal. *But just because it's best for the team doesn't
mean I have to like it.* Angela finished the coach's little speech
for her, "And Shelley looks awesome for the job. You're right,
she should have a chance at it. For the greater good, or something."

Coach Palmer pushed her lips together and nodded.
"Thanks, Angie, for being so understanding. She did look awesome, and I want to keep her there for a while. Who knows,
maybe you can win it back. When Shelley pitches, you'll play
first same as always. But when she's not on the mound, first base
is hers for the time being. I want you to try right field."

"Have you told Liz Hurtz that I might be bumping her?"

"Yes," Palmer said with little enthusiasm. "She's not too
happy about it. I told her when she first got here this morning,
and she cursed you out then turned right around and left.
Between you and me, I almost hope she stays away; she's a troublemaker." Her gaze swept around the field, and she started to
raise her whistle for attention. Hesitating, she looked back at
Angela. "I hope you don't have any trouble with her because of
this, Angie."

"I'll keep it in mind, Coach."

The whistle shrilled and practice started. Infield, outfield,
and subs were split up, and each group had an hour of intense
workout. After a ten-minute break, the starters went to their
positions and the subs batted for game-situation practice. In the
first inning, one batter hit a humpbacked line drive that fell to
the ground in right field a split second before Angela got to it
and scooped it up.

"Throw it here!" Shelley yelled from first base before the
ball even hit the ground. "We got her! Throw it here!"

As the shortstop covered second base, Merrill ran out
toward the outfield and took the toss from her friend. When
Angela looked back at Shelley, the tall first baseman was standing with her hands on her hips, shaking her head.

In the third inning, the same play happened again. Shelley

threw her mitt down on the ground and charged out to Angela, shouting all the way. "What the hell are you doing? Can't you just throw the ball to me when I yell for it? Are you that pissed that I'm playing first base instead of you?"

She reached Angela's spot in right field and stood there glaring down into angry eyes. Shelley could feel the fire boiling in the pit of her stomach. Every place she went she seemed to run into this "shun the new girl" attitude. "What's your problem? Afraid to give me a put out?"

Angela was fuming that Shelley chose to make her weakness the center of attention. The whole team was watching the confrontation, and she could hear their murmuring in the background. Angela's jaw worked back and forth as she struggled to talk past her anger. Clenching her teeth, she finally won the battle. "I can't throw the frigging ball that far," she spit out in an icy monotone.

This unexpected retort provoked a sarcastic reaction from Shelley. "What? You play varsity softball, and you can't throw the damn ball to first base? You've got to be kidding."

"Well, I'm not kidding, Miss Star Athlete," Angela grated. "Not everyone's as perfect as you are." Angela couldn't control her need to be nasty. She wanted to hurt Shelley for hurting her. She felt spurned all over again and that didn't make sense. *This is stupid. She isn't Vicki.* She saw that her words did hurt the first baseman but, contrarily, she felt worse rather than better.

Shelley's eyes narrowed and her voice roughened. "I work hard at trying to be my best. Maybe you should, too."

Angela's chin lifted, and she stuck her hands on her hips. "You saying I'm dogging it?" she retorted.

Shelley mirrored her attitude and actions, sticking her chin out and placing her hands on her hips. She threw each word like a dart. "I'm saying if you can't throw to first base from right field, you need to do something about it."

"Like I haven't tried to for fifty years," Angela said, fuming.

"Really?" Shelley taunted. "If you weren't so damn hardheaded, I could fix that for you."

"Right. I'm sure you're an expert on throwing, especially throwing the bull."

"Stay for an hour after practice. I'll work with you, and you can decide," the taller girl challenged. "What have you got to lose?"

"You're on," Angela muttered.

Sally, one of the subs, had been standing aside, waiting for the fireworks to simmer down. Now she scooted to their side with a jar that wore a label reading, "Cuss Cache." "Okay, Angie, pay up," she gleefully ordered, waving the bottle under Angela's nose.

"Pay up what?" Angela demanded. "I didn't do any cussing."

"Come on, we could tell all the way from the bench that you said the eff word," Sally jeered.

"Me? Get real. I said 'frigging.'" She nodded toward Shelley. "Ask the Star, why don't you?"

Sally turned to the first baseman. The rest of their teammates had become interested in this little act, and they wandered closer to the three players.

"What did she say, Star?" Sally asked.

Shelley snorted at the name, then raised an eyebrow. "You think I'm stupid? I'm not gonna repeat that word and lose five bucks."

With a smirk, Sally brought the jar back to Angela, whose eyes were now smoldering. "Come on, Angie, pay your money like a good sport."

Angela reached into her back pocket, pulled out her wallet and checked inside of it. She had four fives and three ones. She pulled out a five and handed it to Sally. "You satisfied, now, Sal?" she taunted.

"Yeppers," Sally answered.

"Well you better keep that jar open, because all I said was 'the frigging ball,' but this time I am going to get my money's worth." Angela pulled the other three five-dollar bills from her wallet and threw them on the ground one at a time while shouting at the top of her voice, "FUCK! FUCK! FUCK!"

The onlookers chuckled while Sally picked up the money. "You didn't have any trouble throwing the bills," Shelley wisecracked, getting an additional snicker from the team.

Angela took a threatening step toward her, and Shelley's eyes narrowed. Merrill grabbed her friend's arm. "Take it easy, Ange. Nobody wants any trouble. Cool off, will you?" *Wish I could let Angie knock that chip off her shoulder. She'd probably take the skinny smart-ass apart.*

"Yeah, chill," added Marva. "Nothing here worth fighting about."

Their advice helped Angela calm down. "Don't worry, I'm not looking for a fight," she assured her friends, but she waggled a finger at Shelley and gave her a dirty look. "But you owe me five frigging bucks!"

Shelley, biting her lip to forestall any more arguing, threw a rudely dismissive hand at Angela and walked back to first base. Coach Palmer blew her whistle for the team to get back to the business at hand, and they resumed practice.

True to her word in spite of the conflict, Shelley stayed after practice to work with Angela. Merrill, recognizing that they both still held some anger and might need a buffer, offered to help. First Shelley had Angela throw the ball to Merrill about ten times. Then she had her making slight shifts in the placement of her feet while throwing. Finally, they found a stride that vastly improved her accuracy.

Angela threw the ball over and over again until the new placement of her feet became automatic.

"That's good. Now we'll work on your arm movement." Shelley stepped behind her and wrapped her hand around the top of Angela's shoulder. She felt a slight shudder but chose to ignore it. *She obviously doesn't like me touching her. Like I care.* "Throw the ball your usual way," she ordered curtly. Angela tightened her lips but did as directed. She had lived for a long time with the embarrassment of a weak arm, and Shelley's adjustments seemed to be helping. For that, she could put up with a little bitchiness.

Shelley could feel a tiny hitch in the shoulder. She moved Angela's hand a small degree to a different position. "Try throwing from here." After the third slight change, the hitch wasn't there. "Okay, let's work with this spot."

Angela threw the ball about ten more times, then Shelley called a halt. Merrill ran over and clapped Angela on the back. "I can see improvement already, Ange. Looks like ole Star actually knows what she's doing." She glanced at Shelley as she spoke and got a surprisingly cool stare in return.

"Your arm tired?" Merrill asked Angela as the three women walked off the field, towels draped around their necks.

"Not much," Angela said. Her arm could be dropping off, and she wouldn't admit it in front of Miss Know-it-all. Merrill grinned with understanding, then pulled a cell phone out of her bag and called Marva for a ride home.

Shelley glanced down at the redhead. "I think about two

more sessions will do it. We've got your mechanics straightened
out. Now we need to work on your timing. That should take one
session, and when you get it all together, we can spend one more
just using what you've learned over and over until it's part of
you. You'll be throwing runners out at the plate before long."
Shelley nodded her head to emphasize her confidence. "You're a
quick learner," she added almost begrudgingly.

"Thanks for helping me," Angela said with little inflection.

"No sweat, I had a reason for it," Shelley said indifferently.
"I want you to teach me to bat as well as you do."

*I should have guessed she wasn't doing this out of the good-
ness of her heart...if she has a heart. Everyone wants a payback.*
"Can you spare some time tomorrow?" Angela asked.

"I'm going to be pretty busy tomorrow..." Shelley hesitated,
ran her fingers through her hair, then came to a decision. "Three
o'clock?"

"We'll be there," Angela said after Merrill nodded her
agreement.

They had reached the bike rack. "Why don't you toss your
bike in the trunk of the car and ride back with us?" Shelley's
detached attitude rankled, but Merrill's natural good manners
asserted themselves. "Marva should be here in a couple minutes."

"Sounds good." Shelley reached into a hip pocket, pulled
out a five-dollar bill, and held it toward Angela. "Here's the five
I owe you."

"Stuff it, Star," Angela said derisively. "You teach me to
throw, and I'll teach you to hit, but we don't have to pretend to
be buddies."

The eyes darkened and Shelley growled, "My name's not
Star." *But then, it's not Shelley, either,* a voice whispered inside
her mind.

Merrill looked at each of them. "Will you two knock it off?
You guys are teammates." She slipped an arm through Angela's.
"What do you say, Angie? Truce?" Angela hesitated, then
shrugged and barely nodded.

"How about you, Shelley? Truce?"

Shelley glanced at Angela, but the redhead's eyes were
turned away. The taller girl frowned then rasped, "For now."

Marva arrived and they put the bike in the trunk and piled
into the car. The black girl noticed that Angela had pulled Merrill into the back seat rather than share it with Shelley. *Damn!*

Looks like they're still at odds with each other. Maybe I was wrong about the mutual attraction.

"Hey, Shelley, how about telling us what you know about the murders?" Marva reminded her.

Shelley tossed her hair back off her forehead with a jerk of her head. "I don't know much more than I already told you. Both girls were on the junior varsity basketball team. One was a freshman and one a sophomore. They were killed about two months apart. Then everybody started travelling in pairs or groups."

Marva took her eyes from the road and briefly cast them sideways as she spoke. "I found out the girl from Scatsboro U. was killed about four weeks after the first girl at Penlyville. And the second Penlyville girl was killed about three weeks after that, then four weeks later, the girl from Boliss. It looks like he's killing them about three or four weeks apart." Marva shuddered. "What a lousy way to die. I sure hope they catch him in a hurry."

"Are they sure it's a man?" Shelley's query hung awkwardly in the air while the other women exchanged fearful glances.

"My God, I hope it is," Angela said. "I hate to think a woman would cut up another woman like that." There was a murmur of assent from the others, overridden by Shelley's low, silken voice. "There've been women in the past who've done worse. A lot worse."

The dark-haired girl sat in the library, looking through the Scatsboro University yearbook, flipping the pages over slowly and staring at pictures. *Guess it's too early to try Spofford. Don't really want to draw attention there too soon...but this changing from one college to another for my leading ladies is getting to be a pain in the ass.*

The Voice had told her to change, and she always listened to the Voice—but not without some resentment at being yanked around. *How much free time do they think I have, anyway? I can't just walk in and grab these girls; I have to do some reconnoitering, and that takes time. Don't they realize I have studies to take care of, too?*

One good thing: the Voice understood that her leading ladies had to be killed. The girls would never give her the right answer without some persuasion, and how could she use her knife to question them and then let them go? Besides, to her that was the fun part of the whole thing. She was in total charge; she could make them squirm and scream and beg...just as her sister used to do to her. Until four years ago, when she had given her a taste of her own medicine. The woman's lip curled. *Or should I say her own knife?*

Agitated, she reached in her pocket and felt for the knife. Just pressing her fingers against it helped to calm her. Her eyes fell on a face and form that perfectly matched her leading lady preference, and she smiled in anticipation. She rubbed the knife handle, careful not to depress the trigger. *Wouldn't want to cut myself now, would I?* She snorted out a laugh, oblivious to the irritated looks she received from other patrons of the library. Removing her hand from her pocket, she tapped a long finger on the nose of the woman whose portrait she had chosen. *You are next, baby. You will get to play your part soon. Very soon. And you might even be the one who knows the right lines.*

Chapter
3

Sunday's extra batting practice for Shelley was perfectly
timed. The balmy spring weather had held; the sky was azure and
cloudless, and it was a pleasure to be outside playing softball.
An occasional stiff breeze blew dust devils across the scraped
infield, momentarily halting practice as the girls turned their
backs on the stinging mischief-makers. Squat and empty, the aluminum bleachers brought recollections of game days when
cheers echoed from the team's ardent fans. The newly erected
backstop gleamed in the sun and clinked satisfyingly when hit by
a foul from Shelley's strong bat.

On arriving at the field, the girls had dropped their sports
bags and a cooler next to the backstop and pulled out their
gloves and sweatbands. Angela had borrowed an equipment bag
from Coach Palmer, and she and Merrill gathered balls from it
while Marva pulled out catcher's paraphernalia. Shelley had
brought her own bat that she usually kept propped in a corner at
her apartment.

While Angela pitched and Marva caught, Merrill and Kath
volunteered to play the field. Marva was in full catcher's gear,
having learned the hard way that when Angela pitched to any
batter there were a lot of foul tips and the catcher better keep
herself protected.

Shelley worked seriously on improving her batting, and
Angela was a patient teacher. For the first part of her lesson,
Angela showed her that taking a shorter stride, opening her hips

sooner, and swinging the bat in a short, crisp swing with proper follow-through would add to her power. After practicing those three corrections for an hour, they took a break.

Angela laid her glove and ball at the mound, and Merrill and Kath brought theirs with them. Marva pulled off her catcher's equipment, searched in her sports bag for a towel, and wiped her face and hands. When the others hollered, she rummaged in their bags and threw their towels to them, grousing good-naturedly the whole time about not getting a maid's wages. They sat in the shade of one of the trees behind the backstop and had some bottled water and granola bars that they fished from the cooler, sharing them with Shelley.

The tall girl stretched out on the grass and put an arm over her eyes while the rest bantered back and forth for the balance of their break. Angela, sitting nearby, was disappointed that Shelley had covered her face. The girl was so beautiful that just looking at her was a pleasure that anyone would enjoy. At least that's what she told herself.

As they walked back out onto the field, Angela was trying to explain to Shelley how to make better pitch selection. "You are a sucker for a high pitch up around your shoulders," she said. "What you need to understand is that you can't hit a pitch properly if it's so high that you can't keep your wrists higher than the ball."

"But that's one I can really drive," Shelley argued. "I get some of my best hits on that kind of pitch." Her sculptured lips slipped into a pout that captured Angela's gaze.

The redhead had to avert her eyes and get her thoughts in control before answering. "Yeah, but ninety percent of the time you'll drive it right into an outfielder's glove. It's hard to hit the ball on a level line, so you usually hit it too high into the air. That gives the outfielders time to get under it. Let me show you."

Marva leaned against the backstop with her mask and mitt in her hands, having already donned the rest of her equipment. Merrill and Kath walked into the field while Angela and Shelley moved to home plate. "Stand at the plate like you're waiting for a pitch." Angela moved behind Shelley and reached around her to place her hands on top of Shelley's on the bat.

"When you swing up here..." she pushed against Shelley's hands and moved the bat forward, partway through a high swing, "your wrists can't get above the ball. See what I mean?"

"Uh...yeah...yeah," Shelley answered, squirming a bit in the circle of the redhead's arms. *Keep your mind on what she's telling you!*

Marva watched the two, amusement crinkling the corners of her eyes and the edges of her lips. *Yeah, like they really can't stand each other.*

Angela moved the bat lower and swung it forward again. "But here," she waggled the bat then traced Shelley's wrists with a finger, "you can swing with your wrists up. And here," she lowered the bat even further and moved it forward, "if you must swing—for a hit and run, for instance—you can even hit line drives on a low pitch if you remember to keep your wrists up— just drop the bat head. Understand?"

"Yeah, I think I've got the idea." Shelley slanted a look back toward her.

Angela had felt the growing heat coming from Shelley's body once she moved up against her, and it was causing a terribly distracting reaction from hers. Annoyed at her wayward flesh, she stepped back and took a deep breath. "Let's give it all a try now."

Walking back to the mound, Angela picked up her glove and stuck the ball in it. As she lifted her eyes, they met Merrill's frowning gaze. A crooked finger summoned her and she walked over to the second baseman. "What's wrong, Merry?"

"Go slow, Angie. I don't trust her." *I don't want you hurt again.*

"I'm not trying to seduce her, Merry. I'm only showing her how to bat," Angela replied acerbically.

Merrill looked up at her best friend's hazel eyes, and her mouth curled into a dubious smile. She slapped Angela's stomach with her glove. "Just you remember that, okay?"

Angela laughed and shoved her shoulder. "Yes, Mom," she answered, then turned back toward the mound as an uneasy expression flickered across Merrill's face.

Shelley had a rescheduled lab on Tuesday afternoon after softball practice, so she was unable to work with Angela on their joint softball improvement projects. It turned out to be a good thing that Shelley wasn't with them, because Kath had some disturbing news. She waited until they came home from practice and showered, then urged Marva to go next door with her right away.

Expecting them to come over as usual, Angela let them in and was turning away when Kath blurted, "I have some news you guys need to hear. It's important."

"Can it wait till I grab us some sodas?" Angela smiled at Kath's excited expression. She looked ready to burst with her news. When she nodded, Angela hurried into the kitchen and came back with a can for each of them.

The redhead sat on the chocolate-brown couch next to Merrill and made room for Marva to join them. They sat properly on the couch for a change, facing Kath, who stood in front of them. "What's up, Kath?" Merrill prompted as she popped the top of her soda can. The others followed her lead except for Kath. Too anxious to spout her news, she set her unopened can on the lamp table.

"You know I help out in Dean Lohman's office suite on Monday and Tuesday, right?" They nodded. "Well, I was filing in the outer office when some lady came to see him. I think she was a judge—I thought I heard the dean call her that. She had a folder under her arm when she went into his office, and she didn't have it when she came out. Dean Lohman came out with her and they left. I think he must have walked her clear out to her car or something, because he was gone for a long time." Kath paused for a minute to get her thoughts in order.

"Get to the point, Kath, will you?" Marva pleaded. She knew whatever the news was, Kath would probably start at square one and go step by step through whatever had happened. The girl's sense of logical precision was remarkable, but to someone with Marva's lack of patience it sometimes was exasperating. Not that Marva's groans ever made Kath move her story along any faster; she just frowned in mock anger and kept putting one fact after another in perfect sequence.

"I went in to straighten up his office like I always do. The folder—I'm assuming it was the same one the judge had been carrying—was lying open on the desk. I glanced down and guess what I saw?" Kath's eyes were alight and for once she was too impatient to wait for any guesses. "A picture of Shelley!" Everyone's interest perked up.

"What about it? What was it?" Merrill asked.

"I know I shouldn't have read it, but I couldn't stop myself." Kath hesitated, feeling guilty all over again. Marva

rolled her hand in a circle, urging her to keep talking. "Shelley
was a juvenile delinquent when she was fourteen." Merrill and
Marva glanced at Angela as they felt her body tense up.

Kath continued. "She got charged with assault and battery!
Seems she got in a fight with someone and almost killed him—or
her—it didn't say which." The other three girls looked as
shocked as she had been when the words had jumped out at her.

"Damn, I knew I didn't trust her," Merrill murmured. She
took a swig of soda, but it failed to wash out the bad taste that
Kath's news had lodged in her mouth.

Marva leaned forward, rested her arms on her thighs and
voiced the question they all wondered about. "So what's she
doing here?"

Kath was enjoying her moment of attention even while feeling bad that the news had to be disturbing Angela. "She wasn't
convicted of the charge. Instead, she got put in some pilot program for serious offenders where she was in the hands of a court-
appointed guardian. It gives her a chance to continue her education as high as she's able to go. She has to stay out of trouble,
keep a job, and keep her grades at C or better in order to stay in
the program."

"She's a junior, same as we are, so she must have been in
the program for six or seven years," Merrill reasoned. She took
Angela's empty soda can from between her hands and set it,
together with her own, on the lamp table. Marva handed hers,
too.

"Well, get this!" Kath said excitedly, knowing she had
another piece of surprising news. "She's some kind of brain.
She's been put ahead twice and is only eighteen!"

"Eighteen? She's three years younger than we are? Doesn't
seem like she is," Marva said as she turned toward Angela, who
hadn't spoken at all. "But coming from a tough background can
probably age you pretty quickly." Marva found Angela's silence
unnerving. "What do you think, Ange?"

Angela twisted her fingers together and shrugged. "I think
we should keep this confidential, like it was meant to be, and
just judge Shelley on how she acts now, not something that happened four years ago. We don't know what extenuating circum-
stances there might have been."

Now that her news was delivered, Kath sank to a seat on the
green carpet. "Assault and battery is a serious charge, Ange,"
she argued. "I think I'm going to feel pretty nervous around her.

What if she loses her temper and goes berserk? She looks pretty strong."

"It happened once in eighteen years and she's older now. It might never happen again," Angela pointed out. An edge was creeping into her voice, but Kath didn't look convinced.

"Wait a minute," Kath continued. "Aren't we all forgetting something?" Three sets of eyes turned again to her. "How about these murders? Two happened at Penlyville while she was there, and the other two have been practically next door. What if Shelley's involved in them?"

Angela pursed her lips in disgust and shook her head. "Don't be silly, Kath. Let's not jump to conclusions. Do you think Shelley acts like a murderer?"

"Can't say that I do," Kath admitted, "but that doesn't keep me from being leery of her. Do any of us know how a murderer acts?"

Nobody answered. Then Merrill spoke up. "Maybe we'd better not get too friendly with her until the cops find the killer. That would be the safest thing. If she's not involved, great. Full speed ahead. But if she is involved, we'll have saved ourselves a lot of grief, not to mention possible danger."

Angela frowned. "You guys have her tried and convicted already with absolutely no proof."

"You know the saying as well as we do, Angie, 'It's better to be safe than sorry.' I'm not saying we should shun her altogether. Just, please, don't anyone go anywhere alone with her, okay?" Merrill asked, looking pointedly at her roommate.

Angela's smile was ironic. "Why are you all so worried about me? I told you I'm not looking for another relationship right now. Besides, with her looks Shelley could have anyone she wants; why would she be interested in me?"

"That is not a disinterested gaze she is throwing your way when you aren't looking, honey," Merrill said. *And I'll cut her heart out if she's just playing with you.*

"Yeah, and wait till she sees you in shorts and a tank top; I guarantee she'll get weak in the knees," Marva added with a chuckle. "I know I do." She ducked but the pillow hit her in the head anyway.

A message left on Shelley's answering machine had

informed her that she was to attend a special lab session that could not be missed, so she had rushed to the science building right from softball practice. Her sneakers made soft squeaking noises against the hard tile surface as she hurried down a corridor toward the basement lab she had been directed to. It suddenly struck her as odd that she hadn't encountered anyone headed in the same direction.

Becoming suspicious, she halted in front of the closed door, weighing whether or not she should enter. Suddenly, the decision was made for her. The door came open and a hand grabbed her arm and pulled her inside while another hand closed the door and twisted the lock home. Then arms tightened around her body.

Shelley's eyes went wide and a huge grin plastered itself on her surprised face as her arms enveloped the smaller woman who was squeezing the breath out of her. She leaned down so they could kiss each other's cheek.

"Aunt Helen! What a terrific surprise! I thought you were still in Africa," she said.

Judge Helen Ostcott ended her embrace and stepped back from her favorite charge. The judge's average height and chunky build, bespectacled gray eyes, and salt-and-pepper hair gave the impression of a sweetly amiable, motherly type. But upon closer inspection, the set of her chin and her determined mouth warned that this woman was no pushover. Except for Shelley: she loved the girl like she would a daughter.

Tenderly, she reached up and smoothed Shelley's bangs back from her face. "You're always so nice to visit, darling. Too bad we don't get to see each other more often." As she spoke, she took Shelley's hand and led her to a couple of lab stools she had pulled up to a counter. They each picked one and sat down facing the other.

"You're not that far away. We could see each other more often," Shelley said. "This separation is your rule, not mine." She hooked her feet onto the lower rung of the stool and twisted the revolving seat back and forth in a small arc, swiveling her hips.

"I know, but I think it's for the best. You need to develop your independence, and that should be easier for you to do without me around." Helen gazed fondly at the young woman, mindful of how much she had changed in the four years since they had met. Shelley had been beautiful even then, but a tragic past had left her emotions in shreds and resulted in terrible bouts of rage.

Months and then years of psychiatric and psychological help had worked their wondrous ways, and at last an anger management program seemed to enable her to function normally. *At least on the surface.* Helen couldn't be sure that the violent streak had been totally conquered, and she tried to watch for any signs of it.

Judge Ostcott's venue was criminal court, but Jeff Cruz, a close friend, had told her of Shelley's troubles. Jeff had approached her at her home, laying out all the details of Shelley's dismal past. He asked if Helen would be willing to take guardianship of the troubled child if they could get her into a new program for youths accused of serious offenses. Helen deferred judgment, but agreed to be in juvenile court as a spectator when Shelley's case was heard.

As Shelley was brought into court, her striking blue eyes by chance swept to Helen. Helen felt like she was being granted a glimpse of Shelley's soul, and the childless judge lost her heart to the girl. The orphaned Shelley was eventually made a ward of the court and placed under Helen's willing guardianship, and the judge accepted the girl and her problems into her home and her life.

"What happened at Penlyville? I got the message that you were desperate to change schools, but I was on safari when it was relayed to me and I didn't get any details. I just got home."

"Did you get any good shots?" Shelley asked, delaying the requested answer. She twisted the seat more quickly.

"Loads of them," she replied. "I'll send you some when I get them developed." Helen's safari had been a picture-taking one, not a life-taking one. In spite of her somewhat aggressive nature, she would never knowingly harm anyone or anything without good cause.

Helen reached out and halted Shelley's swiveling. "Now, how about answering my question. What happened at Penlyville?"

A rebellious expression flitted across her features, and Shelley looked off into space without replying.

"Shelley, darling, you know I have to ask you these questions; it's part of my duty to know what you are doing and why. Please, just tell me the story. Don't make me drag it out of you a question at a time."

Shelley swung around to the lab table and picked up an empty glass beaker, twisting it around and around. Helen waited patiently, knowing that to push her any harder for an answer could be self-defeating—Shelley might refuse to talk or just ignore her request and change the subject again.

"Aunt Helen..." Shelley set the beaker down, picked it back up, examined it closely, then set it back down. "You know I haven't dated much, right?"

"Yes, I know that. You were always so involved in your studies and sports that you never seemed much interested in dating. I figured when you were ready to, you would. Were you dating someone at Penlyville?"

The dark head dipped in a curt nod.

"And it didn't work out?" *She is making me drag it out of her one question at a time.* Helen sighed aloud.

Shelley's lips contorted and her eyes darted around, but she said nothing.

Helen sifted reasons through her mind for Shelley's obvious discomfort then put a hand over the girl's fidgety one. "Good grief, Shelley, you're not pregnant, are you?" *Surely she would use some precaution.*

Shelley pushed her fingers through her hair, set her elbow on the table, and propped up her head. Nervous blue eyes slanted toward Helen and an odd smile showed on her lips. "That couldn't happen in a zillion years," she rasped, "to either one of us."

Helen frowned at her, trying to make sense of the statement. Suddenly her quick mind picked up on its implications. "You were dating a woman?"

Shelley's tongue wet her dry lips. "Yeah...I...I was." *Lord, help me not to say the wrong thing and turn her against me. I couldn't stand that. She's all I have.*

Helen squeezed and released the hand she touched then turned toward the table, clasping her fingers together in front of her and studying them. She hoped that Shelley would feel more comfortable without her guardian's gaze on her. "How serious did it get, Shelley?"

Shelley shifted her eyes to the tabletop and took two audible breaths before answering. "I was...we were...intimate."

"Did you think you were in love with her?" *I'm no damn psychologist. Yet here I am questioning an emotionally fragile girl about her lesbian love life. Sweet Jesus!*

"Not really," Shelley answered honestly, as her face flushed. "I was curious...and flattered. I had a few dates with guys who kept asking me out. Each time, we got into some heavy petting," she glanced toward Helen, who continued to study her hands, "but that seemed to turn me off instead of turning me on. I wouldn't go all the way...the idea didn't even appeal to me. I couldn't figure what all the fuss was about, and I began to wonder if maybe I just didn't have much sex drive." Shelley tossed her head, but the bangs just fell farther onto her face so she pushed them back with her fingers and glanced beseechingly at the judge.

Helen looked into the eyes she felt on her and nodded encouragement, then she looked away again. "Go on," she murmured, "I need to hear the whole story."

Shelley pursed her lips to blow out a puff of air, then took a deep breath. "A teacher I admired invited me to her apartment for dinner. I thought other people were invited, too, but when I got there I discovered I was the only guest, and I figured out in a hurry what that might mean. I was a little scared at first, but I was curious, too, and like I just said, I was flattered. She was an older, experienced woman..."

She started playing with the beaker again. "I guess I could claim that she seduced me, but actually that first night all she did was kiss me a few times. But that's all it took to awaken the sex drive I thought was missing." Shelley's voice slowed as her mind replayed the wonder of that unexpected discovery. "That was the start of our affair. It went on for about three months, and then I realized that, for me, curiosity wasn't enough to sustain a relationship. I wanted love—I wanted to give love and I wanted to get love, and neither was going to happen with her. She didn't love me; she just lusted after me. So I ended it; or tried to...but she wouldn't let me go. She kept harassing me over and over until I knew I could end it only by leaving the college."

Shelley set the beaker down once more and turned to Helen. "That's why I sent the message to you about changing schools."

With concerned eyes and a sad smile, Helen looked at her beautiful child. "Do you understand you've chosen a very difficult path?"

"I don't think I've chosen it at all, Aunt Helen; it seems to have chosen me. I think I've been on the wrong path up until now and just got on the right one, difficult or not."

Helen nodded solemnly. "With this new knowledge of yourself, it must be tempting to find a meaningful relationship, Shelley, but you better keep a low profile for a while. Getting involved with anyone, male or female, might not be advisable. It could be dangerous for you." *Or them.*

Suddenly angry, Shelley jumped off of the stool and strode fiercely back and forth, gesticulating with her long arms. "First you tell me you want me to learn some independence, then you try to control every damn thing I do! Back off, Aunt Helen!"

"Shelley, listen..."

"No, you listen..."

"Shelley!" Helen's voice carried the full weight of her authority. Shelley gestured wildly with her hands, but she stopped and stared down into her guardian's face.

"Shelley," Helen repeated more quietly, "are you still in your anger management program?"

"Yes," the dark-haired girl answered impatiently.

"Have you been continuing with your drama classes that your doctor recommended as part of the program?"

"You know I started them at Penlyville when he told me to, and I'm taking them here on one afternoon a week. And I'm on the softball team. He said that might help, too." Shelley blew air out through her lips, lifting the bangs on her forehead. "Aunt Helen," she asked exasperatedly, "don't you ever get angry?"

"Of course I do; everyone does sometimes. You've just needed some help learning to control your anger."

"Well, this is one time I think my anger is perfectly justified." Shelley started pacing again, her arms waving. "Do you have any idea what it's like to be yanked back and forth, told what to do and what not to do, what to say and what not to say? I feel like a stupid puppet in an even stupider play." She stopped directly in front of Helen, the blaze rekindled in her eyes. "Well, no one's going to tell me who to see and who not to see—not even you. I'll make that decision myself and whatever happens, happens."

Years of sitting on the bench, reading expressions and body language of all sorts of people from all walks of life made Helen astute at surmising the unspoken word. "You've met someone you care about?" she asked softly.

"No...yes...I'm not sure," the tall girl answered, her belligerence faltering.

"Does she care about you?"

Shelley's eyes dropped for a second, then came back to Helen. Her belligerence had completely faded, replaced by insecurity, and Helen's heart went out to her. "I don't know how anybody really feels about me. I know some people are drawn to me because of my looks, but I don't know if anyone would find me lovable. I just...think she's attractive. I don't really know her yet."

Helen sighed and smiled. "You are definitely lovable, Shelley, and perhaps this young woman is the right one for you. Anyhow, if nothing's even happened yet, I suppose it's useless for me to try to argue against it."

"Are you laughing at me, Aunt Helen?"

Helen reached out and patted Shelley's cheek. "Never, darling. And I don't want to interfere with your new friend or your dreams. I just want you to remember that you have to be consummately cautious...with everyone."

"I understand that," Shelley agreed earnestly. Then her lips twitched up on one side. "Consummately?"

Helen reddened as she laughed, recalling how good Shelley was at using alternate meanings of words or their roots to tweak the user. "Consummately, as in 'very,' no sexual innuendoes intended."

She slid from the stool and opened her arms. "Give me a kiss good-bye; I have to be going."

As Shelley enfolded the judge in her embrace, Helen murmured in her ear. "Please, please be careful."

"I'm always careful, Aunt Helen," she replied.

Chapter
4

The girls decided to keep quiet about Shelley's past for the time being even though the knowledge weighed heavily on their minds. They felt a little awkward around the dark-haired girl at the next practice, but if she noticed any change in their manner she didn't remark on it. The only notable occurrence was the adoption of the nickname "Star" for Shelley by most of her teammates. A couple of times her chin set and she looked as though she might argue, but she refrained and finally accepted the inevitable.

After practice, Angela, Merrill and Shelley stayed for the second session of work on Angela's throwing. Merrill stood on first base and Angela followed Shelley out to right field.

"Let me double-check to make sure your arm is coming through at the right angle, then we'll concentrate on your timing," Shelley said. Stepping behind the redhead, she again put her palm across Angela's shoulder while her pupil threw the ball several times to Merrill. As soon as she entered Angela's personal space, Shelley's imagination soared and her body responded to their proximity. Shelley groaned inwardly, not understanding Angela's power over her emotions, but recognizing that it was growing in strength. *Why does she already have to have a girlfriend?* She took a deep breath, delighting in the scent emanating from the auburn hair beneath her nose.

Loath to release the contact between them, Shelley kept her hand on the shoulder until Angela broke the silence between them. "What do you think?" she asked.

"Strawberries," Shelley murmured.

"What?" Angela turned her head to meet Shelley's eyes and saw a faint blush creep up her cheeks.

"Uh...your hair smells like strawberries," came the slightly flustered explanation.

A smile tickled at the edges of Angela's mouth until she remembered her promise to be careful around Shelley and smothered the smile with a frown. "I was asking about my throws."

Interpreting the frown as a rebuff, Shelley tore her eyes from Angela's face, abruptly dropped her hand from her shoulder and sank to the ground, her legs crossed beneath her.

Feeling a little guilty, Angela looked down at the dark-haired girl who sat at her feet, plucking at the grass. "Do you want me to throw some more to Merrill?"

Shelley didn't look up from her self-imposed chore of picking up grass and tossing it in the air. "Yep, throw ten or twelve times, then we'll try some throws to third base."

While Angela fulfilled the recommended throws, Shelley looked back up at her, struggling to keep her mind on checking the redhead's timing. Angela had an athlete's strong, muscular frame fully rounded in just the right places, resulting in an enviable build that Shelley found was drawing her eyes like a magnet.

She jumped up and dusted off her sweats, using the action to bring some control to her emotions. Straightening up, she hollered to Merrill to move to third base, then Angela shifted her throwing to there. Shelley made a few suggestions to improve the timing of her step relative to her throw, and Angela suddenly felt it all coming together.

Shelley shifted Merrill to home plate to receive what would be the longest throws for a right fielder, and it was soon obvious that Angela had perfected all the necessary moves. Her throw had developed into a stronger one than most outfielders possessed. After fifteen more minutes, the raven-haired girl called a halt to the practice and they gathered their equipment.

Merrill phoned Marva while they walked to the street to await her. Shelley rubbed a towel into her hair, then dried off her face and neck. "I think you're good to go now, Angela. Your throws are really strong."

Merrill, not to be outdone, added her agreement. "Yeah, Angie, you were hurting my hand with a couple of those throws. You look super!"

Angela toweled her face dry and looked up at Shelley. A sudden desire to run her fingers through the unkempt hair tormented her. "Thanks...Star," she said clumsily. "You've helped me to throw better than I ever did."

Shelley shrugged carelessly. "Whatever helps you, helps the team. Now we need to work on my hitting. I'll check with you later to see when we can get together for that, okay?"

"Sure."

"Angela?" Shelley's eyes grew even bluer in intensity and her brows lowered.

"Yeah?" When their glances met, Angela felt a flash of heat. She couldn't deny her attraction in spite of the tall girl's cocky attitude.

"Knock off the 'Star' nickname."

Angela bristled as she quirked an eyebrow. "Okay, but I can't speak for the rest of the team."

"Win some, lose some," Shelley responded with another shrug.

"You want to go to the Steak House... again? Is this getting to be a Tuesday-Wednesday-Thursday-night regular thing now? That could get pretty expensive. I'm holding the entertainment kitty this week, and we're going to have to fatten it pretty soon if that's the case." Kath sat on the couch with one leg pulled up under her. She had been thumbing through a paperback book when Angela made the suggestion. Grimacing as she questioned Angela, she suspected that Shelley's presence at the restaurant was drawing her there.

"You don't have to come, Kath, if you don't want to," Angela replied rather huffily. She had just finished the first draft of an economics paper and felt she had earned a break—at least, that was the excuse she had ready should anyone ask. The truth was she just wanted to feast her eyes on Shelley, and she could do it there without drawing too much attention...or warnings from her friends. She didn't delve too deeply into why she was so anxious to see Shelley. She didn't even like her all that much. Except for that strawberries remark, the dark-haired girl seemed

kind of standoffish. But she always had enjoyed looking at beautiful faces, hadn't she?

In the kitchenette getting sodas, Marva and Merrill heard
the conversation emanating from the living room. "What do you
think, Merry?" Marva collected the sodas from the fridge and set
them on the small counter. Her brow furrowed as she spoke quietly. "Shouldn't we keep Ange from going there while Shelley's
working?"

"Huh!" Merrill grunted. "We would if I had my way, but I
don't think we'll be able to. You know how hardheaded Angie
can be sometimes. If we try to force her to stay away from Shelley, it might backfire on us. Besides, you heard her; she'd go
without us. At least if we're there with her, maybe we can keep
track of what's going on." She was opening and closing cupboard doors, searching for some munchies. She and Angela had a
regular spot to store them in, but when Marva and Kath helped
clean up, no one knew where they might be found.

Marva unconsciously rubbed her arm where the sodas had
chilled her flesh. "We know what's keeping Angie away from
her, but why do you think Shelley has held back? She doesn't
check out the other girls like she does Angie, so there's obviously some interest there. And what the heck are you looking
for? We're going to the Steak House, aren't we?"

Merrill halted her search and grinned. "Yeah, I guess we
are... so we don't need any munchies, right? I don't know what's
holding Shelley back. She's only eighteen, remember? Maybe
she's shy."

"Oh yeah," Marva agreed sarcastically. "No one who's been
that beautiful for eighteen years should be shy. More likely worn
out," she grinned wickedly. Picking up the sodas, she set them
back in the fridge. "Guess we won't be needing these either."

Tearing a paper towel from its holder on the wall, Merrill
wiped up the four wet rings that the sodas had left on the counter
and tossed the towel toward the trash basket. It hit the edge and
bounced to the floor. "Being beautiful doesn't mean she won't be
shy, Marv. But maybe she doesn't have time to get involved with
anyone. She seems to be pretty busy."

"Yeah, I've noticed she's always busy... but busy doing
what?" Marva asked.

Merrill bent down, picked up the discarded towel, and
placed it neatly into the trash basket. As she raised up, her eyes
met Marva's and they just looked at each other for several sec-

onds. Then Merrill shrugged. "I have absolutely no idea."

With a worried frown, Marva shook her head and sighed. "You know, we all wanted Angie to get over Vicki and come back to being her old self. Well, her interest in Shelley seems to have wakened her back up all right, but the girl's past has us all concerned. Now we're worried whether Angie should even go near her. I sure hope everything turns out okay."

"We all do, Marv. But Angie's a big girl, and she has to live her own life. We'll just have to do what we can to stand by her." Merrill laid a hand on her friend's shoulder. "Come on, let's take our lovelorn girl to the Steak House."

The Steak House was crowded but not full, and the girls found a table for four in Shelley's serving area. They had placed their usual order for pizza and beer and chatted away about their latest classes—at least, three of them did. Angela seemed unable to keep up with the running conversation as her eyes followed the tall, dark-haired waitress who kept passing by with trays of food and beer. Her friends needed no further evidence that she was thoroughly captivated, and they were worried about the possibility that Angela could be seriously hurt again. They were signaling their trepidation with their eyes when suddenly someone appeared next to Angela's chair and a rough voice drove the surrounding hubbub into silence.

"Well, well, well, if it isn't Angela Wedgeway, the world's best hitter," the voice grated. "Or should I say the coach's best brown-noser?" Liz Hurtz, the right fielder who'd been replaced by Angela, was several inches taller than she was, with about forty more pounds of solid muscle on her frame. Proud of her size and strength, Hurtz worked out every day in the weight room.

Grabbing the back of Angela's chair, she attempted to dump her on the floor, but Angela's agility enabled her to jump to her feet and twist around to face her foe. Angela followed her first inclination to keep the peace, and smiled. "Sit down and have a beer with us, Liz. Let's talk."

"Talk, hell," the angry brunette blustered. "I'll teach you not to mess with me." With no further warning, she threw a punch at Angela's jaw. An arm came out of nowhere to shove a startled Angela aside while a hand grasped Hurtz's moving wrist and thrust it up in the air. Amazed onlookers winced at the sound of grinding bones.

*If she touches Angela...*A powerful rage erupted in Shelley, shaking her insides. *I'll crush her.* She twisted the wrist she held, forcing Hurtz back against the table. Bringing up her forearm, she put pressure against the brunette's windpipe.

Growling, Hurtz gathered herself to fight back—until her eyes met two slate-blue ones that burned with a cold fury. Nostrils flared above a full upper lip that was lifted in a feral snarl. Hurtz recognized that look. She had seen it on the face of a man who had killed a rabid dog that had attacked his child. With his bare hands he had broken the neck of an animal that no one else would even go near. The growl died in Hurtz's throat, and fear slithered down her backbone, taking the fight out of her like air from a punctured balloon. Shelley released her and watched as she sidled away, holding the sore wrist and muttering.

Angela had lurched against Merrill, who grabbed her and stabilized her balance, preventing a fall. All four women had been in a position to see Shelley's face when she confronted Hurtz, and all four of them felt a shiver of fear go through them.

Angela stepped forward and grabbed Shelley's arm. Shelley's body jerked back toward her, and a fist sliced through the air, stopping a bare inch from Angela's wide eyes.

The dark-haired girl's face crumpled, and she turned away, but Angela pleaded, "Shelley, wait." She took hold of her arm more gently and turned the taller girl toward her, feeling the tension vibrating through her forearm. Angela looked into pain-filled eyes.

"I almost hit you." Shelley's words tore roughly from her throat.

"But you didn't," Angela said. "I shouldn't have grabbed you without warning, and I apologize. Actually you saved me from getting my face rearranged by Hurtz. Thank you. I wasn't expecting her to do that."

Shelley's usually velvet voice was tight and hard, and it jarred Angela. "Always expect an attack. If it comes, you're ready. If it doesn't come, you haven't lost anything."

"I'll try to remember that," she promised.

"I gotta get back to work," Shelley muttered.

"Thanks again," Angela called, watching as Shelley walked away. *That's odd. She won that battle, but she seems upset about it.*

In spite of her puzzlement, Angela couldn't help grinning at her three friends as she sat back down at the table. "Looks like I have a defender," she drawled.

"Yeah, she sure saved your ass!" Marva exclaimed excitedly. "Did you see that look on her face? I would have backed down just like Hurtz did. She looked ready to kill." Marva caught her breath as she realized what she had just said, and her words sobered them all.

"It does make what we've learned about her easier to believe, doesn't it?" Kath asked.

"She didn't even hit anyone," Angela protested.

"I'm just glad Hurtz did back down," Merrill said. "We could have had a damn bloodbath here."

The thought cast a pall over the group as they watched Shelley bring their beer and pizza. Nobody said anything as Kath pulled money from her pocket and handed it to Shelley. When she received her change, she flashed a tentative smile at the taller woman. Shelley could feel the chill in their attitude, and she barely nodded in return.

The foursome hurriedly ate their pizza and drank their beer, each mulling over her own interpretation of the night's events.

"You know, I don't think we're doing right by Shelley," the always fair-minded Merrill said into the silence. The others looked at her, waiting for an explanation. "We concentrated on how scary she looked—and I admit I was scared—but she saved Angie from getting punched in the face, and she risked a lot by doing that. Not to mention that she put herself in the line of fire."

"I know I'm grateful," Angela declared emphatically, happy that Merrill had come to Shelley's defense. "We all know how strong Liz is; she would probably have broken my jaw." The thought brought a wince to her face, and she lifted her hand and rubbed her cheek.

"Yeah," Kath reluctantly agreed. "And Merry has a point; Shelley could be kicked out of her program if she gets in a fight or loses her job. I guess we do owe her something for coming to Angie's rescue."

"Great!" Marva exclaimed. "Does this mean I'm allowed to like her again?"

"We all want to like her, Marv. We're just not sure whether we should or not," Merrill said with a wry grin.

"There's the understatement of the year," Angela muttered.

She raised her mug of beer and took a long, long drink as the others cast concerned looks her way.

The girls continued to transport Shelley to practices with little further mention of Hurtz's attack. The one time Angela brought it up with the intention of thanking her again, Shelley grunted a request to forget about it. As nothing else untoward happened, the four women pushed the memory of Shelley's frightening expression into the backs of their minds and concentrated instead on the fact that she had defended Angela at the risk of losing her job and jeopardizing the court-approved program she was in.

Shelley and Angela held their extra batting session accompanied by the other girls. The dark-haired beauty absorbed Angela's directions like a thirsty desert dweller and soon was pounding the ball in regular practices. Ironically, Angela taught her to be such a good hitter that Shelley's position as first baseman was virtually guaranteed.

School was going well, practices were showing steady improvement, and the team was looking forward to the opening day of the season, only two weeks away.

Shelley stood on the forty-foot-wide stage, looking around. The college theater could hold about 400 people in vinyl-padded folding seats separated by a middle aisle. The outside aisles ran against each wall and led directly to the exits. Footlights, klieg lights, and single spots hanging above the first few rows of seats were controlled by a huge lighting panel mounted on its own console in the wings. Curtains and backdrops loomed overhead on rolls, their ropes dangling out of sight offstage.

Under the guidance of the doctor in her anger management program, Shelley had chosen drama classes as an aid to learning to control her rages. She had started the classes at Penlyville, and when she transferred to Spofford, she decided to continue them.

Though somewhat shy around others, Shelley found herself a natural at pretending to be someone else. At first, that surprised her. Then today, standing on the stage, she realized that she shouldn't be surprised at all, and her lip curled. *Aren't I always pretending to be someone else?*

"Shelley?" A tall, sandy-haired man disturbed her reverie.

Edward Sindbourne, drama teacher, climbed the steps to the stage and joined her. "You are Shelley, right? From Monday's class?"

At Shelley's nod, he continued. "Are you trying to get a feel for our stage? Have you ever acted before?"

"Yes and no," Shelley answered. "I've usually worked more...backstage. Behind the scenes. Oh...I've done some prompting too. Helping the actors with their lines."

Mr. Sindbourne had walked to the lighting panel while she spoke, and he flipped the switch for an overhead spot that shone directly on her. He walked back toward her and circled her. "Pity," he said. "You have a marvelous voice, a natural presence, and an unnatural beauty."

"Unnatural?" Shelley's hackles stirred.

"Sorry, poor choice of words. I meant out of the ordinary." He walked around her one more time, then tucked a finger under her chin and tilted her head up a trifle, disregarding her stiffening posture. "Regal."

He dropped his hand and stepped back. Folding his arms, he lifted a hand to tap his chin as he continued to study her. "Regal, but mysterious...maybe dangerous." Shelley's eyes flashed, and Ed Sindbourne smiled gleefully. "Definitely dangerous. Next class we have, I'm going to pull some scripts for you to take home and look at. I'd like to hear you read for a part."

Shelley looked doubtful, and he hurried to explain. "Nothing major, just a one-act play that we'll work on in class. For experience. Interested?"

Why not? I might learn new ways to be the chameleon I need to be. "Sure, I'll give it a try."

"Super. See you in class Monday. Enjoy the stage." He turned off the spotlight, waved, and left.

Her lips twisted wryly as she spread her arms, quoting Shakespeare to her ghostly audience, "'The stage where every man must play a part, and mine a sad one.'" She walked down the aisle to the exit and flipped the switch, bringing back the darkness.

A cone of pale yellow dropped from the solitary street light, encroaching upon the late-night darkness. The park would have been deserted except for the tall, dark-haired woman dressed entirely in black. Sitting on a bench with her legs thrust out in front of her, she held a long, slim object in her hand, tilting it to reflect the meager light from its glistening surface.

She pushed the blade closed then touched the trigger, delighting in the *snick* it made as it popped open and the feel of its movement against her palm. *Better than sex,* she grinned malevolently. *Or at least more dependable. I know the pleasure it brings me is always available and it never turns me down.* She pushed it closed again and triggered it back open. *And I'm always in control; it never argues with me.*

She closed it again and laid it on her palm, eyeing the intricate pattern that had been carved into its bone handle. Her fingertips caressed the design, moving lovingly across each stroke of the carving. The knife even had a name, but she had bastardized it to match its current occupation. *The Star Maker.* She smiled as pictures of the horrified faces of her victims came to mind.

Her smile broadened as she considered the latest woman she had chosen to act in her play. Tonight her search for new talent had ended; the choice was made, and the props were in place. Soon the play would be ready to begin. She snicked the blade open one more time and slashed it through the air, watching the lamplight wink off its shiny surface. She pondered whether she would start her carving on the left cheek or the right. Or maybe she would start on a breast this time. Her smile turned gleeful. *I think I'll let my leading lady decide that. What fun it will be to discuss it with her.*

She got up from the bench, kissed the knife, and slipped it into her pocket. Grabbing the bike's handlebars, she hit the kickstand with her foot, threw her long leg over the bar, and took off.

She wheeled down the street, the large yellow eyes of an owl her only witness. As she disappeared into the darkness, she smirked at the relevance of its ancient question: "Whooooo?"

Merrill opened her eyes about three o'clock in the morning, wondering what had awakened her. She lay on her back, listening to the night sounds—the quiet *whoosh* of cars passing on a distant street, the chirping of crickets, the far-off clanking of a train. Then she heard a distinct *clink* just outside the window. Curious, she slipped out of bed and looked out. The window opened onto the edge of the parking lot where the bike racks stood next to an area light. Shelley had just slid her bike into the rack and was closing the lock that connected the ends of the chain that she had threaded through the spokes. She straightened up and loped toward the entrance, moving out of Merrill's sight.

What the heck is she doing out at this hour? Nothing in a college town is open at this time of night. Merrill filed the question away for later consideration and returned to bed. Pulling her sheet up around her ears, she went back to sleep.

Chapter
5

The practice had been an especially good one, with Coach Palmer amazed at the change in two of her primary players. She knew Angela Wedgeway and Shelley Brinton had been working with each other, but the results of their collaboration pleasantly astonished her. Angela had changed from an outstanding fielder with a weak arm to one with an outstanding arm to match. And Shelley's progress at the plate was nothing short of phenomenal. The harnessing of that raw power would make opposing pitchers cringe.

Coach Palmer called them together at the end of practice. "Maybe you girls should be helping to coach the team," she remarked.

"I'd be glad to," Angela offered. She looked at Shelley, who had not answered. "What do you say, Shelley? We could work with the batters one night and the fielders another night."

Shelley locked eyes with Angela as she had on their first meeting but still did not answer.

Angela swallowed. "Together," she added.

"Excuse us a minute, Coach," Shelley said as she took hold of Angela's arm and drew her aside.

Shelley stood face to face with Angela and looked down at her tentatively. Her low voice throbbed through Angela's veins. "Is Merrill your girlfriend?"

Angela's mouth dropped open. Had she had a thousand

guesses at what Shelley was going to ask, that would not have
been on the list. She picked her chin up off her chest and shook
her head. "Merrill's my best friend. She's engaged to be married
after she graduates. To Jim Dursik."

Angela couldn't put her finger on what happened in that
instant, but her answer definitely triggered a reaction in Shelley...and in herself, though she couldn't put a name to it. The
dark-haired girl didn't say or do anything unusual, but in some
subtle way her whole demeanor changed. She took Angela's arm
and guided her back to the coach. "Yeah, I'll help too," she told
Palmer.

"Wonderful. We don't have many practices left before the
season starts, so how about if we split the next one and work on
fielding the first half and batting the second half?"

"Sure," Shelley answered without hesitation, earning a
raised eyebrow from Angela. Shelley grinned and shrugged.
"When I make up my mind, I make up my mind."

"I'll hold you to that," Angela said then struggled to keep
from blushing at the look Shelley gave her.

As the girls sat around the apartment after practice, Merrill
told them about Shelley's late night excursion the previous
evening, adding to their suspicions of her behavior.

"Why don't we watch to see if she goes out again and follow
her?" Kath suggested.

"You willing to go first, Kath?" Angela asked scathingly.

"Well, no, not really," Kath admitted. She realized Angela
would champion Shelley's cause, so she was not offended by the
caustic question. "Not by myself, anyway. I thought we had
agreed not to go anywhere alone."

"We could all follow her!" Angela said with mock excitement. "Just think, we could call ourselves the Night Crawlers,
and if Shelley asks why we are following her, we can say we are
looking for bait for fishing."

"Come on, Ange," Kath said, "we're not going to let her
know we're following her."

"You bet we aren't, because we're not going." Angela set
her jaw and glared at each of her friends, daring them to contra-
dict her. "Who the hell do you think we are, the campus police?
It's none of our damn business where Shelley's going. Maybe

she has a lover. You guys are letting your imaginations work overtime."

"Maybe we are, Angie, but I still don't trust her," Merrill admitted. "She never offers any information about herself. She plays softball and works at the Steak House. That's all we know about her. Oh, and she's got a nasty look that could freeze hell over. Usually someone who makes that kind of a look work has earned it somewhere."

"Well, I haven't exactly had to fight off her advances, Merr, so you can come down off Worry Mountain, okay?" Angela was out of sorts today, and this conversation was just making her crankier.

A hard knock came on the apartment door accompanied by an excited voice. Marva, closest to the door, jumped up and answered it. A cute blond stood there, and Marva gave her a big smile, but what she said wiped the smile from her face in a hurry. "Another girl's been killed. From Scatsboro! Last night!"

The news flew around the Brickhouse, and spontaneous groups of students gathered on each floor to discuss the latest information. The newest victim had been found just after day-break by a jogger out for a morning run along the bank of the Broderick River.

The four teammates were mingling with some other students in the first-floor hallway, listening to the same bare details being talked about over and over. Glancing out a window near her, Merrill spied Shelley coming up the walk toward the entrance with a newspaper stuck under her arm. She hurried to the door to meet her.

From her five-foot height, she tilted her head back and looked up at Shelley. "Have you heard the news about another girl being killed?"

"Yeah, I have," Shelley shifted to the side to try to get past Merrill, but the shorter woman moved to block her. Merrill suddenly noticed that Shelley's face looked stiff and her eyes flat and shifty.

"Could we have your newspaper when you're finished with it?" Merrill nodded toward the paper under her arm. Surely the paper would have more details.

Shelley stopped and looked agitated, then annoyed. "Why can't you just buy your own, Merrill? They sell them right outside the damn door." She shouldered Merrill aside and vaulted up the steps.

"Forget it!" Merrill shouted after her. *Damn girl. Just about the time I think I should be nicer to her, she pulls something like this.*

Merrill swung around, her face stormy, and barged right into Angela. The redhead grabbed her shoulders and steadied the smaller woman. "Ange, I swear that girl gripes the hell out of me. Did you hear what she just said?"

Angela grimaced. "Not much worse than I might have said, as grumpy as I feel today. The difference is I'm your friend and you think Shelley's your enemy. Maybe it's the wrong time of the month for her too."

She slipped her arm through Merrill's and led her back into their apartment. Marva and Kath saw them and followed them in, leaving the door ajar. "Hey, Marv," Merrill said, "can you get us a paper? Use the entertainment kitty."

"I already tried to get one. They were sold out."

"Damn," Merrill sputtered. "I'm going to go upstairs and tear that one away from Shelley!"

'No, you're not." Angela laughed and pushed her feisty friend down onto the couch. "Shelley probably eats shrimps like you for breakfast."

"See?" Merrill bounced on the couch cushion in her agitation. "Even you think she's dangerous."

Angela grinned and shook her head. It seemed funny to see Merrill so exasperated; she usually was pretty cool. "Yeah, I think she's dangerous, but not quite the same way you do."

Marva tittered, then someone loudly cleared her throat and all eyes swept toward the doorway. Shelley stood there with the newspaper in question lying in her palm. No one spoke; they just stared.

God, she looks so uncomfortable, Angela thought. *And I feel like a jerk. I wonder if she knew we were talking about her?* At last Angela found her tongue. "Come on in."

Shelley walked in and stopped in front of Merrill. She handed the paper toward her, and Merrill took it. Then the low voice that seemed to caress its listeners said, "I'd like it back when you're finished."

"Sure, thanks," Merrill said through stiff lips. She moved over on the couch and tilted her head toward the cushion next to her. "Have a seat." Shelley sat down and leaned forward, resting her arms on her knees, her head lowered.

"How about some sodas?" Kath had ducked into the kitchen-

ette and now appeared with a six-pack of cans that she handed to
Angela to separate. She and Marva went back into the kitchenette and returned with pretzels and mixed nuts.

Angela pulled the cans from the plastic rings and set them
on the small lamp table, then walked over and handed the last
two to Merrill and Shelley. Shelley's gaze started at Angela's
feet and slowly moved up her body to her face. Angela became
very conscious for the first time that day of having donned shorts
and a tank top. She blushed as Marva's words came to mind,
She'll get weak in the knees. When the crystal-blue eyes met
hers, Angela was the one whose knees weakened.

Marva one-handed a couple of sodas from the table, stepped
past Angela, then reached back and tugged her down to a seat on
the floor, purposely breaking the eye contact between her and
Shelley. "Merry, how about reading us what the newspaper has to
say?" she asked.

Merrill had opened the paper and folded it lengthwise to
make it easier to handle. She read the full description of the
finding of the victim, including a detailed account of the cuts
that had been used to torture the girl. "Apparently, just as in the
previous cases, the wound to the stomach was the cause of
death." Merrill read, then jumped and squealed as Shelley's
elbow hit her.

"Sorry," the dark-haired girl mumbled, drawing everyone's
eyes away from Merrill. She had grabbed her stomach when Merrill read the words aloud, accidentally thrusting her elbow into
Merrill's arm. "That stomach wound... you know it takes a long
time to die from a stomach wound," she barely whispered, her
mouth turning up into a horrible smile. She sat there a moment
before realizing that she was being stared at.

Abruptly standing up, Shelley reached out a hand to Merrill,
who quickly folded the paper back up and gave it to her. Without
another word, Shelley turned and left.

Marva shivered. "That was damn creepy, guys." She glanced
at Angela, whose eyes had widened. The other two women
looked back apprehensively.

Angela bit her lip so hard tears came to her eyes. "Did you
see the same look I saw? She seemed happy about it. Will someone please tell me I am dreaming?"

But no one could tell her what she wanted to hear.

"Listen, Ange," Merrill's usually soft voice sounded ragged,
"you will stay away from her, you hear me? If not for your own

sake, then for mine." She looked at the other girls. "And nobody goes anywhere by themselves, right?"

"Right," Marva and Kath agreed.

Merrill slid forward on the couch seat. Reaching down and grabbing Angela's arm, she jerked it hard. "Right?" she demanded.

Angela looked away, her face and mouth twisting. Merrill tugged again on her arm. "Don't do this to me, Angie," she rasped. "I'll go crazy if I think you're hanging around some demented killer."

Angela stood up then looked down at Merrill, her face hard. "I don't believe that Shelley is a demented killer. Every reason you have for thinking so is totally circumstantial. She's different and maybe difficult. That doesn't mean she's crazy."

Merrill's face got red and she jumped up, shouting. "Goddammit, Ange, you think because she has a beautiful face, her soul can't be warped? Because she rattles your hormones, that makes her okay? You want to bet your life on it? Jesus Christ! What makes you so sure you're right about Shelley? You sure as hell weren't right about Vicki." As soon as the words came out, Merrill sucked in her breath, wishing she could bring them back.

Angela's face turned white, then red, then purple. Her instinct shouted for her to slap Merrill's brazen face, but her love for her friend made her fight so hard to overcome the instinct that she started shaking. Twice she started to raise her hand and twice she fought it down. Finally, Marva, her eyes moist, threw her arms around her in a huge, restraining hug and just held on until Angela's body quieted down, and the red head dropped onto Marva's shoulder.

"Ange," Merrill choked out her name, "I'm so sorry." She put her head against Angela's back and wrapped her arms over Marva's. "I had no right to say any of that, and I'm truly sorry. I'm just really, really scared that something might happen to you, and I'd never forgive myself if anything did. I love you."

The three women stood together for several minutes until Kath intervened. "Okay, you guys, togetherness time is over," she tried to joke, clapping her hands. It was a pitiful attempt, but it did bring a slight smile to each face as they pulled apart.

"Forgive me?" asked Merrill, her remorse plain on her face.

Angela sighed and nodded, knowing Merrill's concern for her had prompted the uncharacteristic outburst. She threw an arm over Merrill's shoulders and gave her a hug. "You know I will...and I won't go anywhere by myself. You have my permission to follow me around like a damn puppy dog. Even to the bathroom."

"Now wait a minute; I never said I would go that far," Merrill protested and they all chuckled, wanting something, anything, to laugh at.

Chapter 6

It was Friday and Shelley was just entering her apartment when the phone rang. She gave the door a shove with her shoulder, dropped her sports bag, and stuck her softball bat in the corner. Kicking off her shoes as she went, she picked up the phone and carried it into the bedroom, trailing its extra-long cord, before answering it. Flopping back onto the full-size bed—the one concession to her size—she lifted the handset. "Hi."

"Hi, Shelley, it's Aunt Helen."

"Like you had to tell me that," Shelley said, grinning into the phone. "How are you? Did you get your pictures developed yet?" She twisted a foot toward her and peeled off the sock, tossing it toward a pile of clothes near the hamper, then did the same with the other sock.

"I was late taking them in, but I should have them back in a few days. Shelley..." she hesitated, and Shelley closed her eyes, waiting to hear the real reason for Helen's call. "I've just learned about the murders that are going on near your school. I'm very concerned."

There was a hesitation and Helen, sitting at her desk in the study at home, leaned her head on her hand, waiting for Shelley's response.

"I know. I've been concerned about them, too."

"They didn't start until you moved into the area, darling." *Dear God, please don't let this be happening.* She could picture

Shelley's beautiful face tightening up, trying to fight her emotions.

The tension showed as Shelley's liquid voice hardened. "That could be just a coincidence, couldn't it?"

"I don't put much stock in coincidences, Shelley. If anything, past events have taught me to be overcautious."

"Look, Aunt Helen, if I notice anything strange happening, I'll let you know, okay?" Shelley's fist opened and closed, again and again, and she finally plunged it into her shorts pocket, wrapping it around the object it encountered.

"Shelley, if anything at all seems unusual in the slightest way, you call me. Don't take any chances, you hear? I can only do so much to protect you." Helen looked at her hand and saw it was shaking. "Do you think you should leave Spofford?"

"I just got here," Shelley said in a grating monotone. "Don't you think changing schools every half hour just might draw some unwanted attention?"

The girl's tone unnerved Helen. "Shelley, are you still taking care of your anger management recommendations?"

"God, when you ask me that, I do get angry!" Shelley flared. "You know I'm doing everything I've been told to do!" Helen could hear her breathing. "Like a good little girl," she finished harshly.

"Shell, I know you don't want me hanging over you all the time. I try not to be too overbearing. But sometimes I have to push you a little, and you know that."

Shelley tangled her fingers in the front of her hair and yanked on it in frustration. "Just because I know it, doesn't mean I have to like it."

"All right, I realize it's a burden." Helen hoped a change of subject would calm Shelley down. "How's your friend? Anything new on that front?"

Just more frustration. A tear squeezed out from under one eyelid and hovered at the top of Shelley's cheek. "You've nothing to worry about there. She barely even knows I'm alive."

"I wasn't asking because I was worried, Shelley. I care about what you do, what interests you. I love you, remember."

Shelley purposely softened her tone. "I'm sorry, Aunt Helen. This hasn't been a good week. I love you, too."

"I have some court work that I must get back to. Good night, darling. I wish I could give you a great big hug."

"I miss your hugs," Shelley murmured with an aching heart.

Will anyone else ever want to hug me? How can anyone love me without knowing me...and I can't let anyone know me. "Good night, Aunt Helen."

She cradled the phone and set it on the rug, rolled off of the bed, and stumbled into the bathroom, shedding her clothes. Dropping them to the floor, she kicked them into the bedroom toward the hamper and jumped into the shower. Afterward, she dragged herself into the bedroom, dropped her towel onto the growing pile of clothes, and leaned back gratefully onto her bed. Stretching one arm above her head and draping one across her waist, she fell quickly into a light sleep.

Downstairs, the women had showered and changed, and were congregated in 112A, lazing around in front of the TV and trying to get up the energy to go out.

"Hey, Angie, Shelley's off tonight. I know I've said that we should stay away from her but we could be wrong." Merrill had trouble admitting that possibility out loud. "Out of common courtesy, maybe we should do something to show our appreciation for her helping you against Hurtz the other night. How about asking her if she wants to take a busman's holiday with us? We'll all be together. Anyone object to that?" Merrill lay sprawled on the rug, and Marva sat beside her with her back against the couch. Angela lay on the couch, while Kath sat at the far end with Angela's drawn-up feet almost in her lap.

Angela threw her arm across her eyes and grunted. "I object. You just want the couch."

"What's a busman's holiday?" asked Kath, who never let an unfamiliar word or expression get by her.

"A tour by bus," Merrill explained. "A busman takes a tour by bus even though he works on one. We ask Shelley to go to the Steak House with us even though that's where she works. Get it?"

"Yeah, cute," Kath grinned. "And I like the idea. We all play on the same team; we can't very well just ignore her. And this way no one is alone with her in some strange place." She reached over and tickled Angela's feet. "So, go get her, Ange, before we all fall asleep."

Angela yelped, then groaned and sat up, swiveling her abused feet to the floor. "Guess I won't get any peace until I do." Marva snickered and opened her mouth, but Angela frowned mightily and pointed a finger at her, silencing her. "Don't you even go there, Marva Derby, or you are in big trouble."

Marva didn't say another word, conveying her teasing thoughts with a wink and a smirk.

"I'm going with you," Merrill said. "You aren't going up to her place by yourself." She started to get up, but Angela rose first and pushed down on her shoulder.

"No way, Merr. Not one of the dead girls was attacked in her room, and you aren't going to make me afraid to visit someone in our apartment complex." She quickly escaped out the door before Merrill could answer.

Now that she was up and moving around, the redhead's energy returned and she took the steps two-at-a-time up to Shelley's floor, enjoying the brush of her bare feet against the carpeted stairs. She was happy that the girls seemed willing to give Shelley more benefit of the doubt. Angela agreed Shelley was mysterious, but she couldn't imagine her as a killer no matter how hard she tried.

Walking swiftly to the dark-haired girl's apartment, Angela halted at the partially open door. Suddenly alarmed in spite of her earlier statement, she pushed it all the way open. The room was far from neat, and clothes were thrown about, but nothing seemed obviously amiss. She told herself not to be spooked so easily, and she walked in. "Shelley?" she called, but when no one answered, Angela considered the possibility that Shelley might be asleep and tiptoed over to the open bedroom door.

The sheer beauty of the sight that met her eyes stopped her in her tracks, bringing to mind a painting of a graceful nude. Though startled by the jolt she felt in her groin and the maddening tingling beginning in her breasts, she drifted closer, drawn by Shelley's exquisite form. Lifting a hand to stroke the glorious skin that beckoned her, Angela fought against the temptation, desperately trying to bring her desire under control. Finally common sense prevailed, and she lowered her hand just as Shelley's eyelids fluttered.

Long lashes swept up, unveiling the sleepy blue they had hidden, and Angela's heart lurched. Shelley seemed unconcerned with her nakedness, but the look on Angela's face quickly heated her blood, filling her eyes with heavy-lidded passion. *Are you really here...or is this wishful dreaming?*

Angela consciously swallowed, and her words came out in a nervous rush. "Your door was open...I came on in. Didn't know you were sleeping. We're going to the Steak House. Do you want to come?"

Shelley's lips turned up, barely showing the gleam of her teeth. "Yeah, I do, if it's with you," she answered, her sultry tone lifting the fine hairs at the back of Angela's neck.

Angela reddened, but she chose to ignore the double entendre. "I apologize for walking in on you like this."

Shelley swung her legs to the floor and sat up, lifting her arms to straighten her tousled hair—an action that threatened to interfere with Angela's heartbeat. "No problem." She chuckled, looking down at her chest. "I don't have much to hide, anyway."

Struggling to restore some equanimity to her thoughts, Angela smiled and dug herself in deeper. "They say more than a mouthful is wasted." *That's "more than a handful," you idiot...either way, she's going to think that you're flirting with her.* In truth, Angela knew she was long past the flirting stage and it terrified her.

Shelley's eyes shifted to the full, enticing breasts right in front of her. Hardened nipples pushed against the stretched cloth, bearing testimony that no bra restrained them. Quickly, but gently, she encircled Angela's waist with her left arm and drew the almost mesmerized woman closer. Her passion-laden voice purred through Angela's heightened senses. "Let's...give that a test." Her mouth enveloped as much of the hot flesh as she could, sucking at it through the T-shirt's cloth, probing with her tongue until she heard Angela gasp. She let go just as Angela's hands buried themselves in her hair but she hadn't given up. Her right hand yanked up the front of the T-shirt and she resumed her pleasure with skin meeting skin.

Hooking her left thumb beneath the back band of Angela's shorts and folding the fingers of her right hand around the front band, Shelley started to tug.

"No!" Angela said urgently, momentarily winning the battle for self-control. "Stop, don't do this." *Oh, God, but it feels so right.* She grabbed handfuls of the raven hair and pulled, trying to detach Shelley's mouth.

While Angela's hands were tangled in her hair, Shelley loosened her mouth. Still holding Angela close, she abruptly stood up, sliding her bare skin against Angela's. Angela's mouth opened as she sucked in a breath, and Shelley bent her head and fused her lips to those below her. But she didn't attack with her tongue; she caressed with it, tenderly exploring until Angela's knees gave out.

Shelley supported her by moving a hand to Angela's buttocks. She began squeezing in a soft, seductive rhythm and Angela again tried to exert some control. She dragged her mouth sideways, away from Shelley's, and put her hands against Shelley's chest to thrust her away. When her pushing palms encountered bare breasts, Shelley whimpered and called her name, "Angela..."

Angela's resolve nearly deserted her but she regrouped, knowing that this was not the time to surrender to her rebellious desires. "Please, Shelley, please stop. You presume too much. I'm not ready for this." She laid her head on Shelley's shoulder and, to her chagrin, began to cry.

Perhaps the tears did it. With a tremendous effort, Shelley stopped her passionate aggression and leaned her head against Angela's. After straightening out the T-shirt, she moved her hand to the auburn tresses and kissed Angela's hair and forehead. "It's okay," Shelley murmured. "I won't push you if you don't want me to." *Oh, Angela, I thought you wanted me as much as I want you.*

Angela, still crying, pushed Shelley's hand away and shoved herself away from her embrace. The rejection hit Shelley's heart like a sledgehammer. She reached across to the lamp table for the box of tissues and handed it to Angela, then slumped down onto the bed with a bruised heart, not meeting Angela's eyes.

Angela knew she had hurt Shelley, but she was too distraught to do anything but run. She dashed into the corridor and shut the door. Leaning against the wall, she wiped her wet face with the handful of tissues she had grabbed, then slowly made her way back downstairs to her own apartment.

"Shelley coming with us?" Merrill asked as Angela entered the apartment. She had been watching television and didn't look up until Marva elbowed her in the side and nodded her head toward their friend. Angela hurried past them with a clenched jaw, strode into the bedroom, and slammed the door.

"I guess that's a no," Marva observed. "I wonder what happened?"

"We may never know," Merrill said with a sigh. "Angie isn't too good at baring her soul. She tends to hold things in."

Kath stood up. "Let's look on the bright side. If they had some sort of falling out, at least we won't have to worry about Angie getting too serious about someone with a bad past." She took the last potato chip from a bowl and crunched it in her mouth. "So are we still going to the Steak House?"

"Why don't you two go ahead," Merrill suggested. "I think I'll hang around, and see if I can lend Angie a shoulder to cry on."

Marva got up and joined Kath at the door. "Tell her we're on her side, okay?" she asked, then she and Kath left.

Merrill knocked on the bedroom door, but there was no answer. She looked down at her hand on the knob and hoped that she was doing the right thing as she turned it and went in. In the soft light of dusk, she could see that Angela lay in bed on her side, staring at the wall and giving no sign that she saw her.

Merrill sat down on the bed next to Angela's stomach. She reached up and swept her hand across her friend's brow then moved it across her hair. "You want to talk about it, honey?" she murmured.

For a while there was no sound from Angela, and Merrill continued to sit beside her with her hands lying loosely in her lap. At last, Angela slipped her hand into one of Merrill's and took a ragged breath. Merrill squeezed her hand and waited.

"I acted really stupid."

"How's that?" Merrill prompted when Angela didn't continue.

Angela had to clear her throat to speak. "Shelley made a move on me, Merry. Lord knows, I wanted her to. But I was too damn scared about getting involved with her, and I made a total ass of myself."

"You sure aren't the first one to do that, Ange," Merrill said soothingly.

"But I hurt her, Merry. I hurt her pretty bad, I think. God, she's only eighteen! And she's so gorgeous. How many people do you think have ever rejected her advances?"

"That's all part of growing up, Angie. Most people don't bat a thousand. How did she react? Did she do something that scared you?"

"No. She just kind of pulled inside of herself like most people do when they're hurt and can't, or won't, fight back. I'm embarrassed to see her tomorrow, Merry. She'll probably be embarrassed, too. I won't know how to act."

"You want me to talk to her?" Merrill asked.

"Oh, Merry," Angela said and chuckled softly, "no, I don't, but you are the best friend anyone could ever have. Lay here with me for a while, will you?"

"Sure, honey. Scoot over." Merrill lay down behind Angela and put her arms around her, pulling her close, praying that her nearness would bring some solace to her lonely friend.

Having Merrill so close did help, but Angela was too upset to be able to calm down very quickly. Her rebuff of Shelley brought back the heartache of Vicki's rejection.

"I don't want to hurt Shelley like Vicki hurt me," she murmured.

For a moment, the words startled Merrill. Angela never spoke about Vicki. Maybe it was time she should. "Angie, tell me about Vicki," she suggested softly.

Angela didn't answer right away, but Merrill felt a big sigh shudder through her and waited expectantly.

"You remember she went home with me," Angela began.

She and Vicki had been together for six months, and Angela was thrilled with her love. Tall, slender, and elegant, Vicki had just graduated. Soon she would be getting an apartment and starting her new job, but she had agreed to go home with Angela for a week at the beginning of summer vacation.

They were packing for the drive home. "Vicki, my folks don't know that I'm gay so be careful around them, okay?" Angela opened a drawer and laid a pile of shirts on the bed next to her open suitcase.

Vicki paused in her packing, put her hands on her hips, and cocked her head at Angela. She asked incredulously, "Are you ashamed of me?"

"Of course not. It's just that I don't feel comfortable yet about telling them you're my lover." She started sorting through the shirts, making a separate pile of the ones she would pack.

"Then why have you invited me to your home?"

"I want you to meet them. And I want them to meet you." Angela returned one pile of shirts to the bureau and put the other pile in one side of the suitcase.

"But they're not going to meet the real me if you insist on telling me how the hell to act," the blonde accused, her voice rising.

Angela had noticed as the end of the school year approached that Vicki grew more bossy and irritable. She had attributed it to the stresses of graduating and starting a new life. But, in her typical reaction, she overlooked her lover's nastiness and tried doubly hard to appease her.

"I'm not telling you how to act, Vick, I'm just asking you to
be discreet about our relationship. Someday when I get my courage up, I'll tell them, but that hasn't happened yet." Angela
grabbed a pile of shorts and began to sort them.

Vicki sat down on the bed and looked speculatively at
Angela. "I'll tell them for you."

"Right," Angela scoffed. "You better get your clothes
packed, or we won't get there before midnight."

"There you go again, trying to boss me around," Vicki
griped, but she got up and finished her packing, and they finally
got the suitcases loaded in her car and set out.

"So this is your hometown," Vicki remarked, checking it out
as they skirted around it. "The air sure could use some attention," she said and wrinkled her nose.

"That's the fertilizer from the mushroom houses," Angela
explained. Ashton, a city of about 60,000 residents, lay sprawled
deep in the heart of mushroom country in Chester County, Pennsylvania. A fresh breeze did its best to overcome the unpleasant
odor, but it was a losing cause. Other businesses had their homes
there, but the mushroom houses just outside the city limits made
their presence known without advertising.

Angela drove on past the edge of the city into the pleasanter
developments of the western suburbs and pulled in front of a
two-story brick and frame house. "This is it," she said. She
loved the home she grew up in and knew her parents were the
major reason for that. They were a close-knit family—except for
one thing. Angela knew they would be distressed if they knew she
was gay, and she had never told them. In fact, the only people
from Ashton who knew were Merrill and her fiancé, Jim Dursik.

Dorothy and Frank Wedgeway welcomed their daughter's
friend and treated her as their own. Almost reaching Frank's
5'10" height, the blonde young woman with cool brown eyes
seemed friendly though a little distant, except with Angela. She
stuck to her like a second shadow.

For most of the week, the girls took off by themselves, but
Dorothy planned one evening near the end of the week for them
to stay home and enjoy a cookout with just the four of them. The
beautiful weather held, and they had the cookout on the back
deck that Frank had built twenty years ago onto their then
brand-new house. They feasted on charbroiled steak, sauteed
mushrooms and onions, green-fried tomatoes with white gravy,
and a tossed salad.

Afterwards, Angela and Dorothy cleaned up while Frank and Vicki chatted over drinks. Angela and her mother were just coming back to the deck as the conversation turned to the rigors of college studies. "I'm kind of glad that Angie doesn't have a boyfriend right now," Frank said. "That could interfere with her study time."

Vicki gave him a rather strange look and made a noise very much like a snort. "You've seen us together this whole week, Mr. Wedgeway, and you still don't get it? I'm Angie's 'boyfriend.'" She glanced briefly at Angela, who had stopped so quickly that her mother bumped into her. "And I don't think us loving each other has hurt our studies at all."

Stunned, Frank slowly set his drink on the table next to him, gathering his scattered thoughts. "Are you trying to tell me you are gay?" he managed to ask.

"We are gay," Vicki corrected him. "I can't believe you didn't know that. Surely you must have guessed...Angie never made any pretense about it at school." She looked at a bewildered Angela with round, innocent eyes. "Did you, honey?"

Dorothy, moaning, stumbled over and sat in a chair next to Frank. Angela turned and ran from the deck, unwilling to cope with this unexpected disaster. She needed time to think.

To this day she could not forget the looks on her parents' faces. The remembrance made her squirm in Merrill's embrace. "They looked so shocked, Merry, and betrayed. I was devastated and so were they."

"What made Vicki do such a thing? She should have known better," Merrill wondered.

"They must have asked her to leave after that. She came upstairs to pack her clothes, and I confronted her. You know what she said? She said, 'You should have told them before, Angie. Here you were living in this lovely little house with this lovely little family and it was all a lie. A lie!' Then she looked at me very calmly and said, 'You might as well come with me now, I don't think you're very welcome here at the moment.'"

"So what did you do?" Merrill asked. Her heart ached for her friend and for Mr. and Mrs. Wedgeway. She could imagine how startled they must have been, and hurt. Merrill knew that Angela had spent some of the summer with Vicki, but the Wedgeways had never breathed a word to her about it.

"Like an idiot I told Mom and Dad good-bye and went with

her. They tried to get me to reconsider, but I couldn't do that. You know I was crazy about Vicki. Even when she was tormenting me, my love for her made me overlook it. We got an apartment, and I sent a postcard home with the address. Same time as I sent you one."

"What finally broke you and Vicki up? Was her telling your parents part of it?"

"In a roundabout way. Several weeks later, she said she wanted to have a serious talk with me. We sat down at the kitchen table..." Angela's voice got quieter and Merrill had to strain to hear her.

"What's so serious, Vicki? Is something wrong?" Angela's forehead wrinkled in a frown.

Vicki stared down at her hands, took a deep breath, and said, "Since we left your house, I've given our relationship a lot of thought, Angie, and it's not working. It's over. Go back home. I don't love you anymore."

Flustered, Angela stuttered, "Wha...wha...what do you mean? You don't...What makes you think you've stopped loving me?"

"You're a nice kid, Angie, and this was a lot of fun while we were at college," Vicki's cool voice pierced Angela's heart like sharp splinters of ice. "But I'm getting ready to start a new job—a new life—and I just can't see you in it. You're a typical small town girl, too unsophisticated to fit with my crowd of friends. I think a clean break is best for both of us."

"No one turns off true love like a damn faucet." Angela's pain was quickly turning to anger at her lover.

Vicki shrugged. If she felt disturbed about this breakup, her manner didn't indicate it. "Then maybe it wasn't true love. Because I sure as hell am turning it off. And you out."

Angela jumped up from the table and slapped Vicki across the face as hard as she could, snapping the woman's head to the side. "You rotten bitch!"

Vicki jumped up as well and bared her teeth in a snarl as she rubbed her cheek. "Look, Miss Goody Two-Shoes, I tried to be civilized about this, but apparently that doesn't suit you. This is just another indication of our differences." She had stuck a knife into Angela, and now she twisted it. "What do you think is so special about you anyway? I won't have a bit of trouble finding someone with more to offer than you have—and probably better at it, too. Get the hell out of here. Now."

"So I did." *With my heart in a thousand pieces.* Angela patted Merrill's hand. She could feel the dampness from Merrill's
tears soaking through her shirt where her friend's head lay
against her back.

Angela might sound accepting now, but Merrill knew the
agony she must have suffered at the time. Her silence for so long
showed that she had been badly hurt. "You were right, Ange, she
was a rotten bitch," Merrill said between sniffs.

"So I'm better off without her, right?" Angela asked almost
wistfully.

"Right." Merrill gave her a squeeze. "You'll find someone
who deserves you, Angie, just you wait and see."

"Right," Angela echoed with a small puff of rueful laughter.

"What happened when you went back home?"

Another sigh escaped Angela's lips. "At first we all just
kind of avoided any mention of what had happened. Then Mom
couldn't stand it anymore, and she called a family conference.
The three of us sat at the kitchen table and discussed my love
life—or lack thereof."

Angela stopped for a minute, remembering the stiffness they
all felt with each other. "We talked for a long time. At one point
Dad threatened to cut off my college money unless I promised
not to 'fool around with women.' But Mom talked him out of
that. Poor Dad. He seemed to think there was some switch I
could throw to 'change back,' and he didn't understand why I
wouldn't agree to do that. Things were just kind of left up in the
air. Who knows how they would feel about this whole bit with
Shelley."

"Oh, Ange, I feel so bad for you," Merrill groaned. She
could imagine Angela's distress. How terrible it would be if her
family insisted that she stop loving Jim.

"Thanks, Merry. Having you for a friend has been a great
comfort to me. Don't worry. Things will work out." Angela
finally quieted and gradually fell asleep.

Just before Merrill drifted off she thought about the other
lonely young woman in the rooms above them, wondering if she
had anyone to offer her comfort.

Chapter
7

Shelley was appalled. *How could I have been so stupid?
She'll probably never even want to speak to me again, and I
don't blame her. Who would want me anyway? Except for one-
night stands, maybe. And I don't want that; I want something
permanent. But no decent person would want to get tangled up
with me. It's too damn dangerous. For me, too. Why the hell can't
I just be like other people?*

She could feel the beginnings of rage flickering around her,
trying to gain a foothold. She stood up and started pacing, needing some physical action to release the murky tension trying to
build a base in her body. She knew that only physical activity
would free the terrible monster building up within her. If she
could just move enough, do enough, she would wear out the rage
before it seared her.

Back and forth, back and forth, endlessly pacing; setting
one foot in front of the other. After half an hour of such forced
effort, she went into the kitchen and stuck a mug of water in the
microwave, hoping a drink of tea would help calm her. The water
boiled, and she added a tea bag then stalked around the kitchen,
cursing herself, impatiently waiting for it to steep. She added
sugar and milk and gulped the mixture, burning her tongue. But
that pain held the rage at bay for a while longer.

She went back to her pacing, concentrating on each foot;
watching as it closed in on the spot she consciously picked out

for it on the rug. Crush...crush...crush against the rug, leaving a fresh imprint that disappeared quickly as the coarse filaments recovered. After another half an hour, she looked around her and became aware that she left no footprints.

Like I was never there. Like I am not here. Like I don't even exist...never have...never will. Like no one gives a damn about me. Because it's true—no one does give a damn about me. Only what I can do for them. And look at what I've had to do. Jumping around from school to school, never making any friends. At least none that meant anything to me...until now. And I've screwed that up too.

She put her hands against her stomach and pushed hard against it, as if she could imprison the rage within her belly so it wouldn't get as far as her mind. But she could feel it creeping past her entwined fingers, up her chest, past her neck, into her head where it hammered against her skull until she couldn't stand it anymore. Tears of pain and frustration ran down her cheeks. She picked up the tea mug and hurled it against the wall. Wicked satisfaction surged through her, accompanied by the gratifying crunch, and a small edge of the sluice gates lifted as the black rage oozed through the dam.

This rage was crafty: *Small, quiet things first,* it whispered; *keep the large noisy ones till last.* She ran into the bedroom and pulled out drawers, tossing clothes every which way, violently swinging her arms to knock things off the shelves and bureau tops, kicking and stomping against what she had knocked to the floor. *Aaaaargh.* Soon she dashed about from room to room, throwing dishes against the floor, kicking lamps into the walls, smashing chairs against tables...no longer caring what it was, or how large, or how noisy—everything was at risk...including her sanity.

BUMP! THUD! CRASH!
Angela and Merrill both jerked awake at the same time. "What the hell is that?" Merrill asked. The two women sat up on the edge of the bed, listening.
THUD! BANG!
"That's from upstairs, Ange."
"Oh, my God, it's Shelley. She must be trashing her room." Angela jumped up and slipped her sneaks on.

Merrill grabbed her arm. "Angie, you're not going up there. If she's that angry she could attack you." Merrill's face was white. She knew she was too small to physically stop Angela from going to Shelley's apartment, but she was fearful for her friend.

Angela tore her arm from Merrill's grasp and started away with Merrill following right behind her. "Don't you see? I have to go up there. It's my fault she's doing this, and she could get in big trouble. If anyone else tries to stop her and she assaults them, she'll lose her college agreement. She'll get kicked out because of me."

"What makes you think you can stop her? Sounds like the girl's gone berserk, for Pete's sake. Doesn't that tell you something?" Merrill was puffing with the exertion of keeping up with the longer-legged redhead.

They skidded to a halt in the midst of a group of students gathered in front of Shelley's door. "What's going on?" Angela asked.

"Sounds like she's tearing the damn place apart," one of the men said. "We've been knocking on the door, but she won't answer. Someone's gone for the superintendent of the apartment complex."

"Shit!" Angela banged on the door. "Shelley, it's me, Angela. Open up." She waited a moment but nothing happened so she tried several more times, keeping up a steady pounding and shouting. "Shelley! It's Angela! Let me in! I want to talk to you!"

After a long minute, a sound of movement came from the other side of the door, and it slowly opened onto a scene of destruction. Merrill grabbed Angela's arm. "I'm coming in with you," she said.

"No, please, Merry. You stay out here and appease the superintendent. Tell him we'll take care of any damage. Ask him to give us 48 hours. Okay?" Merrill nodded reluctantly, and Angela walked through the open door, which then slowly closed and locked.

Merrill put her ear against the door but heard nothing. *At least everything sounds all right.* She heard her name called and looked down the hallway to see a sleepy Marva and Kath coming towards her.

"What's going on?" Marva asked. "A damn herd of elephants congregating up here?"

Merrill grimaced. "Sounded like Shelley was trashing her room. Angela's gone in to quiet her down, and I'm supposed to run interference with the superintendent," she pointed past them, "who's coming down the hall right now."

The super's large, square body was hustling toward them. He obviously had dressed in a hurry and was finding it hard to look authoritative in sweatpants and a sleeveless underwear shirt. "What's the trouble?" he asked, pulling to a stop in front of the girls. Since they were immediately in front of the reported apartment, he ignored the other bystanders who had dropped back at his arrival. He pushed wisps of graying brown hair into some order with his pudgy hand.

"No trouble unless you want it to be trouble, Mr. Squires." Merrill pushed her head as high as she could, trying to make herself look taller, but the superintendent towered over her.

"Guess that depends on just what happened here," the man said gruffly, jingling the large ring of keys he held in one hand, "or what's going to happen."

"A friend of ours got really upset about something and trashed her room. Angie's in there calming her down, and we're going to clean it up for her tomorrow."

Mr. Squires knew the four friends by name, as he did most of his tenants. The friendly giant liked the majority of the students, and they appreciated how fairly he treated them. Occasionally, a bad one came along and upset the harmony of his building, but he tried to nip any trouble in the bud before it flourished.

"That's the new girl's apartment," he stated. "I was a little leery of her the first time I saw her. Too good-looking for her own good and that damn swagger of hers just invites trouble." A few murmurs were heard from the group standing nearby.

"She's okay, Mr. Squires. Just had some bad news and flipped out over it," Marva said, trying to soothe him.

"Yeah," Kath added. "Haven't you ever had any bad news that really upset you?" He looked down at the freckle-faced girl with the cinnamon-brown eyes. She reminded him of his younger sister, the only small person in his family, and one he adored. He wavered when she turned those pleading eyes on him.

He cleared his throat and rubbed his large hand across his upper lip, scrubbing the bottom of his nose. "You say you'll clean it up?"

"Give us 48 hours, and we'll have it good as new," Merrill pledged and the others nodded.

"Well," Mr. Squires hesitated, "I really should report this to the owner." The curious audience stopped their chitchat to hear the outcome of this statement.

Marva measured him with her dark eyes. Back home, a building super would be hinting for some bribe money, but Mr. Squires might consider that an insult. Then she had a flash of inspiration. "We'll cut the grass for you!" she offered.

He switched his gaze to her and pursed his chubby lips in thought.

"For two weeks," Kath added and saw him surrender. "Deal?"

"Deal," he agreed and the three smiles lifted his spirit. "But it better not happen again."

"We hope not, too, Mr. Squires." Merrill held a hand out to him.

He shook hands with each of the girls. "I'll see you this weekend for the grass-cutting," he reminded them. They nodded, and he ambled away down the carpeted corridor.

Merrill put her hands on her hips and stared at her two friends. "Okay, who cuts the grass?"

Kath and Marva looked at her, then at each other, and grinned. "Shelley!" they said together.

Angela stepped further into the room and took a very quick glance at the chaos: the kitchenette door hung halfway off its hinges; furniture was upended and the lighter kitchenette chairs were broken; pictures had been pulled from the walls and smashed across lamp tops; broken dishes, dented pots and pans, and silverware lay scattered throughout; powder or flour coated everything, and Angela could feel a gritty layer of either salt or sugar beneath her shoes. Of the areas visible to her, it seemed nothing was unscathed. The place was a study in systematic destruction.

Completing the survey of the rooms, her eyes came to rest on the nude figure leaning against the closed door. Hair awry and eyes wild, Shelley had several cuts and bruises on various parts of her body. *She looks like hell warmed over. She looks...beautiful anyway.*

The heavy pounding on the door, accompanied by Angela's shouting, had pierced the curtain of rage that enveloped Shelley. Now, Angela's presence was tearing at its remnants, dispersing the rage but exposing the flawed person within. With deep breaths shuddering through her, Shelley looked around wildly, poised for flight like a frightened animal.

Angela lifted her arms to the desolate girl, walked up close to her and stood there, waiting. The eyes slowly changed from wild to hurting, and Shelley ran her fingers through her hair in unconscious habit. Then she stepped into Angela's embrace and started crying in large gasps as though her tears had to fight to get out of her shaking body.

Angela held her and crooned soft noises to her, trying to soothe her agony. When she at last had her calmed, she released one arm and led her into the bedroom, searching for a clear spot to sit. The bedroom had been trashed, too. The closet door was closed, but every drawer in the place apparently had been thrown against a wall and the articles on the bureau top were jumbled as though a giant hand had crushed them. Practically the only empty spot in the whole apartment was the bed.

Unopposed by the robot-like Shelley, Angela sat her on the bed then fished a towel out of the mess. Taking giant steps across the disarray on the floor, she dampened the towel at the bathroom sink, then wiped Shelley's face and cleaned the smeared blood from the larger scratches on her body. She searched through the strewn clothing to find underwear, shorts, and a T-shirt for her and helped her to dress. Then she looked in the fridge, which had miraculously escaped Shelley's wrath, and brought a pint of orange juice to her. Shelley drank it all and placed the empty container on the side strut of the knocked-over lamp table.

Sitting down next to the taller girl, Angela took one long hand and clasped it between hers. "You're coming downstairs."

Heretofore unresponsive, Shelley shook her head.

Angela changed the clasp to a caress, stroking her hand. "You're about ready to collapse from exhaustion, Shelley. I'm taking you downstairs and putting you to bed on our couch. Tomorrow morning we can talk about this if you want to, or, if you don't want to, we won't. But we will help you straighten your place up."

Angela stood up and pulled Shelley up, too. "Come on, no arguments." She marched Shelley outside into the hallway. Her eyebrows rose as she saw all three friends still there, talking with a few other students who had lingered. "Everything's under control now, folks. You can go back to bed." Silently, the other girls followed as Angela continued to the steps and led Shelley down them and up the hall to their apartment. Marva and Kath returned to their own place without a single remark, and Merrill unlocked the door and stepped aside.

She followed Angela in and looked askance at her companion. "Shelley's going to sleep on the couch," Angela said matter-of-factly and marched over to the couch and sat Shelley on it.

Her lips pursed, but not speaking, Merrill collected a pillow and blanket from the bedroom. Angela took Shelley's shoulders, guided her to lie down on the couch, put the pillow beneath her head, and covered her with the blanket. Without a second thought, she leaned down and kissed Shelley's forehead. "Good night."

Angela turned off the living room lamp, followed her quiet roommate into the bedroom, crawled into her bed, and went to sleep, leaving a slightly bewildered Merrill to turn off the overhead light.

Although it was nearly noon, an overcast sky dimmed the morning light, restraining the day's brightness. The weather, though, couldn't be blamed for the cloud hanging over the four friends.

"I can't believe she's still asleep." Kath said.

As soon as Merrill figured Kath and Marva were stirring, she invited them over to the apartment for breakfast. The four women were sitting in the kitchenette, drinking coffee and talking in hushed voices.

Angela twisted her shoulders, trying to loosen the tension that had settled in them as soon as she woke up. "She has to be exhausted. That kind of trashing takes a lot of energy. Wait until you see the place."

"She's probably mentally exhausted, too. She looked like a zombie when you brought her in last night." Merrill took a tentative sip from her mug, then blew into it to cool it down. Realizing the futility of that, she poured more milk into it then turned to her roommate. "You scared the crap out of me, Ange, when you walked into that pit."

"Why would she hurt me, Merr?" Angela asked, as though nothing unusual had happened.

"Maybe because you rejected her? That sounds like a pretty good reason to me. People have gotten killed for that before," Merrill remarked indignantly.

Marva and Kath exchanged raised-eyebrow looks that they didn't even attempt to hide from Angela. "She made a move on you?" Marva was torn between being happy for proof that Shelley definitely was attracted to Angela and being worried that maybe they didn't want her to be. She made a face, understanding to some degree just what indecision Angela must be going through.

The redhead threw them a nasty glance. "Yeah, and I blew her off. You guys have been bending my ear for weeks about how dangerous she could be. Do you think I want to have a serious relationship with an unreformed criminal? I'm scared about these murders, too."

Merrill leaned forward and set her arms on the table. "Well, that's good news to me. I thought you said you didn't believe Shelley could be involved."

Angela sighed. "My heart still doesn't believe it, but my common sense tells me not to take any chances until we know better."

Marva stood up and gathered the empty mugs then set them in the sink. "Let's go up and see what needs to be done. The sooner we start, the sooner we finish," she ended in a singsong voice.

Angela washed the dirty dishes and set them in the drainer while Merrill gathered broom, dust pan, and trash bags. The redhead looked over her shoulder. "Kath, will you stay here with Shelley? I'll help Merry and Marv with the cleanup."

"No way! I'll help clean; you can stay here with Destructa." Kath was already half out the door. Her cautious nature balked at being alone with a girl she was half-afraid of.

Angela made a face at her. "Then get the vacuum, will you? It's in the closet. And you'll need the bucket and some rags, too." Kath eagerly gathered the items, happy that Angela hadn't argued with her.

A few minutes later, the cleaning brigade went out and Angela plopped on the floor opposite the couch. Rather than waste the time, she lifted a textbook from the bottom rack of the lamp table and began to study. In spite of the seriousness of the situation, Angela couldn't restrain the smile that worked its way onto her face as she heard the hum of a vacuum overhead. *Boy, do they have a job ahead of them. I bet Merry will be a drill sergeant up there.*

"Damn!" Marva remarked, "This place looks like a tornado hit it." Her eyes swept the destruction that had once been an apartment.

Kath nodded. "Except a tornado would have carried some of the trash away with it."

Merrill blew air out through her lips. "Let's get started." She made a quick tour of the three rooms. "Marv, how about if you and I pick up all the broken-and-can't-be-fixed stuff and stack it in that corner?" She nodded toward a corner of the living room. "Then we can run it down to the dumpster and make some room here to work."

She stuck her head in the bedroom and crooked a finger at Kath. "If you can shove some stuff out of that side and vacuum it, we can pile the clothes there."

She looked down at her feet. "What the heck is this gritty stuff that's all over the place?"

"I think it's sugar," Kath answered.

"Sugar? What makes you think that?" Marva asked. "It could be salt."

Kath reached down and grabbed a pinch of it and held it out toward Marva. "If you want to taste it, Miss Derby, you are welcome to. But whichever it is, it is going to be one helluva mess to clean up."

"Yeah," Marva groaned, waving a hand of denial toward the proffered taste. "Did anyone bring trash bags?" Marva walked to the closet and turned the handle. "Hey, this is locked."

"Good, that's less we have to clean up," Kath remarked practically. "Merry brought trash bags; they're in the living room in a bucket."

Marva got a bag, picked up the broken pieces of a lamp, and tossed it in. "Watch out for the broken light bulb," she warned her roommate.

Marva and Merrill worked diligently, gathering chairs, pictures, lamps, dishes, and whatever else they found broken and finally had a pile to take to the dumpster.

Kath cleared and vacuumed a place to stack the clothes then gathered all she found in the bedroom, sorted anything that had escaped the grit, folded it and put it away in the drawers she had restored to the bureau. She cleaned off the bed and bureau, straightened the toiletries that had been knocked around, and vacuumed the rest of the floor and made the bed. Then she started on the bathroom.

Merrill and Marva returned from the dumpster, and Marva attacked the kitchenette while Merrill worked on finishing the living room.

Kath came out of the bathroom and stood in the doorway between the kitchenette and the living room. "Have you guys noticed anything weird?"

Each woman shook her head. "Like what?" Merrill asked.

Kath swung an arm, indicating the whole apartment. "There's not one personal item in this whole place. No pictures, no knickknacks, no books, nothing. I find that kind of strange."

"I do, too, now that you mention it," Merrill agreed. "Then again, I find the resident of this apartment a little strange, too. But," she shrugged, "to each his own."

The women went back to work. After a couple of hours they were finishing up, when Merrill picked up a discarded article of clothing to throw in the hamper and something heavy fell out of it.

"Omigod," she muttered then raised her voice to the others, "Look what I just found!"

Angela sat quietly at her studies for a couple of hours before she heard Shelley move. Raising her eyes from the book, she met quizzical blue ones. In seconds the questioning look turned embarrassed and skittered away as Shelley tossed off the blanket and sat up, rubbing her head with both hands. Angela got up, and when the blue gaze came back to her she motioned with her chin. "When you're finished in the bathroom, come on into the kitchen. I'll get you some coffee."

Shelley shuffled from the bathroom into the kitchen and sat at the table. "Cream or sugar?" Angela asked before sitting opposite her.

"Neither, thanks," Shelley mumbled. She accepted the mug, wrapped both hands around it, and took a drink before meeting

Angela's gaze again.

"I guess I was a real idiot," the low voice confessed. "I thought you wanted..." Shelley turned away, emotion choking her velvet voice and twisting her face into an ugly smile.

A shaft of understanding hit Angela. Shelley's horrible smile about the stomach wound hadn't been one of sick humor; it was one of agony. She freed one of Shelley's hands from around the warm cup and captured it in her own, where it shook like a frightened child's.

"Shelley, I—I walked into your room and saw you on the bed, and you looked so gorgeous my good sense went right out the window, and some other senses took over," she admitted with a self-deprecating smile. "I didn't come up there expecting you to..." *Attack me? Jump my bones?* Neither phrase seemed to fit the aggressive but gentle way Shelley had approached her. At a loss for words, she finished with a shrug.

Shelley's head dipped. "You sure are sending mixed signals, Angela. You have me all confused." She sounded like a little child who was being punished and didn't know why.

Angela shifted uneasily, sympathy for the younger girl making her uncomfortable. "Maybe that's because I'm confused too. But mostly I'm scared."

Shelley's head jerked up. "Scared? Of me? Why?" *What could Angela know?*

Angela needed time to think. She released Shelley's hand and stood up. "You haven't eaten yet. I'll fix you some cereal." She pulled a bowl out of the cupboard, filled it with sugared cereal, and poured some milk on it. She set it in front of Shelley and gave her a spoon from the silverware drawer. Sitting back down, she fidgeted with the place mat, then looked at her companion.

Shelley lifted a spoonful of flakes to her mouth and crunched down on it, never taking her eyes from Angela's face. Angela sensed that in a waiting battle with Shelley she would be the loser. But the "evidence" against Shelley seemed flimsy now that it was about to be laid right out in front of her. Her background provided the only hard facts against her, and they weren't supposed to know anything about that. *Where are the others when I need them?*

The irony was that the others were upstairs, diligently cleaning the rooms of a woman they professed to suspect of murder.

Angela struggled to stop her fidgety hands and resorted to
clasping them in front of her atop the mistreated place mat. She
decided to answer Shelley's questions with half of the truth.
"I'm afraid to get involved with anyone right now. I'm just not
ready for it."

Shelley finished the cereal and pushed the bowl aside.
"Someone has hurt you," she murmured.

Angela nodded, and her hands jerked reflexively. She could
see that the whole sorry episode with Vicki was coloring her
reactions now.

"I'll try never to hurt you, Angela, I promise." The younger
girl's brow knit in concentrated sincerity.

Angela took a deep breath as her heart thudded in her chest.
"Shelley, I don't know anything about you: who you are, where
you come from, what family you have—nothing."

A hint of a lopsided smile barely moved Shelley's mouth.
"My name's Shelley Brinton, I come from a small town near
Philadelphia, and I'm...an orphan. My guardian's name is Helen
Ostcott. Judge Helen Ostcott."

Angela's eyebrows lifted as she feigned surprise. "Judge?"

"Yeah. I had some trouble with my temper a few years
back," she pursed her lips and briefly turned her eyes toward the
ceiling. "It wasn't all that serious, but I was made a ward of the
court."

Angela grimaced. Shelley was telling half-truths, too. "I can
believe the temper part."

Shelley blushed and rubbed the back of her neck with her
palm. "I'm sorry about that. I was just so damn frustrated...and
confused and..." *Hurt.* She hesitated for a moment, then came to
a decision. "I'm in an anger management program," she offered
in a subdued voice.

Angela's eyes widened. There was some news Kath hadn't
picked up. "Is it helping you?"

Shelley's eyes shifted away, and she squirmed a little on her
chair before returning her gaze to Angela. "Sometimes yes,
sometimes no. Like last night." Then she said something that
sent shivers along the redhead's spine. "But at least it was a
room I wrecked, not a person." Quickly realizing she had made a
mistake, Shelley groaned inwardly at the look that statement
brought to Angela's face.

Disturbed by the words, Angela took a moment to compose
herself before speaking. "Shelley, I'm very attracted to you. But

I think we should cool any idea of a relationship right now. I'm just not ready to trust anyone yet."

Even though she understood Angela's hesitation, Shelley's eyes clouded with disappointment. "I guess we need to get to know each other better. At least you haven't pushed me away altogether." She tilted her head quizzically, her tone serious. "Or have you?"

"Suppose we just play it by ear, see what develops, okay?"

Shelley reluctantly nodded. Her twisted lips turned into a rueful smile as she stood up. "Guess I better go help clean up."

"Sounds like a good idea," Angela agreed. She followed the taller girl out of the apartment and locked the door behind them, mentally berating herself for the thoughts generated by the ripple of muscles in the long, tan legs and slim hips moving along in front of her.

Shelley walked into her apartment with Angela right behind her and was greeted with a frozen tableau. Marva was leaning against a broom, while Merrill held up a pair of shorts in her hand. After a slight hesitation, Merrill lowered her hand and they both looked a little guilty, like they had been discussing something that Shelley and Angela's entrance had interrupted.

From where she was standing next to the door, Kath waited until Shelley walked past her, then silently pressed something into Angela's hand. The stares of the other friends locked onto it.

Angela looked at the object but didn't recognize it. About six inches long and half an inch wide, it was made of ivory. Its carved surface had a small round area on it that looked something like a button. As Angela's thumb moved toward the circle, Shelley turned around and followed the girls' stares.

Suddenly, a forceful grip encircled Angela's wrist. "Stop!" Shelley demanded, as her other hand closed over Angela's thumb. She extricated the object from the redhead's hand then let go of her. Her initial shock calmed after she had the object in her hand.

Angela rubbed her wrist and frowned at Shelley. "What was that for? What is it?"

Marva answered, her tone ominous. "It's a switchblade, honey. That's something you don't even want to mess with."

A chill shivered through Angela, and she fought to suppress

the alarming question that leaped into her mind: Had she just held a murder weapon in her hand?

"This one's sharp as a razor." Shelley pushed the button, and the girls recoiled slightly as they heard the *snick* of it opening. They watched aghast as the tall dark-haired girl ran her fingers across the edge of the blade. Shelley looked around, finally noticing the apprehensive expressions on the girls' faces. "I'm out by myself a lot," she mumbled. "I carry it for protection." Putting her hand along the side of the blade, she pushed it closed. Her fingers rubbed over the carved handle, then she slid it into her pocket.

"Aren't they illegal?" Kath asked, then turned red as Shelley beamed her blue eyes onto her like a beacon.

The taller girl shrugged. Her lips turned up in a sly smile, and she half-whispered, "Not if no one knows you have it."

This newest turn of events confused Angela. The newspaper accounts of the murders had described the victims as being cut with a "razor-sharp blade." She didn't want to think that Shelley might be a killer, but evidence seemed to be mounting against her. There was not enough to go to the police with, but the decision to be as careful as possible made more and more sense.

"Having that in your possession could get you in a lot of trouble," she warned.

"Or get you out of trouble," Shelley stated, raising her eyebrows. "Depends on your point of view, I guess."

Merrill kept glancing from Angela to Shelley. She saw Angela's confusion but didn't know how to help her friend. In fact, she was frightened for her. Merrill leaned strongly toward believing in the possibility of Shelley's guilt, but didn't want to arouse the girl's suspicions. All she wanted to do right now was finish with the cleaning and get out of the apartment, so they could discuss the situation in light of the new development. "Come on, let's finish up here," she said into the awkward silence.

"Right," Marva agreed and started to sweep with the broom she held in her hands. "Kath, grab the dustpan, will you?" Kath came to life and held the dustpan while Marva swept up the debris from a small area the vacuum had missed. Merrill took the shorts to the bedroom and shoved them into the stuffed hamper.

Angela tore her eyes from Shelley's and looked around the rooms. The women had worked wonders in the short time they had been cleaning. The broken chairs and lamps would need replaced, but they had cleaned up the wreckage, put everything else back in reasonable order, and vacuumed the furniture and rugs.

A subdued Shelley apologized to all of them for the mess and thanked them for their generosity. The four friends gathered their cleaning materials and returned to Merrill and Angela's apartment, about to burst with the need to talk about the knife.

Chapter
8

"Aunt Helen?" Shelley grew nervous as her guardian answered the phone. "I thought I better let you know before you heard it somewhere else. I trashed my room last night." Too tall to stretch out comfortably on the couch, Shelley was lying on the floor with her feet propped up on it, and the phone resting against her shoulder.

"Shelley," Helen's voice sounded more sympathetic than disappointed, which bolstered the girl's spirits a bit. "What happened?" Helen laid the brief she had been reading down on the end table, next to her tea. She removed her glasses and rubbed her hand across her eyes, then resettled the frames over her ears.

"I told you about the girl I was attracted to. I tried...I made...She rejected me. And I went berserk." Shelley sucked her lips between her teeth and closed her eyes.

Alarmed, Helen raised her voice. "You didn't hurt her, did you?"

"No!" Shelley protested vehemently, her eyes flying open. "She wasn't even in the apartment then."

Helen sighed. Shelley had reason to feel rejected in so many ways. It would have been nice to have her find acceptance in this. *But possibly dangerous.* "I thought we had agreed that you wouldn't pursue this relationship?"

It was Shelley's turn to sigh. "I know that's what you wanted, but I never agreed to that. If you remember, I argued about it."

"You do agree that it could be dangerous for you—and for her—don't you?" The judge sipped at her tea, but it didn't seem very soothing at the moment.

"Yeah, I do," Shelley sounded discouraged. "I don't think I have much chance with her anyway. She and her friends seem suspicious of me."

Helen's antennae went up. "Suspicious? In what way?" She hurriedly set the teacup in the saucer, rattling the spoon that sat there.

"Angela keeps saying she doesn't know anything about me. I gave her some background, even told her about my anger management program, but it didn't seem to be enough." Shelley heard the china rattle and briefly closed her eyes. "Then, her friends were cleaning my rooms for me, and they found my knife. They started to look at me kind of funny after that, leery like."

"You promised you would keep that knife out of sight," Helen said uneasily.

"Well, I didn't hand it to them, Aunt Helen." Shelley's impatience was beginning to be evident. She sat up and began running her fingers through her hair.

"No, but if you had been more circumspect, they wouldn't have found it," Helen chided her ward. She shook her head and laid it back against the chair.

"And if I hadn't lost my temper none of this would have happened. But I did, and now I have to cope with it," Shelley said, her voice flat. "But if they report me, I might need some help. From someone with legal authority...like a judge."

"You know I'll help you as much as I can, Shelley. I always do, don't I?"

"Yes, you do...and thanks, Aunt Helen. You're the one person I can always count on. I love you. Good night."

"I love you, too, darling. Good night." Helen laid the phone down, took another sip of her tepid tea, and made a face. *Will it ever end? And just how involved is she?*

Helen picked the phone back up and dialed Jeff Cruz, the man who had introduced her to the troubled girl four years before. He and Helen had kept in constant touch. "Jeff? I just talked to Shelley." She explained their conversation and emphasized that she might need to intervene for Shelley if the police arrested her. "I'm getting very disturbed by the situation that

seems to be developing. I can't continue to move her from college to college—that would be too noticeable. I think we need to
go to the next step."

Helen removed her glasses and laid them on top of the brief,
too agitated to keep her mind on work. She listened intently to
Jeff's suggestions. "Yes, that sounds like the best possible solu-
tion. Thanks, Jeff. Keep me informed of your progress."

"So what do you think about the knife?" Merrill started the
discussion as soon as the cleaning materials were put away, and
everyone had grabbed a soda and flopped in the living room. The
girls could have used a beer, but they had mutually decided not
to keep beer on the premises except for special occasions. Too
many students drank their way through college instead of studying their way through, making a mockery of the education they
were paying for.

"Scares me just to look at it," Kath said, clasping her arms
around her body. Marva and Angela sat on the floor, granting the
couch to Kath and Merrill.

Marva reached over and tugged on Kath's ankle. "I won't let
anyone hurt you, darlin'. They'd have to go through ole Marv
first."

This declaration of loyalty brought a sweet smile to Kath's
freckled cheeks. Then her face clouded. "A knife like that would
be hard to stop."

"It sure would," Merrill agreed. "And what really scares me
is that it's in the hands of a woman who went berserk and trashed
her rooms. What if someone had walked in on her?"

"I did walk in on her, and she never touched me," Angela
declared. "At least not in anger," she added softly.

Merrill's eyes darted toward her, and her brows lifted as a
slight blush diffused across the redhead's complexion. "I helped
her get dressed," Angela asserted, provoked by Merrill's gaze.
She could see Merrill's brain assimilating this information, and
it bothered her.

"Ange," her friend exhorted, "we have to face the facts
here."

"What facts, Merry? A new girl shows up. She takes off at
odd times of the night, and nobody knows where." *But I don't
think it's to meet a lover.* "She doesn't tell us anything about her

background, and that's no surprise because we find out—illicitly, I might add—that she has a criminal background of assault and battery." Angela held the cold soda can against her forehead, attempting to minimize an incipient headache.

"She saves me from getting smacked in the chops by Hurtz which, instead of being a point in her favor, turns you all further against her. Then she makes a move on me, and I am so paranoid about the suspicions you have that I turn her down, and she goes berserk from frustration and trashes her room." Angela paused before the next sentence, shaken by its implications.

"And then we find a knife," she continued, "but we know she was a juvey, so why are we so appalled?"

"A juvey?" Kath asked.

"A juvenile delinquent," Marva answered.

"Oh," Kath replied, then frowned. "Isn't that more reason why she shouldn't carry one?"

"Exactly," Merrill answered. "Angie, we know our suspicions have no really incriminating facts to support them. I for one believe they are enough to indicate—certainly not definitely but at least possibly—that Shelley is the killer. I think we should report the knife if only to get it on record that she has one. How do you all feel?"

All three women looked toward Angela, who sighed. "What if she's just a lonely kid who has a bad temper?"

Merrill slid down off the couch and sat next to Angela. She picked up her best friend's hand and held it. "Angie, I sure as hell will be happier if we're wrong than I will be if we're right. If we're wrong, we'll explain everything to Shelley, including the fact that you didn't believe us. If we don't do anything, and we are right, I think we all would have trouble living with our-selves. We have to report her. We have no choice."

Angela bowed her head, then nodded, and Merrill patted her hand. "Good girl. I'll call the campus police."

A terrible feeling of betrayal surged through Angela. She turned her head away and wiped her palm across the tears that trickled down her cheeks as Merrill reached for the phone.

It wasn't the campus police who came for Shelley. Because of the notoriety of the murders on nearby campuses, they had contacted the township's police chief. He sent four officers, two male and two female, to arrest her. Word spread quickly when the patrol car pulled up in front of the Brickhouse. Half the complex was in the halls or standing outside, providing a backdrop of murmuring students, curious to see what was happening.

When the dark-haired beauty came down the steps with her arms pulled behind her back and handcuffed, her eyes skipped to Angela, conveying pain and disbelief. Angela swung around and went back to her room, too disturbed to continue watching.

After a while her other friends joined her, and they all sat around in silence, the TV on just to fill the void.

Kath couldn't stand it any longer. "What do you think they'll do to her?" she asked.

"Question her, no doubt," Angela answered. Her voice sounded weary. "Maybe even keep her."

"I felt kind of bad that everyone in the place saw her being led away. What if she is innocent?" Kath knew that she'd been just as afraid as the others that Shelley could be a killer. She had believed that the girl should be turned in, but now her soft heart was fighting against her fear.

"Let's leave that to the police, Kath," Merrill pleaded. "That's the whole idea, isn't it?" Merrill's chestnut curls bounced as she shook her head and looked into each girl's face. "We all agreed to this, remember? We've no reason to feel guilty about it. We're trying to protect people."

Marva's vibrant voice shook with emotion. "I feel like I'm being torn apart. One minute I hope we're right and have saved some innocent lives, and the next I think of Shelley and I hope we're wrong."

Angela stood up, walked to the door, and left the apartment, stunning the remaining three. Merrill reacted first. "You think this is tearing you up, Marv, how do you think Angie must feel? She's got to be tired of us going over and over the same things about the situation. To tell you the truth, I'm tired of it myself. I wish Shelley had never showed up here."

"Me, too," Kath added.

"Well, I'm not," Marva surprised them by saying. "Angie was going through her days like a damn zombie before Shelley came. At least the girl changed that."

Merrill considered the thought-provoking idea. "She did, didn't she? Maybe some good will come out of this, after all."

"Yeah," Marva agreed, staring toward the door their friend

had left through, "but I wonder if Angie feels that way?"

The police station was just off the center of the town of Spofford on a short side street. Made of the same greenish-gray stone that was prevalent in the area, it stood stolid and square, two stories high. Polished slabs of darker stone formed five steps, twelve feet wide by eighteen inches deep. The steps reached a walkway of the same dark stone that ended ten feet later at twin doors made of heavy double-paned glass.

Shelley stepped out of the car at the request of an officer and was led up the steps into the building. The entourage passed by the reception area, past the sergeant's desk with a nod to the blue-clad man seated there, and into the processing center, where they removed her handcuffs. After being fingerprinted, photographed, and relieved of her personal effects, she was taken to an interrogation section. Shelley was told to sit in a chair at the only one of the three desks manned by another officer. Her escort handed him some papers and left.

"Miss... Brinton," the studious-looking man said, checking her name on the papers he had been handed, "were you read your rights?" He bit his words off as though he were a drill sergeant.

"Yes, I was, and I want to make a phone call." Shelley was sitting with her back straight as a board, her bowed head staring at the hands she was twisting in her lap.

"You'll get a chance to make a phone call, miss. First we have a few routine questions to ask you."

"I don't answer anything until I have legal representation."

"These are just the usual background questions, Miss Brinton. You don't need a lawyer yet." The officer picked up some other papers and began to shift them around.

Shelley lifted her head and pinned him with her eyes. "Where can I make my phone call, Officer... " She switched her look to the nameplate on his desk then back again, "Gibbons?"

The officer stared at her for a moment, debating whether to enforce his authority. But something in her gaze made him suspect he would be wasting his efforts. There would be time later to let her know who was in charge here. *These beauties think the world revolves around them.*

"Suit yourself. You'll just be paying for an extra half-hour of your lawyer's time." He stood up and came to her side. "Come on." He took her arm and steered her to a windowless room that held only an empty desk and a phone. "You got ten minutes," he said and left.

Shelley sat down with her elbows on the desk and dropped her head into her hands. Long fingers spread through her short hair, mussing it. "Damn, damn, damn," she intoned, then shivered. After a minute, she raised her head, pulled the phone to her, and dialed a very familiar number.

"Aunt Helen? We've got a problem. I've been arrested."

At the other end, Helen Ostcott unknowingly mirrored her ward's actions, putting her head in her hand and rumpling her gray-streaked hair.

"I know you were expecting this, Shelley, but I'm sorry it happened. I hate anything that draws unwelcome attention to you. But I made a few contacts after your last call, just in case, and everything is set up. Give me a few minutes to put it in action, and you'll be out of there in a half-hour or so. How are you, otherwise? Anything strange going on?"

"No, I'm okay. Thanks, Aunt Helen, I really appreciate this. I love you."

"You're welcome, dear. Keep your eyes open. I love you, too." *I just pray that this doesn't work against you.*

The women hung up and Shelley went to the door and knocked. When the officer opened it, Shelley gave him a cool smile. "You'll be hearing from my lawyer shortly."

Officer Gibbons led her back to his desk and motioned for her to sit. He sat behind the desk and picked a piece of paper out of the bunch spread across his desk. His eyes moved down its length then he looked at Shelley, who sat there with the same cool smile on her face. Irritated, he snapped at her. "You know you are facing a charge of possessing an illegal weapon."

Anal guys like you give good cops a bad name. Shelley put her elbow on the chair arm and set her chin on her hand, saying just to bait him, "I have a permit."

Gibbons snorted. "There's no such thing as a permit to have a switchblade."

Shelley shrugged just as the officer's phone rang. His irritation carried into his voice as he answered, "Officer Gibbons." His eyes flicked to Shelley. "She's right here." He picked up his coffee mug, intending to take a sip. "Do what?" he shouted and slammed the mug down, sloshing coffee onto the papers on his desk. "Says who?"

Helen's voice stayed soothing. "I repeat. This is Judge Ostcott. I have an order in hand for Shelley Brinton to be released at
once and any charges dropped."

"No way. You have to come in here with those papers...
Your Honor." He tried to sop up the spilled coffee one-handedly
with tissues.

Helen's voice hardened. "Very well, Officer Gibbons, the
next voice you hear will be Police Commissioner Dougal's." She
hung up on Gibbons' reply and dialed the commissioner.

"He won't listen to me, Pete. Says I need to bring the order
in to him. Take care of it, will you, please?"

"Sure will, Helen. And don't forget you owe me some of
your homemade chocolate chip cookies."

"I'll remember, Pete. You'll get some of the very next
batch. And thanks."

Officer Gibbons dried the coffee from his hands and
smirked at Shelley. "Could have been anyone who made that
phone call. I guess some people think all they have to do is
threaten me and I'll give in."

Shelley's cool smile never changed; she pointed at the
phone when it rang, irritating Gibbons further. *Cocky bitch.*

"GIBBONS!" The angry voice pulled Gibbons up straight in
his chair. He had heard the commissioner's voice often enough to
recognize it even when he shouted.

"Yessir?" he quickly answered.

"You just had a call from Judge Ostcott?"

"Yessir. But how did I know if it really—"

"GIBBONS!" Pete Dougal didn't wait for his reply.
"Release Shelley Brinton and drop all charges. Now."

"Yessir, I will, sir." He winced as the other phone crashed in
his ear, then mumbled curses under his breath as he felt Shelley's
arrogant gaze on him.

He fought for a moment to get his anger under control,
which really tickled Shelley. *Been there, done that,* she thought.

"You are released from custody, Miss Brinton," he said
through tight lips.

Shelley stood and held out her hand. "My knife, please," she
asked, laying on the politeness.

Gibbons swallowed a sly smile. "What knife? I haven't seen
any knife." He signed a paper and handed it to her. "You can pick
up your personal effects at the front desk."

Had Shelley known where the knife had been put, it would

be back in her hand. But she hadn't seen where it was, and she knew Gibbons would just love for her to start something. She could get another one, but she would ask Aunt Helen to retrieve this one for her—because of its sentimental value.

Oh, well, might as well let the jerk have the last word, give him a chance to save a little face. She started to turn away, then swung back. *But not today!*

She leaned over closer to Gibbons and said very quietly but distinctly in her throaty voice, "When you find my knife, stick it up your tight ass...and hit the trigger." She straightened up, and her face broke into a genuine, cheek-splitting smile as she watched Gibbons turn several different shades of red.

"Ta-ta," she waved and walked out.

Angela, fleeing the well-meaning but painful discussions about Shelley, had wandered around the building and found a seat on one of the wrought-iron benches in the rear courtyard area, not even noticing the coolness of the metal against the bare skin of her legs. Paved with decorative stone in varying shades of gray, the yard boasted several Japanese maple trees ringed with beds of daffodils and hyacinths. The benches had tables set near them where many students ate their meals or studied, but for now the place was empty.

The fresh air, scent of hyacinth, and lovely ambience were lost on Angela as she sat there with her head bowed. Her mind teemed with thoughts about the whole sorry situation and her even sorrier part in what had happened. An occasional tear tracked its way down her cheeks until finally she searched the pockets of her shorts for a tissue. Coming up empty-handed, she used her palm to smear the dampness. Through the blur of tears she saw a hand offering some tissues to her, and she took them, wiped her face and eyes, then looked up, expecting to see Merrill.

Shelley stood there, her expression unreadable. "Omigod, you're back!" Angela said. A wave of relief swept over her. "I'm so happy that they let you go. I had visions of your having to stay in jail. How did you get out so fast, anyway?"

Shelley had noticed before that Angela talked almost non-stop when something upset her. *Well, she should be upset.* She sucked in a deep breath and let it burst out through her lips, then plopped down on the bench a couple of arm lengths away. "My aunt made a phone call and said all the right words. They kept the knife."

Shelley stared at Angela for a long time, and Angela returned the stare, the two of them lost in each other's eyes. Shelley shook her head to break the connection, flopping a shock of raven hair onto her forehead. Her gaze darkened and she ground out her words. "Angela, why did you turn me in to the police? You could have threatened me with telling the campus police about the switchblade, and I would have gotten rid of it." *Or at least hid it better.*

Angela turned red and her voice sharpened. "It wasn't just the knife. We've all been nervous about the killer who's in the area. Then you come along, tall, dark, and mysterious. You sneak around at night, and nobody knows where. You tell a bare story about your background that could easily be a fake. You forced Hurtz to back down with such a fierce look it scared all of us. Then we find the switchblade, and all that other stuff looms larger in our minds." She stopped and caught her breath, then admitted the truth. "We're afraid."

Shelley looked at Angela and her eyes widened. "You guys are afraid of me?"

Angela nodded, her jaw clenched.

Shelley frowned. Suddenly understanding what Angela was getting at, she barked, "You think I'm the killer!" She jumped up, and Angela flinched. "Damn, damn, damn." Shelley strode back and forth waving her arms, her face showing anger and hurt. "You mean to tell me that you've been friendly to my face and all along you've been thinking that I'm a killer? I don't believe this. I know we haven't been hanging around much together, but at least I thought you girls were my friends."

She swung back to Angela and roughly shoved the hair from her eyes, betrayal eating at her like a burrowing worm. The rasp in her voice scraped along Angela's nerves. "That's what this was all about all along, wasn't it? Is that why you pushed me away? Because you think I'm evil?"

Angela's jaw set, and she shook her head. "I don't know what to think. We hardly know anything about you. For instance, where do you go at night?"

Shelley's eyes shifted, and she looked away. "I...can't answer that."

Angela's heart fell. She had been sure Shelley would tell her some plausible reason for her nocturnal wanderings, something the other girls would accept. "Good God, Shelley, help me out here. Everyone's wondering where you disappear to."

Shelley's chin jutted out. "I don't have to make excuses. It's nobody else's business where I go."

Angela found Shelley's lack of cooperation exasperating. "That doesn't do much to make us believe in you."

Shelley winced. "I can't tell you. It could get someone else in trouble. Can't you just trust me?" She sat back down, closer to Angela than before, and laid her arm across the back of the bench behind Angela's shoulders. Even with her anger at Angela, it was a struggle to keep from putting her arm around her. She leaned forward. "Angela, look into my eyes. I... am... not... the... killer."

Angela was very conscious of the warmth of Shelley's arm behind her, Shelley's bare leg almost touching hers, Shelley's gorgeous face so close, so close...

"I don't trust you," she said, surprising herself. "I can't. There are just too many coincidences, too many unanswered questions." *I don't trust myself either. Merry's right. I was wrong when I believed in Vicki; I could be wrong to believe in Shelley. I can't take that chance.*

Shelley straightened up and pulled her arm back, her face a granite mask. "Until the killer is found, I can't do anything about that doubt in your mind."

Angela let the silence grow. She felt torn apart and had no idea how to mend the breach.

Shelley sat a while, staring at the ground, then turned back toward Angela. Her voice grew intense and her eyes glistened. "I want to get to know you, Angela, to give us a chance to find out what we can mean to each other. There's not much likelihood of that while you're not sure of me." She stood up. "When that doubt is gone, I'll come after you." She turned and walked away.

The sun went behind a cloud, and Angela shivered, only partly due to the unexpected chill. *When that doubt is gone, I'll come after you.* Shelley's voice seeped into Angela's consciousness, but with so many questions, she just couldn't muster the trust to believe the words wholeheartedly. *She'll come after me? Surely that must be a promise, not a threat?*

Angela's gaze followed the retreating figure with the wide shoulders, slim hips, and slight swagger that had caught her eye that first day at the softball field. Her initial attraction was deep-

ening into something more whether she wanted it to or not, and it
frightened her. She brought her hand to her chest and rubbed it,
trying to ease the ache Shelley's departure had planted there.

Chapter 9

On her way to drama class, Shelley strode down the crowded corridor of the Performing Arts area, seemingly oblivious to the stares and double takes she received from both male and female students. She used to be comfortable with her beauty, but now she perceived it as possibly dangerous to her.

She knew it was prudent for her to remain unnoticed, unremarkable, and better yet, invisible. She shrank from being in any plays that might be shown publicly or even to the student body. If fewer people saw her, fewer would be able to identify her. Because of this she wasn't too sure of the wisdom of being in a drama class, but her anger management doctor had recommended it. She thought she better stay on his good side, or he could report her to the court.

Mr. Sindbourne had given her several one-act plays to look at and allowed her to choose one she would like to read for. He assured her that they were only for presentation in class. One play concerned a woman running for public office who had a terrible secret in her past; in the second one, the protagonist was in charge of a military outpost about to be overrun; and in the third, a woman was debating whether to run away from her abusive boyfriend or kill him before he killed her. *Three great choices there, Ed,* she thought derisively.

But she could see the dramatic opportunities in each scenario, and she read each one several times before she told Mr.

Sindbourne she had chosen the abusive boyfriend one. Today, she and another student, Ted Hoffman, would read the parts from the script, and next week they would present the act.

Shelley and Ted took center stage and began to read. The play was going well until Ted was shouting at Shelley and, following the script, threw a fake punch at her. Shelley had her head down, and without thinking she stepped toward him and caught the half-punch full on her jaw. She threw her script on the floor, grabbed Ted by the throat, and pushed him across the stage, up against a backdrop. Seething, she drove her hand into her empty shorts pocket and made a fist. She stood there a moment, fighting her anger, while Ted just watched her, his dark blue eyes wide open.

Mr. Sindbourne had reached them by this time and he spoke to her. "Shelley, calm down. It was an accident. That punch was part of the script."

Shelley's rapid breathing was audible to the whole class. Gradually, it slowed down and she released Ted's throat. "Sorry," she mumbled and dropped her gaze.

"No problem," Ted grinned and massaged his neck. "If somebody slugged me, I'd fight back, too."

Shelley raised her eyes and observed his sincerity then quirked a quick smile. "Thanks."

"Okay, folks. Let's try that fake punch again... only this time don't move, Shelley." Mr. Sindbourne tilted his head and smiled until Shelley smiled back at him and nodded. "Good, let's get back to work."

After class, Ted came up to Shelley. "Do you think we could find some time to practice the play together before next week? How about coming to my apartment and we can give it a try?"

Shelley grinned sheepishly. "Well, if you're going to trust me not to choke you to death, how about you come to my place instead? Friday after softball—about 7? 212A Bricker Apartments."

"Hey, I live at the Brickhouse too. Even the same floor, down at the end--236A. I'll be there Friday."

They walked out to the bike rack. "You ride a bike too?" Shelley asked.

"Yeppers. That one over there," Ted answered. "I have a car, but sometimes a bike is easier." They unlocked their bikes and rode back to the apartments together, chatting idly, mostly about Ted having grown up in a small town.

He had Shelley laughing at some of his anecdotes, especially the ripe tomatoes one. "I was twelve years old. In my current fantasy world, I was a demolitions expert in charge of saving the world. I had a sack of overripe tomatoes—my bombs—and police cars were the tanks of the enemy invaders. I hit all three cars on the local force before I got caught. For punishment I had to wash the three cars every week for the rest of the summer. It was more embarrassing for my dad than for me. I was the savior of the world, but he was the Chief of Police."

Shelley decided he seemed like a pretty nice guy. And Ted decided Shelley seemed like a gorgeous but mysterious girl who hadn't told him one darn thing about herself.

With those pleasant thoughts, they steered homeward.

A quarter moon hung in the black sky as Shelley pedaled her bike toward her destination. The night air carried the light chill of spring, and she hunched her shoulders against it, glad that she had decided to wear her jeans. Nocturnal insects played their symphonies, and the scent of early flowers and mown grass floated through the air. Shelley took a deep breath, recalling Aunt Helen's words about the season: Spring smells like new beginnings.

The raven-haired girl slowed to turn onto the boulevard lined with oak trees and rhododendron bushes that passed near the entrance to Spofford College. She heard a sound and turned her head to the left, but it was a planned diversion. Several bodies hit her from the right. One grabbed the bike's handlebars, and the others pounded on her, knocking her onto the ground. The attackers had to come around the bike, and that gave Shelley the chance to roll away and flip onto her feet.

Six hooded people were coming at her. She straight-armed the first one in the nose with her left fist and caught the second in the jaw with her right one. She flung her leg out and struck another face trying to get her from the side, then pirouetted and kicked another under the chin. Her foot caught under the edge of the hood, tearing it from the attacker's face. Shelley recognized the attacker a split-second before something hard struck her in the side of the face, and she went down. The last she remembered, the bodies were gathered around, kicking her...

She woke up curled next to a rhododendron without any

idea of how she got there. She only knew she was in pain. She lay there for a while, giving her mind a chance to absorb what had happened. Gradually, her memory returned, filling in the missing details. She struggled to her knees and began to crawl around, hoping that her bike had been left unscathed. Luckily, she found it undamaged behind the next bush. It took every bit of willpower she had to stand, lift the bike up, and put a leg across it. Her face, head, and body screamed at the damage that had been done to them.

Grinding her teeth so hard they squeaked, she pedaled very slowly homeward. She rode the bike right up to the door of the Brickhouse and fell rather than climbed off of it, letting it clatter to the walkway cement. She crawled to the door and opened it from the telescoping key chain attached to a belt loop of her jeans. She crawled inside and took one discouraged look at the stairway before turning right and moving slowly down the corridor to 112A.

Merrill was already asleep, and Angela had changed into her pajamas but was putting the finishing touches on a paper for statistics class. She lifted her head when she heard a strange noise—a sort of scratching—but couldn't determine its origin. She turned toward the window when it came again, more like a knock this time, then realized it was coming from the door. Walking over, she looked through the peephole but didn't see anything. She was about to turn away when the sound came again. Perplexed, she opened the door on its chain, bracing a foot against it for safety. Her eyes dropped to the damaged face peering up at her.

"Omigod, Shelley! What happened?"

"Hurts," the dark-haired girl managed to say.

Appalled, Angela slid the chain loose, opened the door, and reached for her.

"No...crawl." She pulled together what energy she still had and crawled past Angela, toppling over onto her side in the middle of the green carpet, her arms wrapped around her middle.

Angela, her stomach churning with concern, knelt next to her and tried to assess her injuries. "Shelley, you need a doctor."

A long hand fell over hers and squeezed her wrist. "No. No Doctor. Promise." A smile faltered on her bleeding lips. "Not unless I start to die."

"My God, Shelley, this is nothing to joke about. You need help."

"You help. Ice."

Angela jumped up and ran to the fridge. She collected several ice packs that she, like all athletes, kept in her freezer and grabbed some dishtowels to wrap them in. Hurrying back to Shelley, she wrapped the packs in towels as fast as she could, placing them on various parts of the injured girl's body. She saved the last one for her face. Tears came to Angela's eyes as she looked closely at the damage. Something blunt had hit the right side of her face, making it swell out of proportion and blackening her eye. Her lips were swollen and bleeding from the inside where her teeth had cut into them. Her nose and left eye were undamaged, but her chin had a nasty bruise.

Judging from the looks of her face and her inability to stand, Angela reckoned her body must be in just as bad shape. She pulled the afghan from the back of the couch and covered Shelley, tucking it gently around her, then placed a soft pillow under her head. "Who did this to you? Do you know?"

"Hurts," Shelley mumbled.

"I'm sure it does, honey." Angela frowned with concern. "Can I do anything to stop the hurt?"

Shelley's body quivered, and she moaned. "Please don't make me laugh. Hurts as in Liz Hurtz."

Angela's eyes widened. "Liz Hurtz did this to you? Because you defended me? How many people helped her?"

Shelley's body quivered again. "Five, I think."

"That Goddamned bitch!" The unusual outburst revealed the depth of Angela's outrage.

"Angela...stop, please." Shelley quivered a third time. The anger that had been building in Angela left her as she began to chuckle, too, struck by the ludicrous sight of a battered Shelley lying there chortling at her predicament.

"You're in pretty sad shape, kiddo. Do you think I can help you to my bed?"

"That an invitation?" Shelley struggled for a sultry glance.

Angela had to grin at the girl's grit. "You know it isn't."

"Then I better stay here. Tired. Cold."

Angela lifted the afghan and curled up against Shelley's back. "I'll keep you warm and watch the ice packs. You go ahead and sleep."

Shelley went to sleep with a smile, even though it hurt her lips.

The next morning, Merrill was met with the unsettling sight of her best friend wrapped around their suspect. She tiptoed into the living room and sat on the couch. She put her elbows on her knees and bent her head onto her hands, sitting that way for several moments, close to emotional shock. Then she lifted her head and met a single blue eye staring at her from a black and blue face. The other eye was swollen nearly shut.

"My God, you're hurt!" Merrill's compassionate heart forgot for a moment about the cloud of suspicion hovering over Shelley. She dropped to her knees next to her. "What happened to you? Why aren't you in the hospital?"

When she heard her roommate's voice, Angela woke up. With a jolt she realized she was plastered to Shelley's back, and she scrambled to sit up. "That damn Hurtz jumped her. There were about six of them, and they stomped the hell out of her. She wouldn't go to the hospital."

Merrill's raised eyebrows made Angela blush, and she quickly stammered, "She...was cold...and hurt. She came to us for help. I wanted to stay by her to make sure she was all right."

Wouldn't go to the hospital? Merrill's compassion was waning as she looked back down at the woman who had yet to say a word. "And are you all right?" she asked bluntly.

"Dunno, haven't tried to move yet," Shelley answered.

Her voice sounded stronger to Angela, which she took as a good sign. The redhead crawled from under the afghan and stood up. "You want me to help you try?"

"Let me see if I can straighten my legs first." Shelley slowly moved her legs until they were straight. "Well, that worked pretty well." She pushed the afghan away. Then she rolled onto her stomach, put her hands flat on the floor, and pushed herself into a kneeling position. She reached a hand to Angela for balance and stood up, facing her.

Angela got a good look at Shelley's face. The swelling in her cheek had mostly gone down and it was bruised, but her eye was definitely blackened. The cracks in her mouth no longer bled and were already starting to heal. "I kept changing the ice packs during the night and that really has helped. Your face looks ten times better."

"Thanks."

Shelley squeezed her hand and Angela realized she had not

let go of it when Shelley stood up. She placed the taller girl's hand in the crook of her arm. "Let's try walking, shall we?"

Shelley took several tentative steps. "I'm fine." She patted Angela's arm, and the redhead removed it. "I think I can make it upstairs now." She knew Merrill wasn't too happy that she was there.

"What are you going to do about Liz Hurtz? Report her to the police?" Merrill watched Shelley's expression carefully. For some reason the girl wanted to stay away from authorities, and Merrill wondered why. No hospital, and she was willing to bet no police either.

"No, I'll worry about Liz Hurtz later." She limped to the doorway, in more pain than she would admit. "Thanks, Angela. I owe you one."

She went out the door, and Angela moved as if to follow her, but Merrill grabbed her arm. "Stay here, Ange. Can't you see she's using you? Why didn't she go to the hospital? What's she hiding?"

Merrill's questions stopped her dead. Angela couldn't deny it any longer; Shelley was hiding something, and Angela was determined to find out what, whether she liked the answer or not. *I have to know. But right now, she needs me.*

Angela lifted Merrill's hand from her arm. "I'm going to help her upstairs, Merry. And I'm going to stay with her as long as she needs me."

"Whatever happened to good sense?" Merrill looked into her best friend's determined face and knew she had lost the battle. Angela was past listening to good sense. She was following her heart. Merrill sighed in defeat as Angela went out the door.

The redhead hurried around the corner of the hall and saw Shelley standing there with one hand on the banister, looking up the stairs. She turned as Angela reached her, and her face began to light up, but she quickly squelched it and took on a guarded expression. One eyebrow crooked up in inquiry.

Angela picked up Shelley's closer arm and put it across her shoulders. She wrapped an arm around the taller girl's waist. "Come on, let's give it a try." Slowly, Shelley mounted the stairs, relying heavily on Angela's help. Angela guided her to her apartment and used Shelley's key to open the door. She took Shelley straight into her bedroom and helped her onto the rumpled bed, then removed her sneakers and socks.

"Where are your sleep shirts?" she asked the quiet young

woman.

"Third drawer."

Angela pulled out the drawer and chose a rose-colored T-shirt. She took it to the bed and laid it on Shelley's stomach.

"Am I supposed to use this for a sheet?" the dark-haired girl asked.

"Oh, you are really funny. Put it on, and I'll help you get cleaned up."

"You're the funny one. I can barely move, let alone dress myself. Not to mention undress myself." She thrust her bottom lip out in a pout, which got Angela's immediate cooperation.

"Okay, I'll help you." She assisted Shelley in sitting up, then carefully took her shirt off, one arm at a time. Gritting her teeth, she unhooked the snowy white bra and lifted it off. Then she undid the button on her jeans and unzipped them. She lowered Shelley gently to the bed and pulled off her jeans and panties.

She rustled up a basin of warm water, soap, a washcloth, and a towel, and gently bathed her battered body, cringing at sight of the ugly bruises. She dried Shelley and carefully sat her up again. Quickly slipping the sleep shirt over the dark head, she helped to maneuver each arm through its proper hole. She laid her back down and pulled the shirt to the tops of her long legs, which also had suffered bruising.

Through this whole undertaking, Shelley kept her eyes closed, and a slight smile tugged at the corners of her mouth. When Angela was finished, Shelley opened her eyes and looked deeply into the hazel ones above her. "Thank you," she whispered, "for helping me."

Moisture stung Angela's eyes, and she quickly looked away. She pulled a brand-new desk chair up next to the bed and sat on it, then clutched her courage to her and looked again at the gorgeous woman she was losing her heart to. She swallowed hard then asked, "Can I do anything else for you?"

In obvious invitation, Shelley opened the hand that was lying on her stomach, and Angela scooted the chair closer and put her hand in Shelley's. "Having you here with me is enough...for now," Shelley said. "I just need some more rest." She closed her eyes, squeezed Angela's hand, and smiled as she drifted off.

Later she woke up and Angela was gone. The lamp table had been loaded with cookies, cheese, fruit, and bottles of water.

Shelley lay there, disappointed that Angela hadn't stayed, but accepting the inevitability of it.

Her mind replayed Angela's actions in helping her, from the time she crawled to the apartment up to falling asleep in her own bed. Her body's reactions to Angela's ministrations were expected, but she was pleased to note that Angela's reactions were just as heated—and unhappy that the redhead would not admit it aloud.

Chapter
10

Their first practice game was a runaway. The score was already 18-3 in favor of the Spofford Jaguars, and the three runs had been a gift from the coach. She had put a pitcher in who would at least let the fielders have some practice. The one bright spot happened in the bottom of the fourth inning when Angela threw a runner out at third base. It was the third out, and the team loped toward the visitors' dugout.

"Hey, Wedgie, good job on the throw," Barb Olanti hollered to Angela as they neared the dugout. Angela stopped short and turned around to face the olive-skinned third baseman, disgust and amusement fighting to take over her expression. The result was a rather attractive grimace.

"Thanks, Barb, but knock it off. You know my name's Angie," the redhead said pointedly. A name like Wedgeway was a magnet for hecklers and Angela had had her share of them at opposing fields. She didn't intend to let it slide by with a team-mate.

Barb grinned wickedly. A freshman and new to the team this year, she had noticed the good-looking redhead from the first day of practice, but she had stayed in the background, just observing, waiting for a chance to get to know her better. When Star had first appeared, she thought there might be something between the beauty and Angela, but she wasn't sure. She wouldn't let it stop her from trying anyway. Hoping that Angela could take some teasing, she took the opportunity to garner some notice. "What's wrong, you can't take a little ribbing?" Angela opened her mouth to answer, then inexplicably closed it as her eyes flicked towards Barb's left shoulder.

A hand clapped firmly on the shoulder, and Barb's head swiveled to meet steel-blue eyes on the same level with hers. The curve on the full lips did nothing to offset the ice in the narrowed eyes.

"Angela doesn't like that nickname," Shelley purred, "so we don't call her that. Right?"

Barb's gaze narrowed, too, as she debated how to handle this intrusion. She tilted her head slightly toward Shelley's healing eye. "You look like you had a little run-in with someone, Star."

"You should see the other six guys," Shelley responded softly as her hand tightened on Barb's shoulder.

Angela's voice interrupted their dangerous duet. "Hey, Barb, we don't call you B-O, do we?"

The third baseman snorted a short laugh, but her eyes never swerved from Shelley's. "You got a point there, Angie. Guess we better both back off...on the names." The hand dropped from her shoulder and Shelley moved on past her without another word.

Barb watched her pick up a fresh ball and stick it in her mitt, then sit on the far end of the bench. The third baseman followed Angela into the dugout. "Sorry, Angie, I just meant to kid around a little. Didn't mean to set Star off."

Angela stopped in front of the bench the rest of her team was sitting on. "No problem, Barb. Just stay cool around her, okay?"

"Right. I should know better than to tangle with an older woman." The freshman raked the listeners on the bench with a roguish smile. "Usually more fun being friends with them."

"An older woman?" Kath laughed. "Shelley's only eighteen," she blurted.

Marva poked her in the ribs with an elbow, and Kath turned to her with a questioning glance. The question was answered when she heard Shelley's silken voice. "How do you know how old I am, Kath?"

Kath was dumbstruck as she realized she knew Shelley's age from the file she shouldn't have read. She opened her mouth to answer, but nothing came out at first. On the second try, she blurted, "I work in the Dean's office—"

"She saw your birth date on a class list," Marva said, coming to Kath's aid.

"Yeah, it kind of jumped right out at me," Kath resumed when her thudding heart slowed down. "It was later than anybody else's by several years. How come you're a junior, anyway?" she asked, relieved to hide the truth about her errant eye.

Seemingly satisfied with the answer, Shelley shrugged. "I was put ahead a couple of years."

"Wow!" said Marva with a grin, happy to have rescued Kath from her blunder. "Beauty and brains, too. Aren't you the lucky one?"

Shelley's eyes turned to Marva but they seemed to be looking far past her, and the odd expression on her face belied her next words. "Yeah, that's me. The lucky one."

Seated on the far side of Marva, Angela had been watching Shelley's face during the exchange, and the look this last remark evoked disturbed her. The same old refrain jangled through her head: *I don't believe she's a killer. What if she's just a lonely kid?* She forced herself to get up and move to the seat next to the raven-haired first baseman, making her break eye contact with Marva.

As she sat between Shelley and Amber, her eyes fell on the sketch Amber was working on. It was an arresting full-length picture of Shelley at first base, prepared to field her position. "Wow, Amber, that's terrific!" *I'd love to have one of those. Maybe I'll ask Amber privately for one.*

"Yeah, Allie asked me to do it. And one of you." Amber sneaked a glance at Angela and smirked. "Guess she can't make up her mind."

Allie, seated on the other side of Amber, jogged her with a forearm. "Don't go putting ideas into people's heads, Amber," she said, and leaned forward to look at Angela. "I'm ordering the whole team. You two are the best players on the team, so I asked for you first."

Angela smiled at the compliment and nodded. "I thought you were an artist, too. How come you aren't doing them?"

"I do a different style, mostly scenery. Amber's better at people than I am."

"That's a great idea to get the whole team. I might order some, too, Amber. I'll talk to you about it later, okay?"

"Sure, Angie, whenever you want."

Angela turned toward the dark-haired girl sitting silently

beside her. "Shelley?"

Shelley had leaned her head back against the boards of the dugout, intensely aware that Angela was sitting next to her. The hooded pale eyes swept to Angela's, and the redhead berated herself for the effect they had on her in spite of her friends' suspicions. She could feel Shelley's lips, her hands, her... *Stop! This woman could hurt you!*

Angela wet her lips. "This thing with Barb? I'm big enough to fight my own battles, okay? Lots of people have teased me about my name."

"I don't like it. She's a teammate. She should have more respect." That chivalrous thought tickled the edges of Angela's heart, but she brushed it away.

"That's not your call, Shelley. I could have handled Barb. Back off, will you?" She watched in dismay as the warmth that had started to rise in Shelley's eyes receded.

"Sure, Angela. Whatever you want." Shelley picked up her mitt and stood up. "Inning's over," she said and sauntered out onto the field, her shoulders and hips swaying in reciprocal rhythm.

Angela locked her eyes on Shelley and followed her slowly, wondering how long her heart could stand the terrible wrenching it was going through. It was pure hell being attracted to a girl who came under such heavy suspicion, especially when she knew that Shelley wanted her, too. How much longer would the pain continue—both hers and Shelley's?

How much longer until the killer is caught? Even that thought caused wrenching pain.

Shelley opened the door to Ted Hoffman's knock and invited him in. As she watched his appraising blue eyes check out the apartment, she was glad she had spruced it up a bit in advance of his coming.

He held an offering out to her. "I brought a six-pack. Thought we might work up a thirst." Shelley was a little leery of inviting a virtual stranger into her apartment, but she trusted her instincts that Ted was okay. Just in case she was mistaken, she didn't lock the outside door. She thanked him for the beer and put it in the fridge, retaining two for them to work on.

"Okay, let's get started," she suggested, picking up her

script from the lamp table. Ted pulled his copy from the thigh pocket of his mottled fatigues.

Parts of the script called for furniture to be overturned while the abused woman was screaming. The two kitchenette chairs, one draped with Shelley's black windbreaker, had been brought into the living room to serve as props. In their zeal to stay true to the action, Shelley and Ted caused more commotion than they realized. There was a pounding on the apartment door, and Angela and Kath came tearing in.

Angela's heart froze as she saw a strange man with his hands around Shelley's throat. She grabbed Shelley's softball bat out of the corner and started toward him. Ted immediately let go, and Shelley stepped between them, raising her hands. "Angela, there's no problem. Ted and I are rehearsing a play."

Angela had the bat raised, ready for a blow, when Shelley's words penetrated the rage that had overcome her. Shocked by the abrupt change of purpose, Angela slowly lowered the bat, keeping her eyes on Ted. "Rehearsing?" she echoed in a daze.

Shelley removed the bat from the redhead's shaking hands and propped it against the wall. She led Angela to a seat on the couch, then sat next to her. "Kath," she said, "there's some beer in the fridge. Grab one for Angela, will you, and one for yourself."

Trying to be helpful, Ted went with Kath to get the beer and followed her back into the living room. Ted offered a can to Angela, who grasped it with both hands. She looked up at the tow-headed man. "I could have killed you," she said, her voice shaking partly from shock and partly from anger. She turned toward Shelley, who was looking at her uneasily, her black locks falling over her forehead.

"Didn't it occur to you that we would think something was happening to you?" she demanded. "Especially with all the other crap that's going on?"

Shelley lifted her hands and shrugged, distress plain on her face. "I never gave it a thought," she admitted.

Ted and Kath righted the toppled chairs, and Kath picked up Shelley's windbreaker from the floor and laid it over the couch arm next to Angela. Ted jumped into the conversation in Shelley's defense. "Neither one of us did. But we should have, and I apologize." Kath was divided between feeling bad for Angela and watching the attractive young man who had seemingly noticed her, too.

"And just who the hell are you?" The jar to Angela's system had made her uncharacteristically brusque.

Shelley recognized this and was even more disturbed that Angela had been so upset. "This is Ted Hoffman. He's a class-mate from my drama class. We're practicing a little play that we're in."

She turned toward him. "Ted, this is Angela Wedgeway and Kath O'Brien. We're all on the same softball team. Angela and Kath live downstairs. Everyone's kind of jumpy because of the killer who's around this area."

Ted nodded to the girls. "I don't blame you. All the women around here should be worried. Better make sure you stay together and don't go anywhere alone." Ted picked up his beer before sitting next to Kath in the chairs they'd set back up.

They started a quiet conversation as Shelley looked apolo-getically at Angela. "I'm really sorry this happened, Angela. I would never purposely upset you like this."

Angela took several sips of beer, then one long drink, and finally let her eyes seek Shelley's. "I guess I should be happy that it was a false alarm. I thought he was hurting you, and I went a little crazy."

Shelley ached to take her in her arms and soothe her, but she settled for brushing Angela's arm with a forefinger. "My guard-ian angel," she murmured.

"Right. More like a misguided one," Angela said with a snort. She gulped the rest of her beer and stood up, trying to recapture some dignity. "I guess we can safely leave you two to your thespian pursuits." As she talked, she unconsciously lifted Shelley's windbreaker from the couch arm and took it the few steps into the bedroom to the closet. She opened the closet door just as a startled Shelley bolted into the bedroom shouting, "No!"

A blinding shaft of light seemed to engulf Angela and the inside surface of the door, bringing time to an abrupt halt and shutting out the rest of the world. The inside of the door was plastered with pictures and news articles. As though in a dream, her eyes slowly moved back and forth across the items taped there. A chronological history of the coed murders was laid out precisely, with some parts circled and others underlined in red ink. Blurred newspaper pictures of the five girls, their names captioned beneath, were aligned side-by-side across the door slightly above Angela's eye level.

If it were possible for human beings to freeze from the inside out, Angela would have. The other two visitors were speechless too. They had followed Shelley into the room, then moved to stand behind Angela when they saw the layout of death.

Shelley glanced from one to the other and licked her lips. Angela looked like her world had ended, and Kath and Ted were horrified. "I... I've been keeping a record of the murders. I'm concerned about them," she tried to explain. But only silence met her. *Oh, God, what can I say?*

"Look, Angela. Look at all those girls. Read their descriptions—I've underlined them. Doesn't something strike you right away?" Shelley groped for a way to lighten Angela's dark expression.

Angela read for a moment, then as her mind compared the descriptions, she spoke in a flat voice. "They're all white... tall... black or dark-brown hair... blue eyes... athletes." Her voice gained some life. "And eighteen years old. They all resemble you."

"That's right," Shelley's low voice got even deeper, "I noticed it right away, and no one's even mentioned it. Maybe the police are suppressing it—though God only knows why they would." She looked from Angela to Kath. "No redheads, no sandy-haired, no blacks, no short ones, and only eighteen-year-old girl athletes. While you have been scared to death that I might be the killer, there's no one in your group who fits the description of the victims as closely as I do. I'm the one walking around with a target on her chest. Doesn't that tell you that I'm innocent?"

Angela reached into the closet for a hanger and put the windbreaker on it, then hung it up, stalling for time to think. What Shelley said made sense on the surface. Still, Angela could hear what Merrill would say: There was nothing to stop a tall, dark-haired, blue-eyed, athletic maniac from killing people who looked like her. And there were questions Shelley hadn't answered.

Angela turned to face her and lifted, then dropped her arms. "I don't know. I just don't know. If I were you and knew that I fit the description of all the victims as closely as you do, I sure as hell wouldn't be tooling around at night by myself. Tell us why you do that, and maybe then I can be sure of you."

Shelley stomped her foot and jerked away. She doubled up

her fists and then shoved them into her pockets to keep from striking out. Her voice was so intense it burned like lava. "I told you I can't answer that because someone else is involved. But it's not important. It has nothing to do with these murders. If you can't accept my word on that, then there's nothing more to say to you. Please leave."

Angela opened her mouth, then snapped it shut. Kath spoke softly to Ted before taking Angela's arm and practically dragging her out.

Shelley frowned at the young man. "I don't feel much like practicing now, Ted. Give me a call tomorrow; maybe we can find another chance, okay?"

"Sure, Shelley. Take it easy." From the conversation he had overheard, Ted realized that the other girls thought that Shelley might be involved in the killings. After seeing the bizarre collection on the closet door, he could understand their suspicions. *Maybe we can work together to keep an eye on her.* But for now, he just needed to get out of her apartment. Shelley let him out and locked the door.

She went into the bedroom, closed the closet door, and leaned her forehead against it. *You idiot! Why did you ever do something so stupid? You should have kept the damned door locked, or you could have put this stuff in a drawer. You might as well have gone to the police and confessed.* She banged her head against the door, hard, once for each girl who had been murdered, while tears of frustration laid trails down her cheeks.

Angela and Kath came into the apartment arguing. "You could have let me have a chance to reason with her," Angela was saying. "You didn't have to almost yank me out of there."

Merrill and Marva had just come back from shopping and were in the kitchenette putting Merrill and Angela's share of the groceries away. When they heard the raised voices, they hurried into the living room.

"Right. From the looks of you two, you would have come to blows in about ten more seconds," Kath rejoined. "It might have been interesting to see which one of you won, but I really wasn't in the mood for bloodshed."

Angela cast a nasty glance at Kath, and Merrill purposely

interrupted the exchange. "What happened?"

Angela clamped her lips shut and looked at Kath, who shook her head and looked apologetic. "Ange, I only know what I saw." She turned to Merrill and Marva. "Remember we wondered why Shelley's closet was locked when we cleaned her room? She has newspaper articles and pictures of the murdered girls pasted all over the inside of the closet door."

Merrill and Marva looked shocked. "Just like you see in the movies," Marva muttered.

Merrill plunged further toward acceptance of Shelley's guilt. "Ange, what more proof do you need? Do you have to see her with knife in hand, mutilating some innocent girl?"

"She doesn't have her knife any more. The police kept it," Angela said stubbornly.

"Good grief, Angie, you know she could buy another one. I think we need to make a move." Merrill looked to the others for some support.

"You mean call the police again?" Marva asked as she sat down on the couch. Following her lead, the others settled themselves. Angela dropped onto the floor, unconsciously sitting slightly apart from the rest.

"I don't think that's the answer," said Kath. "Look what happened last time—nothing!"

Marva glanced down toward Angela. "Did she tell you how she got away with that, Ange? I never saw the cops turn anyone loose that fast."

The redhead was sitting on the floor, playing with a lace on one of her sneakers. She glanced up and grimaced. "Her court-appointed guardian is the judge. She got her off somehow."

Merrill sighed loudly, drawing everyone's attention. "Looks like we are going to have to follow her on these nightly excursions of hers after all, like Kath suggested earlier. What do you think?"

"I don't like the idea, but I don't see any other answer," Marva conceded. When she saw Kath nod, she made an offer. "Kath and I can take a night, then you and Angie, and we can alternate."

Merrill stood up, went into the bedroom, and got a pencil and paper from her desk. Bringing them back to the living room, she sat on the couch, rested the paper on the lamp table, and drew a chart with days and times blocked out. "Okay. Let's figure out who will watch on what nights."

Angela put her elbows on her knees and her head in her hands. "You pick our nights, Merry. I'll go with whatever you decide."

Marva moved down to sit beside her. "Whatever happened to the famous Wedgeway faith? We're going to prove your girl innocent, aren't we?"

Angela turned her head toward Marva and smiled ruefully. "Sure wish I could be certain of that, Marv. But thanks for the vote of trust in Shelley."

Marva shrugged. "It's more a vote of trust in you, Angie. It's tough for me to believe that you could fall this hard for a murderer."

Merrill reddened. "It's tough for me, too, Angie. I just wouldn't be able to live with myself if we ignored the evidence and we were wrong. You understand that, don't you?"

Angela looked at the woman who had been her best friend for the last fifteen years. She did understand. Merrill was relentless. She wouldn't let go of this mystery until she found the answer, one way or another. But maybe that was good. If they could prove Shelley's innocence, Angela knew that Merrill would be right there, cheering for them both. She nodded and even managed a half-smile. "I understand, kiddo. Do what you have to do."

"Speaking of what we have to do," Kath pointed out. "Someone has to cut the grass tomorrow."

As Merrill and Marva nodded, Angela gave Kath a puzzled look. "Cut the grass? What are you talking about?"

"Marv and I bribed Mr. Squires not to turn Shelley in for trashing her room. We offered to cut the grass for two weeks in return for his silence. We thought Shelley could be persuaded to do it, but that's out of the question now. So we have to get it done."

Angela winced. "Well, thanks for getting Shelley off the hook. I'll cut the grass. Tomorrow?"

"Yeah, he said Saturday." Kath looked at Marva and Merrill as she spoke next. "We'll help, Ange. Won't we, guys?"

The other two nodded and Merrill suggested, "How about if Angie and I cut it tomorrow, and you two cut it next weekend?"

"Sure," Marva agreed as Kath nodded.

"Wish everything could be solved that easily," Marva said wistfully.

Chapter
11

It was opening day, and the whole team was excited. Their first game was away against the Scatsboro Pumas, last year's champs, and would give them a good indication of whether they had the makings of a winner. A good-sized group of softball fans had showed up, quite a few of them rooting for Spofford.

Shelley was the starting pitcher, Angela at first base, and Bobbie Sue in right field. In the first games of the season pitchers often tired, so the coach's plan was to have Shelley pitch the first four innings, then switch to Bobbie Sue. It would mean position changes at first base and right field in the latter innings, but those changes would strengthen both positions. The girls were ready and hopeful.

Spofford's team sported their new kelly-green uniforms with shorts that were just about as short as they could get. Walking back to the dugout after warm-ups, Angela had a difficult time keeping her eyes off of Shelley; the green set off her tan, making blue eyes bluer and long legs longer.

Shelley had been the first into the dugout and was sitting at the far end watching the others come in. As she caught the glimpse of Angela she had been searching for, her heart leaped. With her red hair, the green uniform made her look...Shelley couldn't think of a word to describe exactly how she looked or how she caused her to feel. She only knew that the excitement of the upcoming game made her heart race, but the vision of Angela raised that movement to a thud. She thought it might burst right out of her chest. *Good thing she plays behind me in the field. Don't know if I could keep my mind on what I need to do otherwise.*

Coach Palmer called the team together at the dugout entrance, and they jointly touched their hands together and yelled, "Go, Spofford!" The first batters in the line-up got ready, while the rest sat on the bench or stood close to the fence, prepared to cheer for their teammates.

"Play ball!" The umpire's call signaled the start of the game, and the teams went at it.

In the bottom of the third inning with the game tied 0-0, Scatsboro's next batter, their pitcher, stood near the plate waiting for Shelley to finish her warm-up tosses.

"Hey, Marv." The girl was 5'8" and solid, one of the best pitchers in the league.

"Yo, Jodi." *Whap!* Shelley's pitch slapped into Marva's catcher's mitt with a satisfying jolt, and she fired it back.

"Where'd you get your pitcher?" Rubbing a wristband across her forehead, Jodi soaked up the perspiration threatening to run into her eyes.

"She came here from Penlyville." *Whap!*

"They aren't on our schedule, so I wouldn't have seen her, but damn, she looks familiar. Not exactly a forgettable face," Jodi said and grinned at Marva.

Whap! "That's for sure, but she's taken, so stick your eyeballs back where they belong." *Not quite a lie—she would be taken if things were different.*

"Not what I meant, Marv. I think she was at Scatsboro for a while—maybe only a month or so. Didn't play on the team. Got there too late."

Whap! Marva frowned as she took the last pitch. Shooting up from her squat, she threw the ball to second base, then straightened out her chest protector. Jodi picked up the catcher's mask from where it lay on the ground, dusted it off against her hip, and handed it to her as the umpire moved into position behind Marva. "Batter up!"

Marva had a million questions bouncing through her mind about Shelley, but knew she had to forget them for the moment. She settled her mask, squatted down, and smacked her mitt. "C'mon, Star, show this puny runt what a real pitcher can do!"

The first four innings belonged to the pitchers: the score was 0-0. Bobbie Sue came in for Shelley as planned. She pitched well but gave up one run to Scatsboro in the sixth.

The top of the seventh was approaching, and Coach Palmer called the team together for a quick pep talk. "We're only one run down. We've stayed in the game because of our super pitching and fielding. Now it's time to reach down inside for that something extra that separates winners from losers. Get those bats working! Remember, when we beat Scatsboro, we can beat anybody. Go get 'em!"

The Spofford Jaguars had gone through their lineup twice, and the leadoff batter was starting things off again in the top of the seventh. Merrill, the smallest player on the team, was an excellent spray hitter in any direction and a swift runner, so that position belonged to her. With a good eye and great patience, she slapped the close pitches foul and worked the pitcher for a walk.

Barb Olanti, the third baseman, bunted Merrill to second base. Teammates, urging Barb on with shouts from the dugout, gave her additional impetus and she almost, but not quite, beat out the bunt for a hit.

Anxious to do her part, Marva hit a screaming line drive that Scatsboro's third baseman timed perfectly. Jumping high into the air, she speared it in the webbing of her glove. Merrill dove swiftly back to second base, barely avoiding being doubled off as the whole team and their fans breathed sighs of relief.

Angela stepped up to the plate, and the outfielders backed up several steps. The opposing coach weighed the advisability of walking the clean-up hitter—the last thing she wanted was a home run—but with Shelley Brinton batting next, she decided against it. As fourth and fifth batters, both women were home run threats, but Brinton had that whip-like build that sometimes signaled more raw power. If they could get Wedgeway out, Brinton's power would be a moot point—the game would be over and Scatsboro would register its first win.

Angela worked the count to 3-2, then hit a scorching grounder in the hole between third and short. Against any other team she would have had a run batted in, but Scatsboro's shortstop was the best in the league. She couldn't get to the ball in time to catch it, but she knocked it down with a stretching dive and prevented the run from scoring.

Next came Shelley. She had a count of 1-2, and the pitcher threw a high fastball just a fraction above the strike zone that looked as big to Shelley as a beach ball. Angela held her breath. She saw Shelley's hands start to move, then jerk back, taking the pitch for ball two. The next pitch was a nasty curve that started outside but curved back in toward the plate. Shelley's fast reflexes saved her. She swung late, but slammed the ball just fair down the first-base line and it bounced around in the corner.

The sweet reverberation of the solid hit coursed up Shelley's arms, through her shoulders, and down her body, powering her feet as she flew past first base, charged toward second, and hit the bag with a stand-up double. Both Merrill and Angela scored, giving Spofford the lead. The team cleared the benches as soon as Shelley's ball hit fair and they jumped up and down with joy, high-fiving the runners as they entered the dugout. The fans in the bleachers made up for their fewer number by stomping on the aluminum stands and screaming prodigiously.

The left fielder, Allie Monroe, hit a long fly ball, backing the center fielder to the wall for the third out. She threw the bat in disgust that she had stranded the runner, but that didn't dim the jubilation. As Shelley came in off the field her teammates slapped her on the back and gave her high-fives. She swiveled her head to answer one of them and walked right into Angela. Grabbing her shoulders to steady them both, Shelley reveled in the chance to touch her, even so briefly.

"Great hit," Angela said. She hesitated, then forced herself to step away from Shelley's grasp. "I saw you flinch at that high pitch and I nearly died."

"It sure was tempting, but I knew from your lessons that I might just pop that up. I thought I better wait." She was drowning in Angela's eyes until the shortstop, Roz Carrow, swung her around and handed her first-baseman's mitt to her. Roz was one of only three seniors on the team and was considered one of their leaders. "Let's go, guys. Take the field."

"Oh, how fleeting is fame," Shelley groused, but the few words from Angela had her flying high.

Scatsboro was at the plate for their last chance to tie or win the game. They had a runner on first with two outs and their heaviest hitter at the plate. She swung at a pitch that should have been a ball but caught it squarely and with her strength hit it over Kath's head in center field. Kath chased it to the wall and, with it so deep, Angela came running over to give her an extra relay person. Kath hit Angela's glove perfectly, and she wheeled to throw it to Merrill when she heard Shelley's distinctive voice slicing through the screams of Scatsboro's fans: "Home! All the way home!"

Without a second thought, Angela let it fly and the ball sizzled into the infield and made one hop to Marva, who threw her shin-guarded leg alongside the plate and tagged the blocked runner out. Spofford players and fans erupted in jubilation, the stomping in the stands reaching fever pitch.

Coach Palmer was jubilant, too. True, it was only their first win, but it was a sweet one. Scatsboro always led the league, year after year, and maybe, just maybe, the Jaguars could change that.

"Nice throw," Shelley congratulated Angela as they left the field, basking in the win.

Angela blushed. "Thanks...guess those lessons did us both good. And thanks for the tip. If I had thrown to the relay, the runner would have been safe and we could have been in extra innings. Good game, Shelley." The tall girl nodded and blazed a full smile.

Kath had been walking behind them next to Marva and Merrill. "Well, I for one am glad we didn't go into extra innings. I have a date tonight." Her friends looked at her with big grins. "Who with?" Merrill asked.

"Would you believe Ted Hoffman? You know the guy I met at Shelley's the other night?"

"Hey, you're a fast worker, Kath—or he is," Merrill said with a chuckle.

Marva nudged Kath in the side. "I have a date, too," she smirked.

This time the women stopped in their tracks. "And who might that be?" Angela, overhearing, dropped back with them.

"Our illustrious third baseman has asked me out," Marva answered.

"Barb Olanti? No kidding?" Angela said. "She's a freshman. Better watch that cradle robbing."

Marva threw an arm over Angela's shoulder as they resumed walking. "Shelley's almost underage, too, you know. Is this the pot calling the kettle black, or what?" Marva murmured, returning the teasing.

Angela reddened and gave her a shove. Then Marva bubbled a laugh out. "Hey, I am black, no matter what you call me."

"Crazy?"

"Goofy?"

"Cute?"

"Thanks, Kath, now I know who my one true friend is,"

Marva whined, and all three women laughed and pummeled her with their gloves.

Shelley's wistful glance went unnoticed.

It was dark, but not as black as some moonless nights. The lone rider sailed smoothly down the incline of the bike path, the air swishing softly past her ears and blowing her hair off her face. The night dampness magnified the mingled smells of the earth, the nearby river, and scattered vegetation.

The path flattened out at the bottom and stayed parallel to the river road, though set back enough to be inside the trees, providing a more picturesque ride. *In the daytime, that is.* She grinned because she liked the night—no inquisitive eyes, no stupid questions, no suspicious people. She came alive at nighttime; it was her friend.

Friend. Oh, Angela, I've waited but you haven't made up your mind. Do I keep waiting? You're so beautiful and your body is so perfect...how many nights I've ridden around thinking of you. Maybe someday... The rider heard a noise and quickly pulled into the undergrowth, hunching down out of sight.

Two bike riders went by pumping furiously. *Racers in training, looks like.* Relieved, the rider got back onto the trail.

Well, Spofford, looks like you finally get your turn. I've already picked my leading lady. Now all I have to do is trail her for a while, find out her habits, and I will have her in the palm of my hand.

The rider slowed and turned off the trail, working through the underbrush, which was sparser on the roadside. She rode down to the beginning of the riverbank and stopped, looking in all directions. Three trees bunched closely together gave the spot some privacy from the road. *Perfect.*

With a satisfied smile, she turned back toward Spofford, taking her time, drinking in the total freedom that she found only under the concealing cloak of stars.

Helen Ostcott wore her apron with pride. She had always been a good cook; born with the knack, some said. Chocolate chip cookies not only were her favorite to bake, but also one of her favorites to eat. And Shelley loved them, too. But the first batch of these would go to Commissioner Pete Dougal, as promised.

The eggs had been beaten into the sugar and butter; flour, salt, and baking soda had been added; and now it was time for the semi-sweet chips and the nuts, which she had cut up ahead of time. As she reached for the chips, the phone rang. Wiping her hands on her apron, she picked up the receiver. What she heard made her drop into a chair.

"No, Jeff, that never entered my mind. Surely not." Helen closed her eyes. *You're not being exactly truthful, Helen. Admit it.* "Yes, Shelley's had many, many psychological evaluations and no, she probably will never be completely 'cured.' She's come a long way, but even the experts admit that the mind can be very strong or very fragile. With the terrible trauma in her background, it's a wonder she's as sane as she is."

Helen listened intently as her eyes roamed her neat kitchen, touching on the hidden refrigerator/freezer; Italian marble counters, specially ordered to match the floor; the sparkling pots and pans dangling from the ceiling rack; the built-in oven, microwave, and dishwasher; the flat-surfaced electric range. Cupboards jutted proudly from every wall with utensils and towel racks hanging beneath them. A blender, can opener, bag sealer, and coffeemaker stood near at hand.

This was her best-loved room, but her eyes saw nothing in it at the moment. Instead they were looking into the past at the beautiful young girl with the ravaged soul whom she had worked with, and prayed for, for years, trying to help her return to a world she hated. And they had succeeded.

Or had they? Tears rolled from her eyes as she pondered the implications of what Jeff was proposing. *No, not my Shelley— never. Never.* But saying it didn't make it so. Only time would tell the true answer. And they had to think the unthinkable...just in case.

"Do what you have to do, Jeff," she said softly, and hung up the phone. Jeff had been about to say something sympathetic, and she hung up abruptly before he could say it, but he understood. He had known Helen and Shelley for years, and he realized how hard it was for her to face what had to be faced. *Maybe. There's no solid proof yet. But it doesn't look good.*

The four usual cohorts gathered at Angela and Merrill's table the morning after the game.

Merrill looked in the fridge. "Hey, Angie made a pitcher of iced tea last night. Good girl! Anybody want some?"

She poured a glass for each of them in response to their affirmative answers while Angela cut some coffee cake and got out the paper plates and napkins. When she returned the pitcher to the fridge, she got the butter out, shut the door, and gathered a few knives, laying them on the table.

"So how were the big dates last night?" Merrill asked. She sat down next to Angela on the padded red bench that formed the dinette corner.

"Mine was okay," Marva replied. "We went to The Barrister for a couple of drinks." She scooped a piece of coffee cake onto a plate and took a bite.

"The Barrister? That's a private club, Marv." The answer had surprised Angela.

Marva washed the cake down with a swallow of iced tea. "Barb's registered to study pre-law, so she was allowed to join. Besides, they don't check her age there, so we were able to have some mixed drinks."

Kath looked up from buttering her piece of cake. "What's she like? Any chemistry there?"

Marva considered the question as she licked coffee cake crumbs from her tapered fingers. "We only had a few drinks and left. We were both pretty worn out from the game, especially me. Up and down with every pitch is a real workout. Too early to tell if there's any chemistry. We have another date next week." Marv winked at Kath. "How about you and Ted?"

"We went to a movie..." Kath began. She had meticulously buttered both sides of her coffee cake and cut it into bite-sized chunks. She daintily picked one up and popped it into her mouth.

"Adventure or love story?" Merrill interrupted.

"Adventure," Kath answered after she swallowed.

"Uh oh," Merrill said.

"What's the difference?" Angela inquired with a frown. She picked up a napkin and brushed powdered sugar from her lips, then folded the napkin and put her sweating iced tea glass on it. She handed a folded napkin to Merrill, who set her glass onto it. Taking another napkin, Angela wiped up the wet rings in front of them.

Marva had been watching this action with a smile. With a

small shake of her head she muttered, "Damn neatniks," then did the same thing for her and Kath.

"Adventure means he thought of himself first; love story means he's feeling romantic," Merrill answered. "Of course, that's only my own opinion."

"I picked the movie, and I like adventures. I think it's too early to be trying to be romantic," Kath said. "We just met."

Merrill didn't feel brave enough to attack that line of reasoning, so she digressed. "Did you have a good time?"

"Yeah, we did." Kath's face lit up. "After the movie we walked for a while, just talking. Ted said he was totally shocked about all those clippings Shelley had."

"We were, too," Merrill said needlessly. She rose and cleared the table, dumped the paper products in the trash can, and washed out the knives, then refilled their glasses.

"He wants to help us keep tabs on Shelley. I think it's a great idea. We'll have another set of eyes." Kath gazed around to see if the others agreed.

Angela took a sip of her fresh tea and looked sour. "What makes you think he couldn't be the killer, Kath? Maybe he just wants us to help set Shelley up."

"He didn't seem to be hiding anything, Angie," Kath responded. She leaned toward the table and her long wavy hair swung forward from her shoulders. "We talked for a long time about our backgrounds, and he answered every question I asked him. He grew up about fifty miles from my home and knew a lot of the same places I did." She looked at Merrill, the natural mediator. "It would be easy enough to check him out. He said his dad's the Chief of Police and his mom's a teacher at the local high school."

Angela rolled her eyes, but Merrill spoke up as she sat back down. "I like the idea. It won't hurt to have the extra help. We can't be everywhere."

Kath looked at her redheaded friend with concern. "Besides, Angie, if she really is innocent, we might find out that much sooner."

Kath turned to the others. "Maybe Ted could take a night. I could double up with him." She quirked an eyebrow at Marva. "You think Barb might help out?"

Marva considered it for a moment then declined. "I don't know her that well yet. We don't want the whole team knowing we suspect Shelley of this." Her thoughts turned momentarily to the team, and what Shelley's loss would mean. Then she felt guilty. The damage to Shelley, and even to Angela, far out-weighed anything the team might suffer.

"Okay, guys." Merrill retrieved her chart from the lamp table and made some adjustments. "Kath and Marv take tonight, Ange and I will take tomorrow night, and Kath and Ted can take the third night. Then we start all over. How's that sound?"

Marva looked over Merrill's shoulder at the chart to make sure she wasn't scheduled for the night of her date with Barb. "We can take turns with the car," Marva suggested, "but we'll have to be careful because Shelley knows it."

"Ted has a car, too," Kath informed them. "Shelley might not recognize his."

Merrill sucked the inside of her cheeks in thought. "Maybe we should begin by following her on our bikes since that's the way she always seems to travel."

The others nodded in agreement, and the plan went into effect that night.

Chapter
12

Shelley carefully glanced in every direction, then removed the chain from her bike and pulled it out of the rack as quietly as possible. A sliver of moon lay against the starry curtain of night like a golden bangle surrounded by carelessly strewn diamonds, but she was too intent on her mission to notice the night's beauty.

She pedaled several blocks to the woods and angled off the street into the darkness of the trees. The black slacks and windbreaker that she wore while riding her black bike made her blend invisibly into the forest background. It took only a moment for her eyes to adjust to the meager light diffused among the growth. Branches hunched overhead as the bike's tires found one of the many paths, some of which were becoming increasingly familiar. As she started to coast down a hill, she heard the swish of another bike somewhere behind her. Turning sharply off the path, she maneuvered down through the trees onto another path and continued on her way with no further disturbance.

"Damn! I think we lost her," Marva called softly to Kath. She could hear Shelley's bike going down the hillside.

"We can follow her noise," Kath said. "Come on." She steered her bike toward the thicket of trees, but Marva grabbed her arm as she passed her.

"There's half a dozen trails down there, Kath. Our bike lights don't brighten the ground enough to figure out which one

she took in this darkness. We should have brought a flashlight."
Marva was as brave as the next person, but the idea of being in a
dark woods with a demented killer running around did not appeal
to her at all.

Kath was rummaging through her backpack, but came up
empty-handed. "I thought I had one. We'll have to remind Merry
and Angie to take one with them."

Marva cupped her hand around her ear, but no more noise
reached her. "Let's go back. No sense in wasting the whole night
out here."

The next morning, Marva and Kath reported their lack of
success and advised the others of the necessity of carrying a
flashlight. Three times out of the next six nights, Shelley went
out but evaded the followers.

"I have an idea," Ted said. The girls had invited him in for
something to eat, and they sat around the apartment living room
afterward, discussing their plan.

"What is it?" Kath asked.

"We keep losing Shelley. I think she knows someone is following her, and she could be suspicious that it's us. We know
what general direction she's heading, right?"

The girls nodded.

"How about if we station ourselves in strategic places in
that same direction? If she passes any of us, we can get a further
idea of which way she's headed and keep doing that until we've
mapped her progress."

"Sounds like a plan," Merrill said and the others agreed.
The third time they implemented the new plan, they saw someone go by who looked like Shelley. The next night, Marva and
Kath placed themselves near the path, so they could establish
that it was Shelley, and that she used that way more than once.

The moon cast a little more light tonight, giving the underbrush more definition. Marva wasn't sure whether that was helpful or not. After a long while of staring, the brush gave the
appearance of moving, and she kept jerking her head around,
thinking someone was near.

After some whispered discussion, they picked two trees
right near a bend in the trail, so the rider would have to slow
down, and they would be able to get a good look at her. About
twenty minutes later, Shelley passed them. Kath jumped on her
bike to follow her, but Marva stopped her. "Let's go back and
report and keep following Ted's plan. It seems to have the best

chance of working. If you try following her now and she hears you, she might start using another path."

"Good thinking," Kath conceded. She and Marva turned back the way they had come.

After a moment, Marva halted and raised a hand for Kath to stop. "Did you hear anything?" she whispered to her roommate. Kath cocked an ear, listening, but heard nothing and shook her head. "Thought I heard another bike," Marva murmured. "Couldn't tell whether it was behind us or in front of us." She swiveled her head uselessly, frustrated by the spurious movement of the silvered bushes. "Damn, it's creepy out here. Let's go home." The two pedaled away, oblivious to the dark-haired woman watching from deeper in the trees, her lips turned up in a mocking smile. When they left, she resumed her travels.

Abandoning her other plans for the time being, the dark-haired girl pedaled to the old house and put the bike in the dilapidated garage, next to the car—the car that was reserved for special uses. Thinking of those uses brought a crooked smile to her lips. She lifted a small package from the bike's carrying basket and used the outside entrance to go directly down several broken wooden steps to the pitch-black cellar.

Orienting herself in the open doorway, she blindly crossed the dirt floor with her arm bent overtop her head. When the arm came in contact with a hanging chain, she pulled it and turned on an overhead light that was nothing more than a bare bulb screwed into a ceramic plate. Two old dowel-backed wooden chairs—one showing dark stains—sat on the packed floor just beyond the light, facing each other. Further past them squatted an ancient picnic table and against the wall stood a heavy metal laundry sink with deep double basins.

The house's ancient coal furnace had never been replaced, and it took up the other half of the cellar, with its hot water tank for the radiators suspended from the ceiling and its radiator feeder pipes reaching along the subflooring like round, fat arms supporting the house. In the corner nearest the furnace was the coal bin, formed by a half-wall of old timbers. Long empty from disuse, the bin held a few scattered, broken lumps of coal that were lonely witnesses to the atrocities performed in the outer cellar.

The tall woman emptied her package, dumping several small boxes and a ring of metal measuring spoons onto the dented picnic table, next to an assortment of bowls and utensils. A coil of rope and a roll of duct tape lay near one end of the table. Reaching into the left pocket of her windbreaker, she pulled out a much-folded piece of paper and sat down at the table, pinning the paper down with sundry knives and spoons. She sorted the small boxes in the order she would use them, then opened them to reveal several different powders. Referring to the pinned-down paper, she used the measuring spoons to place the proper proportion of each powder into one of the bowls, stirring them together after each addition.

When she got to the end of the recipe, she reached for a bag that had been sitting on the table, opened it, and took out a paper straw. She bent one end of the straw up and, using a rolled piece of paper as a funnel, poured a half-teaspoon of the powder into it. Tearing off the straw just above the highest level of the powder, she folded the top down to form a small cylinder. She pushed her dark hair back from her forehead, then stuck the packet into her left pocket. After making five additional packets from the straws left in the bag, she put one more in her pocket. The other finished packets she dropped into the bag and left sitting on the table.

There were liquid substances she could have used for her purpose, but she found that the powder was simpler to handle. She could hide a straw in her hand, flip one end open, and pour the powder into a drink without anyone noticing her. Then she could just drop the straw in a trash receptacle and no evidence would be found on her. The second packet was for insurance, but if she didn't need it she would drop it into the trash, too. The powder began acting on the chosen victim within ten to fifteen minutes, making her nauseous, then disoriented, then unconscious.

So far, the dark-haired woman had been lucky. Because of the queasiness, each victim had gone to the ladies' room where the disorientation started to take effect. The tall woman had been waiting there to offer her assistance, suggesting some fresh air might help. When she had the nearly unconscious victim outside, she had hurried her into the car before she passed out. After that, everything else continued to fall into place exactly as planned.

Pleased with herself, the woman smiled and patted her pocket where she usually carried her knife—her "Star-Maker."

The smile turned into twisted lips as she remembered the knife was no longer there. She rose, turned out the light and made her way in the dark to the exit. *But I'll have it when I need it,* she smirked, and went up the outside steps two at a time, returning to the blackness of the night.

Merrill threw her arms around Jim Dursik's neck and squealed as he straightened up, lifting her off the floor. She melted into his embrace and their lips joined in the sweet assurance of love. The other four occupants of the apartment—Ted had joined them—smiled at the result of Merrill's opening the door to Jim's knock, then went on with their conversation.

"When did you get here?" Merrill asked when Jim returned her to the floor and she could catch a breath. "I had no idea you were coming."

Jim's devilish grin, coupled with deep dimples and sparkling blue eyes in a tanned face, made Merrill's already ensnared heart jump with excitement. "I didn't know until the last minute. One of my labs was canceled and I wanted to surprise you. I jumped right in my car, and here I am."

Jim intended to be a doctor. His science courses and their required lab hours left him with little extra time, but he had managed to free up Friday and Saturday and couldn't wait for the chance to see his fiancée.

He lifted his foot and pulled up the leg of his sweatpants, displaying a walking cast. "Unfortunately, I broke my ankle."

"Aw, honey, what happened? Does it hurt?" Merrill looked properly sympathetic, and Jim squeezed her shoulders.

"I slipped yesterday running down a pair of steps and no, it doesn't hurt much, just kind of a dull ache. A buddy got ice on it right away for me and kept the swelling down. They gave me a walking cast so I can get around, but it's still pretty awkward."

As he explained this, Merrill took his hand and led him into the room where he got a big hug and kiss from Angela—and some more sympathy. He smiled and nodded as the other girls greeted him then Merrill introduced him to Ted.

"Ted, this is my fiancé, Jim Dursik. Jim, Ted Hoffman. Ted's helping us follow Shelley." Merrill had been keeping Jim informed of their worries about the murders. He was worried, too. A psycho going around murdering coeds stirred every decent person's desire for his capture—or, as was possible in this case, her capture.

The men shook hands, and Jim sat on the couch seat offered by Angela, who grabbed him a soda from the kitchen then dropped to a seat on the floor.

The group thoroughly explained the problem, and Jim was convinced of its serious implications. "You say these killings are three to four weeks apart. How long has it been since the last one?"

"Three weeks," Kath answered, "and we're really getting antsy about it. We need to find where Shelley is going at night— and soon."

"We've been working on that," Ted said, "and we think we may be close to discovering where it is."

"Following her there could be pretty dangerous," Jim cautioned.

"Yes, it could," Merrill said as most of the others nodded. "But we're only following her in pairs, and once we find her base of operations, we intend to inform the police and let them take over from there."

Jim knew Angela well, and he noticed that she stayed aloof from the conversation. Merrill had told him that their friend was sweet on their suspect, and he knew she had to be hurting. He reached down and squeezed her shoulder. "Hey, Ange, we don't want your girl to be the murderer, but from what the others tell me, I have to agree that we need to find out for sure. You okay with this?"

Angela reached up and patted his hand. She and Jim and Merrill had been pals since first grade, and Jim was like a brother to her. They all looked out for each other. "I'm trying to be, Jimbo. I don't believe that Shelley is guilty, but I don't dare assume that she isn't. The sooner this is straightened out, the better."

Angela's expression told how distressed she was more than her words did. Jim turned his hand over and clasped hers briefly, and the gesture warmed her heart. He glanced from one to the other. "Merry told me about your tracking arrangements. Whose turn is it tonight?"

"Angela and I are scheduled for tonight," Merrill answered.

"Great! How about if I go with you?"

"Just try not to," Merrill teased. "But first, we are going out to eat. We want to celebrate how well our team is doing—we're

3-0—and now that you are here we have an extra reason to celebrate. We're going to the Steak House, and Shelley is coming
with us, so you'll have a chance to meet her."

"You're still hanging around with her even though you suspect her?" Jim was surprised.

Merrill looked defensive. "We thought it would be easier to
keep track of her if we kept her close. Besides, we ride back and
forth to the games and practices all the time, and it would look
kind of strange if we didn't invite her to join us. Other members
of the team will be there. I don't think Shelley takes our suspicions all that seriously, but that could be to our advantage."

Angela had a strange feeling, almost a premonition, that
events were coming to a head. She knew that some resolution
would occur sooner or later, and she suddenly felt that it was
coming shortly. *But what will that resolution be?* She shivered
then abruptly stood up. "Let's get moving. I'll go get Shelley."

The group piled out of the men's cars and trooped into the
Steak House. Amber Zorno had arrived ahead of them and was
holding places. Two tables had been pushed together to accom-
modate their number. As they arrived, Barb Olanti joined them,
and all were introduced to Jim and Ted.

"Where's Allie?" Marva asked when they had gotten settled.

"She had a couple of errands to run," Amber answered.
"Said she would be a little late but would be here. She told me
what she wants to order."

Jim and Merrill sat on one side of Shelley with Angela on
her other side. Shelley had been particularly pleased to meet Jim,
especially when she found that he was the man Merrill was planning to marry. That sweet fact erased any lingering doubts she
might have had about the relationship between Merrill and
Angela and put her in a good mood. Although naturally reticent,
she held her own in the conversations going on around her.

A student band had offered to play at the Steak House just
to get the exposure, and their surprisingly entertaining music
added to the festivities as the group enjoyed a long, leisurely
dinner. Afterward, the pitchers of beer continued to flow as they
toasted the team several times and Merrill and Jim several more.

The evening was winding down with about forty-five minutes to go before closing time when Barb Olanti pointed out that

it was so crowded they would have to go to the bar to be sure of getting their last round of beer in time. She jumped up to go after the beer, and Allie offered to help her. Ten minutes later they returned with four bottles of beer.

"Would you believe they ran out of draft beer and are down to bottles?" Barb sneered. "And you're only allowed two bottles per person." She set an opened bottle in front of Shelley. "Here, Star, you've earned this more than the rest of us have."

"Thanks, but I have one." Shelley had just poured the last mug of beer from the pitcher, so she handed the bottled beer to Ted, who promptly handed it to Kath. Barb set the second bottle in front of Marva and winked at her.

Allie set one of her bottles in front of Shelley. "You sure make it hard to reward you, Star. Have a cold one and pass that warm mug to me." She set the other bottle in front of Amber, who grabbed it gleefully.

Shelley cupped her hand over the top of the mug as if to refuse, then apparently changed her mind. "Okay, you take the warm one." Allie swapped with her, and Shelley immediately handed the bottle to Jim. "Let's not ignore one of our guests," she said, and refused to take the bottle back. "I've had enough to drink, anyway. I have things to do tonight."

Aided by the amount of drinking they had done, the whole group thought the bottle passing was a great joke, and they all got involved in the game, laughingly urging the bottles on everyone else. Even the mugs of beer got shifted around. *Shit!* One person saw her plans go awry in the playful shambles. *Now I'll have to follow her when she leaves.*

"What kind of things?" Jim asked. Even in the midst of the boisterous confusion, a few people heard Jim's question and held their breath waiting for the answer.

Shelley slanted shining eyes at him, tossed her hair off of her forehead, and smiled mysteriously. "Just things."

Wow, Ange, Jim thought, *if this girl is innocent, you sure have picked a beauty to fall in love with.* Merrill had told him that Shelley was beautiful, but seeing it for himself was a lot more impressive than hearing about it. Then his thoughts sobered as he wondered how Angela would react if Shelley weren't innocent, especially after the Vicki fiasco. *Sure hope you have better luck this time, kiddo.*

Finally the commotion settled down, and the party started drinking the final round of beer. Soon the friendly chatter was interrupted by a loud groan. "Oh, God, I feel awful," Kath said. She stood up and headed away, calling over her shoulder, "Marv, come with me, please."

Marva had already jumped up and followed right behind her. Ted, concerned about Kath, had stood up, too, and now he doubled over. "Christ, something's hitting me, too," he grunted, heading toward the men's room.

The others sat staring at each other, somewhat startled at the sudden sickness of their friends. They'd all had about the same amount to drink, and they only felt a pleasant buzz. Angela had almost nothing to drink, as she wanted to keep a clear head for following Shelley later that night if it became necessary. She noticed that Shelley had spaced her mugs of beer far apart, too.

When the closing of the bar was announced, the group settled their tab and Barb, Allie, and Amber all left, leaving Merrill, Jim, Angela, and Shelley still at the table. "Jim, maybe you should go check on Ted, see if he's okay," Merrill suggested, "and I'll go check on Kath and Marva."

"Sure," Jim agreed, and he and Merrill went off to the restrooms.

"This was a fun evening," Angela said to Shelley. For the past few hours, they had talked with the rest of the group but both hesitated to address each other specifically. Happy just to be near Shelley, Angela caught a few stolen moments of gazing at her gorgeous face. Meanwhile Shelley worked hard at being sociable, wanting Angela to see her in a good light.

"Yeah, I had a good time," Shelley said. "Jim's a nice guy. He and Merrill are lucky people." She looked deeply into Angela's eyes, but didn't say what her feelings urged her to reveal. Reluctantly, she pulled her eyes away from Angela. "I've got to get going. See you at practice tomorrow." As she left, she felt the redhead's gaze following her out. *Wish I had time to stay, Angela, but I have some business to attend to.*

Jim returned just as Angela was wondering how they could follow Shelley. "Ted's in pretty bad shape, and so is Kath. Merry thinks someone slipped something into their drinks, though God only knows who it could be." He wasn't about to tell Angela that Merry suspected Shelley. *After all, she was the one who started shifting the drinks.*

He ran his fingers through his already tousled hair. "She's calling an ambulance, just in case, and she and Marva will wait with them. She said you and I need to follow Shelley. We can meet her at the hospital if we find out anything. "

"Right," Angela said. She was concerned about her two friends, but the need to continue shadowing Shelley loomed large in her mind. She couldn't do anything here to help, and she didn't want to erase the progress they had made so far in tracking Shelley's movements. She jumped up, and the two hurried toward the exit, with Jim hobbling a little on his cast.

They climbed into Jim's car, and Angela directed him to the last place they had sighted Shelley, where one of the trails crossed a street. They were on the edge of the main part of town, sitting amidst the cheaper retail stores, hock shops, and garages. At this late hour, everything was closed. They sat in the car, waiting for Shelley to pass, secure in the knowledge that she wouldn't recognize Jim's ancient Plymouth.

Jim glanced at Angela, whose eyes weren't leaving the trail. "You pretty well stuck on this girl, Angie?"

Angela took a deep breath and let it out noisily. "Yeah, Jim, afraid I am."

"What are you going to do if she's the killer, Ange?" Jim averted his eyes from the agony that crossed his friend's attractive face.

"I don't believe she is, Jim. I'll have to see her in action with my own eyes before I'll believe that she could torture and kill anyone."

"She sure is beautiful. You haven't let that influence your judgment, have you?"

"I've seen other beautiful people, Jim, and they haven't made my heart jump the way one look from her does. I wasn't planning to fall in love, you know. Didn't even want to. It just happened, and I couldn't seem to stop it." She threw a quick look at Jim; he was watching the trail, too. "Merry's a good-looking girl. Did you fall in love with her because of her looks?"

"No, I fell in love with her because you wouldn't have me." Jim chuckled at the look this statement garnered from Angela. "I'm only kidding." He threw his hands up in mock surrender when she punched his shoulder.

"You're right," he admitted. "I fell in love with something inside Merry that seemed to fit exactly inside some special place in my heart. And there was no stopping it."

He started to turn his head when he saw a movement on the trail. Angela saw it at the same time, and they instinctively ducked below the dashboard. "Look! There she is!" They strained to watch her as she crossed the street and re-entered the trees. "She's bearing left."

"Where does that trail go?" Jim asked. His fingers itched to start the car, but he wanted to wait until Shelley was far enough away that it wouldn't arouse her suspicions.

When they had first arrived, Angela had opened a trail map and placed it on the seat next to her. Now she pulled it onto her lap and flashed a penlight on it. She quickly found the red X that marked their current location at Shelley's last sighting. After a moment, she looked up at Jim. "It comes out at the bottom of the entrance drive to Spofford. Let's get over there."

"Why would she be going to the college?" Jim inquired.

"I have no idea. Maybe it's just a coincidence. She could take any one of several trails at that point."

They arrived at Spofford's entrance much more quickly than a biker could. "Let's go on up the drive on the chance she may be headed there. If we wait and she goes up, we'll have to be right behind her to see where she's going, and she'll see us following her."

"Good thinking," Jim agreed and steered the car up the hill, along the tree-lined drive. The drive emptied into a large parking lot surrounded by the manicured lawns of the campus and edged with several large clumps of trees. He chose a part of the lot that gave a view of several buildings and parked in a shadow formed by some of the trees. There was one other car in the lot, and they hoped that would keep from drawing attention to theirs.

Jim fiddled in the glove compartment and brought out a roll of electrical tape. Angela watched curiously as he tore two short strips from it. "What's that for?" she asked.

Jim grinned at her. "You evidently haven't watched enough cop shows, Ange. Or you're not used to old Plymouths." He cautiously opened his door, intercepting the finger-like protrusion that automatically turned on the inside light whenever the door opened. Pushing it back into its hole, he taped over it, then closed the door.

"Great idea," Angela commended him, accepting the second strip of tape. She fixed her door the same way. Afterwards, as they sat in silence, Jim felt tension pouring from Angela like a brewing storm.

Ten minutes into their waiting time, Shelley showed at the top of the driveway. "Wait here, Jim." Angela slipped from the car without closing the door. Disregarding the order, Jim slid out, too.

Running from tree to tree, Angela easily kept Shelley in sight until she pulled her bike up near some bushes next to the red brick science building.

Angela stopped a building away, throwing out an arm to halt Jim's progress as he caught up to her. He bent over and put his hands on his knees, puffing to catch his breath. "Damn, Angie, it's hard as hell to run with this cast," he whispered.

"Shhhh," Angela admonished him. "She's climbing in a basement window. Wonder why the darn thing's open?"

"Maybe she opened it during the day," Jim suggested. "Why do you think she's going in there?"

"I haven't the slightest idea," the puzzled redhead admitted. "Look, you go to the hospital and tell Merry and Marva where she is. I'll stay here and watch to see if she leaves."

"No way, Angie. I'm not leaving you here alone. I'll wait while you go."

"Jim, she's in the building. I'm out here. If she comes out, I'll hide from her. Better yet, unhook your bike from the back of your car and leave it for me. If she leaves, I can still follow her."

Jim shook his head, knowing that Angela could be stupendously hardheaded at times. "I don't like that idea. I'll stay."

Angela snorted. "Jimbo, you have a broken ankle. You can't even ride a bike. Now stop arguing and go. Just follow the road we came in on, only in the opposite direction. You could have been there by now." This was an exaggeration—the hospital was on the far outskirts of Spofford.

"Why don't we just call the police?" Jim asked.

"And tell them what? That we are following a student who just sneaked into the science building? I don't want to get Shelley in trouble if she's not the killer. She could lose her chance at college." Angela was trying to cover all the bases.

"And even if she is the killer, who is she killing in the science building? She has to go somewhere else, and you have to bring some reinforcements, so we can follow her when and if she leaves. We've been following her for days. I don't want to lose her now." Angela put her hands on her hips and tilted her head at Jim. "Got all that?"

"Yeah, I do," Jim said. "At least most of it," he added with a grin. He wasn't happy, but Angela's reasons for staying did make sense—and she was pretty resourceful. He started to turn away then reached back to put a hand on her shoulder. "You wait out here, Angie. You won't do anything stupid, will you?"

Angela's mouth curved up in a humorless grin. "I already got the stupid prize for falling in love again."

Jim turned completely back, put his arms around her, and kissed her cheek. "Don't be so quick to judge yourself, kiddo. Nothing's been proved against your girl yet. Keep the faith."

Angela hugged him back. "Okay, pal, I will. And thanks."

"Anytime," Jim promised, gave Angela one last squeeze and left.

Angela crept closer to the science building. She couldn't see any sign of a light and wondered what Shelley could be doing in there in the dark. She couldn't make any sense out of it. *What could she do at night that she couldn't do in the daytime?*

The redhead got edgier and edgier as time ticked by. *I keep saying that I believe in Shelley. Well, do I or don't I? If she truly is innocent, what harm will come to me if I follow her inside? We're on the college grounds, for Pete's sake.* Determined to put her belief into action, Angela climbed in through the same window that Shelley had disappeared through.

Trying not to give their presence away, Jim drove slowly out of the parking lot with no headlights and coasted down the hill. As soon as he reached the main thoroughfare, he turned on the lights and floored the accelerator. Zooming in and out of the sparse late-night traffic, he jumped red lights in his haste to get to the hospital. Maybe he was wasting his effort, but he felt really upset about leaving Angela alone at the college with a possible murderer inside.

After what seemed like an eternity, he pulled into the hospital's emergency area, jumped from the car, and hobbled inside. It took him only moments to find Marva and Merrill in the waiting room and explain what he and Angela had discovered.

"Why would she be at the school?" Merrill wondered.

"Ange and I couldn't answer that one either," Jim said. "Maybe she stopped there to pick something up."

"The labs are all closed this late at night. Wasn't there a night watchman around?" Marva questioned.

"We didn't see anyone." Jim looked around as Ted came staggering through the emergency entrance, a nurse trying to halt his progress by pulling on his arm. He looked white and drawn and half-stumbled as he entered the waiting room.

"Where's Shelley?" he demanded. "Did you follow her?"

Jim frowned at the man's pushy questioning. "Yeah, we followed her to Spofford College. She sneaked into the science building through a basement window. Angie's there watching her."

Ted said something under his breath and ran into the emergency room office, closing the door before they could follow. They could hear a commotion inside and Ted's raised voice, but couldn't make out what he was saying. In a few moments he ran back out and headed for the exit.

"Ted, what's going on?" Merrill shouted.

He slowed down just a fraction and looked back at them. "I'll take care of it. You stay here!" With that order, he dashed out.

The three friends looked at each other in bewilderment. "Like hell we will," Jim offered, and he and the two women hurried out.

Chapter
13

Backing through the basement window, as she had noticed Shelley doing, Angela held onto the inside ledge for a moment, gathering her courage, then let go. She bent her knees to cushion her fall and was relieved to find that the drop was a short one. Turning around to face the room she had entered, she was met with a nearly impenetrable blackness. She knew from the unrecognizable mix of somewhat acrid scents in the air that she must be in a chemistry lab.

She waited for a moment, giving her eyes time to adjust, then started to wend her way between the lab counters that became barely visible as she approached them.

She heard a small thump and shivered as she wondered whether she was alone in the room. *Don't be silly. Shelley wouldn't be sitting here waiting for you to show up.* But she stopped and tilted her head, listening to what sounded like quick breathing that suddenly stopped. "Shelley," she said in a low voice, "is that you?" She felt a presence. Her eyes darted back and forth, but the blackness hid everything except the counter she was standing at the end of. Angela never had liked the dark.

Why isn't she answering me? Maybe she's mad that I followed her. Have I pushed her too far? The thought raised goose bumps on her arms, and she rubbed them hard, trying to chase her fear away.

Angela took one more hesitant step forward when a strong arm suddenly flung itself around her neck. She jerked in startled reaction and felt something round and hard push against the side of her head. "Shelley, what are you doing?" She wheezed as she struggled to get the words past the arm pressing against her windpipe. As her legs weakened, she sagged.

"An...ge...la," the word was drawn out and syrupy-sweet. "The question is, what are you doing?" The voice changed into a snarl. "And the second question is, should I shoot you for your damned meddling or not?" The query rasped along Angela's heightened senses. Shelley's breathing was labored, as though she were fighting for control of herself. *Oh, my God, what will happen if she loses control? What can I say to calm her?* Angela was just shy of panic as visions of Shelley's trashed room caromed around her skull. *What was it she said? "At least it was a room I wrecked, not a person."*

"I was following you," Angela admitted, taking short gasps of breath, yet trying to speak soothingly. "The others are convinced that you're involved in these murders, but I don't believe it. I was following you so I could prove it."

The arm tightened for a moment, then returned to its former hold. The grating voice had lost all semblance of Shelley's silken timbre. "Your friends were right, Angela, you've been betting on the wrong player. In fact, you may have just lost the game."

The deep chuckle sent burning vibrations along Angela's nerves. "Shelley, you're making a big mistake. Stop now and I'll help you. We can get a doctor for you. Your Aunt Helen will help you."

"Quiet! You haven't the slightest idea what you're talking about—or what I need. You're going to have a real treat, Angela. You're going to get to watch a play that's about to start. A nice, gory, exciting play that is soooo much fun. I have a mission to accomplish, but no one said I couldn't have some fun doing it. Maybe your presence there will force my leading lady to say the right words. Maybe this time she's the real thing."

As the babbling went on, it woke a voice that screamed in Angela's head. *Wake up, Angela. Shelley really is crazy! Get away from her before she kills you too!* Angela forced her body to relax, and as she had hoped, she felt a slight easing of the arm clutched around her neck. Quickly she threw up a hand to grasp the wrist that held something—was it really a gun?—against her head, and twisted it away. The distraction enabled her to escape from the restraining arm without releasing her hold. She heard an object clatter to the floor and skitter some distance beyond them.

She kept twisting, trying to bring the other girl's wrist up behind the muscular, squirming back. The point of her elbow collided with the corner of one of the lab counters, and her arm fell useless as the captive wrist freed itself from her grasp. She tried to back away, but something hard struck the side of her head, and she tottered. A second strike knocked her to the floor, unconscious.

Flipping Angela over onto her stomach, the taller woman reached into a bag fastened to her waist and pulled out some rope and duct tape. Worried someone might have heard the noise of their tussle, she rushed to tie the redhead up and tape her mouth closed. *You'll make a good audience for my next play, Angela, darling.*

The dark-haired woman scrabbled about on the floor, searching unsuccessfully in the dark for the gun. With a curse, she hurried out of the room, intent on finding the person she originally came looking for—her current leading lady. .

Running as quietly as possible along the corridor, she spied a light coming through the transom of one of the labs ahead of her. She gently turned the door handle and entered a brightly lit laboratory. With a grin, she noticed that the basement windows were covered with black curtains. *Clever. And very useful. Black curtains can conceal more than light.*

She walked further into the room until the figure leaning over one of the counters looked up, startled to see someone else had come in.

"What are you doing here?" she asked the intruder. *And how did she get in?* A caution bell rang in her head.

"I have some lab work to catch up on. I figured this late at night would be a good time—no one else is here—so I sneaked in a window. I see you had the same idea." She stuck her hands in her pockets and sauntered over next to the other girl, craning her neck to look at the experiment set up on the countertop. "What are you working on?"

The woman working the experiment shook off her apprehension. *Relax, Shelley, you're seeing monsters behind every shadow. This is just Allie, trying to keep up with her work same as you.* Heedlessly, Shelley turned her head back toward the workbench and suddenly was grabbed from behind. Allie had a chokehold around her neck and held a switchblade against her throat. Shelley stiffened but stood her ground. "You know what this is against your neck, Star? It's a Star-Maker. Isn't that cute?"

Shelley automatically felt for her own switchblade. Her heart dropped as she realized she hadn't retrieved it from the police yet. *Damn that Officer Gibbons for a fool!*

"Other people know I'm here, Allie. Someone might come in at any moment," Shelley bluffed.

Her heart plummeted when she heard Allie's sneering retort. "If you're waiting for Angela, you'll have a long wait. She's lying in the lab where we all came in, trussed up like a pig waiting for a roast. Maybe I'll let her watch while you perform in my play." Allie snickered. "I like Angela. Too bad I'll have to get rid of her, too."

At Angela's name, Shelley's insides twisted and she could feel the familiar black rage building in her. She fought to control it, knowing that losing her temper could mean losing her life and Angela's too. But if she could harness that rage, it would give her extra strength and right now she needed all the extra power she could get. Allie was as tall as she was and considerably huskier, so it was a good bet that she was stronger. *But maybe not as quick.*

"What are you going to do, Allie? Slit my throat?" Shelley was gambling that Allie would have to let go of her neck to pursue whatever "play" her demented mind was considering. And her gamble paid off.

Allie released her and gave her a shove toward the far wall. "There's a desk in the corner of the room. Pull the chair out into the aisle, and sit in it."

Shelley slowed her walk so that Allie came up to her and pricked her in the middle of the back with the knife point. As soon as she felt the sting, Shelley swung around with her elbow, knocking Allie's hand away from her back. Quickly she kicked the hand, sending the knife flying across a lab counter into another aisle.

As Shelley's leg followed through, Allie flung a counterpunch at the side of her head. Shelley jerked her head back, but the punch landed at the edge of her forehead, staggering her. Allie threw out a boot and swept Shelley's feet from under her, making her fall heavily against a counter, then the floor. Before Shelley could move, Allie stomped her several times. The beating she'd taken was almost enough to put her out of commission, but Shelley's rage came to her rescue, magnifying her strength. She seized Allie's foot and twisted until the heavier woman grabbed the edge of a counter and pulled her foot away. Shelley did a back roll and came up onto her feet, the surge of adrenaline making her unmindful of how her body was bruised and straining for air.

Allie ran around the end of the counter into the next aisle, hurrying toward the switchblade. Shelley came running behind her and shoved her in the back, forcing her to stumble past the knife. She reached down for it herself, but before her hand could close around it, Allie had recovered her balance and kicked at it, sending it underneath a low-slung credenza, out of reach for both women.

Shelley hit Allie with a straight-arm left and a right hook, jarring her. Allie backed away as fast as her stumbling feet would take her, finally edging around into another aisle. "Why are you doing this, Allie?" Shelley asked, panting. She bent over with her hands on her knees, pulling in great gasps of air, fighting to recover her breath. Her rage was working well for her. She had been able to harness its increased physical strength while keeping its destructiveness under control, a new experience for her. "Why are you...killing all these girls? Why do you...want to kill me?"

"I have a mission...to save some lives. I'm looking for someone," Allie shouted angrily. "She looks just like you and the other girls. But I don't know her name."

"Why does she...deserve to die? What did she...do to you?"

Allie's face turned crafty. "If you're the right person, you know the answer to that. You are the right one, aren't you, Star?"

Allie was between her and the door. Shelley's breathing had recovered, but she needed a few more moments to rebuild her strength so she could get past her. "Maybe I am, Allie. Tell me how you worked it. How did you choose which girls to kill?"

"I found their pictures in the yearbooks. I judged their age by their class. But that wouldn't have worked with you, would it? Kath gave away your age at one of the games, remember? And you were never in a yearbook, were you? Why is that, Shelley? Hiding?" Allie sneered and went on with her bragging.

"I had to check each of them out on the sports listings to see if they were the right height. If they were, I followed them and found out their habits. I waited until they went out somewhere, and then I dumped knockout drops in their drinks. When they went to the ladies' room, I helped them outside for fresh air, but I put them into my car instead," she smirked. "It was so easy. I just drove them to the house on Farmdale Lane and put them on stage in the cellar. But they wouldn't say the lines I wanted to hear."

Good God, she says she has a mission, but she's half demented too, Shelley realized.

"What lines did you want to hear?" Shelley asked.

"A name! They need to tell me the right name!" The talking had increased Allie's anger. "But they never did, so I had to kill them. And I'm going to kill you too," she yelled and charged at Shelley, who sidestepped and caught her with an uppercut as she went by. Shelley decided this might be her last chance, and she better throw everything she had left at her assailant. She shoved Allie's shoulder to bring her face to face and pummeled her with constant punches, shaking off a few hard hits on her own body. Finally, she stepped back and swung a foot at Allie's jaw, making her sag to the floor, unconscious.

Shelley stood for a minute, chest heaving, a red fog numbing her mind. Then it cleared enough to wonder how she could restrain Allie—where could she find something to use to tie her up? Then she remembered Allie had boasted of tying up Angela. *If I hurry, I can use those same ropes—and get Angela out of here. Then we can call the police.*

She stumbled out of the lab as quickly as possible, determined to find Angela and get her out of harm's way.

Angela came to, not knowing for a moment what had happened to her. As she regained her memory, she realized she was bound. Sudden clarity hit her and threatened to freeze her heart. *Shelley's the killer! Shelley really is the killer.* Tears rose in her eyes and coursed down her cheeks even as she struggled with her bonds. Eventually the tears slowed and the ropes, tied too hastily, loosened. She slipped her hands free and tore the duct tape from her mouth, wincing as it pulled against the sensitive skin of her lips. She almost welcomed the pain; at least it showed that she was still alive, even though her heart felt dead.

As she rubbed the tears from her face, the grim reality of her situation hit her. *She said she's coming back for me!* Hurriedly, Angela flipped a light switch, bathing the lab in a fluorescent glow. She dashed around looking for the dropped gun and finally found it. Picking it up and checking it out, she found the safety was already off. Angela gasped. Shelley had been holding a loaded gun at her temple. She really would have killed her.

Angela shook so badly she leaned against the wall and slid down it to the floor. In a daze, she heard someone running down the corridor. She braced her back against the wall and sat there, holding the gun with both hands and aiming it toward the door. She jumped as the door was thrown open, and Shelley came barreling in.

"*Stop!*" Angela shouted in terror, waving the gun for emphasis.

Shelley grabbed the end of the lab counter to slow her momentum, but she didn't stop. "Angela, it's okay. It's me, Shell..."

Boom! In the close quarters of the lab, the gunshot sounded like a cannon. Shelley's mouth gaped open, and her eyes widened in disbelief as the force of the shot slammed her body against the doorjamb behind her. She bounced off and fell facefirst onto the hard tile.

Angela's jumbled thoughts seared jagged paths through her shocked brain, struggling to grasp the enormity of what had happened. *I...shot...Shelley.* The words sounded too simple to explain the horror she felt as she looked at the body lying on the floor. A slow flow of blood painted a thin red line against the dark-gray tile.

Angela crawled most of the way down the aisle toward the still form before she realized the odd *clump* that she was hearing was the gun, still in her hand, hitting against the floor. Stunned by the damage she had wrought with it, she flung the weapon away, not caring where it landed.

Crawling the remaining distance, she reached Shelley's side and was trying to gather the courage to touch her, too dazed to notice when another figure entered the room. Her first knowledge of the person's arrival was when a foot slipped under Shelley and turned her over, exposing the oozing entrance wound on her upper chest, near her left shoulder.

Shaken and confused, Angela looked up, not comprehending what she saw. "Allie? Wh...why are you here?" she stammered. "Can you go for help?"

Allie, seeing that Angela was unarmed, laughed out loud through her bloodied lips and couldn't pass up the chance to boast. "You still think Shelley's the murderer, don't you? Well, I'm the one who claims that honor, sweetheart. You just shot an innocent girl."

Angela's battered senses slowed her understanding. *Shelley's innocent...and I shot her?* The truth suddenly blasted through her heart like an exploding shell, and Angela slumped back against an open cupboard. "No!" she wailed. "No, no, no..." She covered her face with her shaking hands, grief-stricken by the sight of Shelley's fallen body.

"Ah, but yes." The whole situation tickled Allie's warped sense of humor. "I'll just bet your girlfriend came dashing in here to save you, and you shot her. I couldn't have written the script any better myself. Though I have much more fun with the kills I get to participate in."

Angela cringed at the sickening thought, but it helped to clear her brain. She looked toward Allie and in her peripheral vision saw Shelley's eyelids flutter. Her heart lifted. *She's alive! I've got to do something to get us out of this. Keep Allie talking. Find the gun.* She raised her head and forced her voice through her constricted throat. It came out a hoarse whisper. "What do you mean, she tried to save me? From you?"

"Of course from me, An...ge...la. You don't think I can leave you alive, do you? Hell, I'd kill you just for robbing me of my fun." Her evil grin reinforced the meaning of her words, and her cunning mind noticed Angela surreptitiously peeking around.

She looked up the aisle past Angela and saw the gun. They moved for it simultaneously. Angela dove on her belly, and Allie ran toward it. Both hands closed on it at the same time. Angela butted her in the face, but Allie's strength was too much for her. The dark-haired woman slammed both their hands against Angela's already bruised head, stunning her. Allie easily wrested the gun from her and stood up, panting furiously.

"Michelle Stella!" Shelley's voice rang out, but Allie was too enraged to heed it. She pointed the gun at Angela and pulled the trigger.

The gun didn't fire. In their tussle, Angela had pushed the safety on. But now Shelley's words filtered through Allie's anger, and she switched her attention in a hurry. With a wide grin on her face, she pushed off the safety and sauntered back to where Shelley still lay bleeding.

"Michelle Stella," Allie echoed with a satisfied grunt. "Finally." She aimed the gun at Shelley. "Too bad I have to waste such a gorgeous girl, Shelley, but that's just the way the game is played." Her finger tightened on the trigger. "Say good-bye," she sneered.

Angela pushed herself up onto her hands and knees and shook her head, fighting to clear her vision. She could hear Allie at the end of the 30-foot aisle, talking to Shelley, and she knew that time was short. Her eyes cleared and at last she could see the husky killer. And she saw something else that gave her hope. On the shelf in front of her rested a softball-sized crucible made of heavy stoneware. As quickly and quietly as she could, Angela grabbed it, stood up, took a step forward, and launched it at Allie's head.

There was a split second between the thud of the missile hitting Allie and the roar of the gun. Horrified that Shelley had been shot again, Angela dashed down the aisle, grabbed the fallen crucible, and leaped onto Allie's back. Twice she slammed the stoneware against Allie's unconscious head before a hand grabbed her wrist and the loveliest voice in the world called her name.

"Angela, that's enough," Shelley said softly.

"You're alive!" Angela shrieked. "She missed you!" She hastened off of Allie's back and knelt next to the wounded girl. It had taken all of Shelley's energy to crawl over to halt Angela's attack. She slumped back onto the floor, lying out flat and closing her eyes.

"Oh, God, Shelley, how bad is it? I'm so sorry I shot you. I could have killed you." Angela touched Shelley's ashen cheek with shaking fingers. "Allie grabbed me when I first came in the window, and she threatened me. I thought it was you. I didn't think you were guilty until that happened. I wanted to prove you were innocent." Angela's words were coming as fast as her tears. "It was dark. I couldn't tell, and I knew you had come in..."

"Shhhh," Shelley said and slowly smiled. Her eyes opened and met Angela's red and swollen ones. "Maybe you better call an ambulance, huh? And the police?"

Angela put her fingers against her trembling lips, smiled through her tears and nodded. "Yeah, I guess I better," she agreed and sniffled.

To their astonishment, the door burst open and several policemen hurried in, their guns drawn. Angela and Shelley were surprised to see Ted with them. He beckoned to the paramedics who were heading toward Allie. "Take care of this girl first," he

ordered, pointing to Shelley. "The next two can see to her," he
said as he gestured toward Allie. While they attended to Shelley,
he squatted down next to her. "How are you?"

Shelley frowned. "I have a bullet in me and it hurts like
hell, but I'll live. How are you mixed up in this? What are you
up to?"

Ted stood up and removed a case from his hip pocket.
Squatting back down, he opened the flap and showed Shelley an
ID card, which elicited a grimace. "Guess you know I have to
take you out of here."

Shelley closed her eyes. When she opened them, they were
filled with a different kind of pain. "Can I please just have a
minute of privacy with Angela?" Ted bent over and whispered in
her ear then stood up. The medics had finished bandaging Shelley's wound and had put her on a stretcher. He called them away
with him. Two other medics put Allie on a stretcher and carried
her out.

Angela looked totally confused, and Shelley held out her
right hand to her. When Angela put her hand in Shelley's, the
dark-haired girl pulled her close. "Would you please bend down
here and give me a kiss? I sure could use one."

Angela tried to wipe her cheeks. "I'm a mess," she sniffled.

"Wait a minute," Shelley said. She let go of Angela's hand
and reached into her pocket, pulling out a wad of tissues and
handing it to her.

"Thanks," Angela mumbled as she wiped her face and blew
her nose.

"No problem," Shelley answered. "I carry them just for you,
you know." This prompted a small snort from the redhead that
made Shelley's heart sing.

She moved her arm up just enough to allow her to caress
Angela's hair. "I love you, Angela," she said, her velvet voice
wrapping itself around Angela's soul.

Angela tilted her head down. The moisture remaining in the
hazel eyes made their yellow and green highlights glisten. Now
she could say the words that had been carved on her heart for
weeks, words that she had dared not admit even to herself. "I
love you, too, Shelley."

Their lips met and magnified the sweetness of the words.
Fire that had smoldered in both of them burst into flame, and
they clung to each other, drawing strength and healing from its
heat.

At last their lips parted. Shelley touched Angela's face with her fingertips, slowly tracing her cheek and lightly brushing her lips. "I made a mistake the last time...grabbing at you. I was too hasty. I want to court you slowly and thoroughly," Shelley said, her eyes burning with passion.

Angela swallowed. "Yes, I would like that." Then a grin tweaked the edge of her lips. "But not too slowly," she said, chuckling aloud at the excitement that flared in those blue, blue eyes.

Ted's voice interrupted them. "Hurry up, Shelley!"

The excitement in Shelley's eyes dimmed, and her voice took on urgency. "Angela, I have to go away for a while. Will you wait for me?"

Angela's confusion returned. "Yes, but why? Where? When will you be back?"

Ted suddenly became very businesslike as he heard another commotion in the corridor. Someone yelled that a TV crew was arriving. *How the hell do they find out about things so quickly?* he wondered. "Sorry, ladies," he interrupted, "but we just ran out of time." He nodded and two men grabbed the stretcher and hustled Shelley out. Angela stared after them in bewilderment, watching as the dark-haired girl struggled to keep her yearning eyes on Angela as long as possible.

Merrill, Jim, and Marva arrived soon after Shelley's departure. Although they weren't allowed on the scene, Angela was given a couple of minutes to talk to them.

When Merrill saw the look on her best friend's face, she opened her arms and Angela walked right into a hug. "Oh, God, Merry, I shot Shelley."

Astonished, Merrill pulled back a little. "You what?" Jim and Marva looked as startled as she did.

Fighting back her tears, Angela quickly gave them all hugs and explained that Shelley was innocent, Allie was the real killer, and Shelley had almost been killed because of Angela's confusion. The three friends had a hundred questions to ask, but Angela had to go to the police station to give her statement. She assured them that she would fill in all the details when she got back home. Just before she left, she grabbed Merrill's hand. "See if you can find out where the ambulance took Shelley," she begged.

"I'll do that, Ange; you just worry about you," Merrill answered.

Chaos had seemed to descend on the lab as the departure of the ambulances and arrival of more police and the TV crew coincided. Angela gladly allowed the police officer to lead her to his patrol car and take her away. She hoped that she would be reunited with Shelley soon, but the heaviness in her heart raised doubts about such a simple outcome. *Where did she go? Where did Ted take her? What's going on?* This relationship had been frustrated from the very beginning, and somehow Angela felt that the frustration wasn't over.

At the police station, Angela was up all night answering a thousand and one questions about the events of the night. She replied to questions about Shelley, Allie, herself, and all their friends, then had to go through it all over again. Finally she was released and escorted home. When she dragged herself into her apartment, Merrill was waiting for her.

"Did you find Shelley?" were the first words out of the redhead's mouth.

Merrill shook her head, sadly. "We checked all the hospitals around, and she's not in any of them. No one would tell us anything, honey. Do you feel up to talking about what happened?"

Angela waved a weary arm at her and begged off. "Please, Merry, just let me sleep, then I'll answer everything. I can't even think straight right now." Merrill nodded and Angela staggered into the bedroom and flopped onto the bed, not even taking time to shower or change.

Physically and emotionally exhausted, Angela slept for 24 hours, and Merrill wouldn't let anyone bother her. She finally awoke, ravenous, on Sunday morning. Merrill heard her in the shower and greeted her with bacon and eggs, toast and juice— and the mainstay coffee. Marva and Kath were already there.

"This is great, Merr, thanks." She wasted no time beginning to eat. "Guess I kinda messed up things with you and Jim the last couple of nights, huh?"

"Not at all," Merrill said, grinning at her best friend. She was anxious to hear the whole story but knew Angela would tell them in her own time. "Kath was held overnight in the hospital, and Marva slept in my bed. Then last night Kath took the couch. You were too zonked to notice. They let us have their apartment for the two nights. It killed Jim that he had to be back at school.

He wanted to hang around and get the whole story, but I convinced him I would let him know about it as soon as I found it out."

"Ah, that's great. There's just no substitute for friends, is there?" Angela looked up from her food and smiled at the three women. "How are you, Kath? Your stomach okay now?"

"It's fine, Ange. The doctor said apparently it was knockout drops. Ted and I split the bottle of beer we had, so we both got sick, but not as bad as we would have if one of us drank the whole thing."

Angela was half afraid to ask the next question. "Have you heard anything about Shelley?"

Merrill looked at her friend's hopeful expression and felt like crying. "God, Ange, we thought it was an answer to a prayer when we found out that Shelley was innocent. And we were thrilled to find out that you were okay. Then a couple of women came yesterday and took everything from her apartment."

"They wouldn't tell us anything; they just closed the place down," Marva added.

"And Ted hasn't shown up since he left the hospital, either," Kath admitted with a disappointed look. She remembered Merrill telling her how distressed Ted had been when he found that Angela and Jim had tracked Shelley to the college and Angela had stayed there alone to watch her. As soon as he could walk straight, he'd dashed out of the hospital and taken off. "Do you think there's any connection?"

"I think I need to tell you everything that happened Friday night," Angela said. She told the girls the whole story, stopping constantly to retell some of the scariest parts. She had to piece some of Shelley's part of it together since they hadn't been able to explain everything to each other.

The girls were stunned all over again when Angela recounted her shooting of Shelley. "Wow," Marva exclaimed. "So you thought Allie was Shelley at first? That must have really shook you up."

"I was devastated to think that Shelley was the killer," Angela admitted. "Then I was convinced that she was insane, and I was alone with a murderer. When she came rushing back into the lab, I thought she was coming to kill me. I was so terrified that I pulled the trigger...and shot her." *Will I ever get over that guilt?*

Everyone was quiet for a moment, realizing how close

Angela and Shelley had come to real tragedy. Then Kath frowned and broke the silence. "Angie, you know I'm glad that things turned out well and Shelley's been cleared of the murders, but I'm disturbed about Ted. Do you think he was some kind of undercover policeman pretending to be a student?"

Angela patted Kath's hand. "I'm afraid so, Kath. I just can't figure out why he took Shelley away." She looked around at the others. "Do you think maybe she was wanted for some other criminal activity? I'm just totally confused."

"We're all confused, Ange," Merrill said. "Guess you'll just have to wait until Shelley gets back to you and fills you in."

Angela nodded and blinked, trying not to cry the tears that welled in her eyes.

Kath was upset too. Her relationship with Ted hadn't passed the dating stage, but she had been greatly attracted to him and had believed that he was attracted to her, too. Now her self-esteem and self-confidence suffered. *Was he just using me to stay close to Shelley?* She wondered if she and Angela would ever find the answers to what had transpired.

"Merry's right," she said to Angela with a sigh. "We'll just have to wait."

They had no idea how long that wait would be.

Chapter 14

Three months later.

Spofford had finished the softball season second in their league, behind Scatsboro. Their only two losses were by one run each, and Angela felt certain that Shelley's presence would have meant the difference. But as much as she loved softball, that was the least of her worries.

Angela struggled daily with her emotions. She thought the rejection she had experienced when Vicki left was earthshaking, but that was nothing compared to how she felt now. She didn't believe Shelley had rejected her; on the contrary, she believed in their love. But how could she express her love to someone who was totally inaccessible? No, rejection wasn't bothering her. She ached to put her arms around Shelley and to feel those long, tanned arms wrapped around her. She was mentally, physically, and emotionally frustrated—and that was driving her crazy.

Apparently there hadn't even been much progress made toward a trial for Allie Monroe. Angela knew murder trials took a long time, but usually the newspapers ran an occasional article about them. Once the initial furor was over, however, there hadn't been a peep about Allie Monroe or her trial.

The discovery of the killer had been played up big in the newspapers when she had first been caught, and coeds in all the nearby schools had felt enormous relief. According to the papers, no motive was established. Angela vaguely recalled Shelley calling out a name to Allie, but for the life of her she couldn't remember it. At the time, she wasn't hearing too clearly and her mind had been totally occupied with struggling with Allie.

It seemed to Angela that if Allie had been looking for a name, there had to be some motive to the murders other than just some psycho playing out her macabre fantasies. She sighed...so many unanswered questions. And the biggest one still was—where was Shelley?

She remembered that Shelley had told her that Judge Helen Ostcott was her guardian. Several times Angela had thought about calling her, but lost her nerve. One day when she was home for summer vacation, she gathered her courage, searched for the judge's office telephone number, and made the call.

Angela had a private telephone at home that sat on a desk in her bedroom, and she called from there. "May I speak with Judge Helen Ostcott?"

"May I ask who is calling?"

"My name is Angela Wedgeway. I'm a friend of her ward, Shelley Brinton."

"One moment, please." Angela drummed her fingers on the desk while her eyes nostalgically roamed the room. This was the room she'd grown up in, and it still reflected her younger self. Its slightly frilly flowered bedspread carried a blue-and-white morning glory motif intertwined with green vines on a pale yellow background, and matching drapes hung at the two windows. The green of the vines was picked up by the darker green carpet that blended softly with the maple furniture.

Her bed doll, Suzy, dressed in a long, old-fashioned green gown with a bonnet on her yellow pigtails, shared the bed with Angela's favorite teddy bear. Other stuffed animals adorned the bookcase, while a couple of family pictures sat on the two bureaus. A small entertainment center held a TV, VCR, and CD player, and a stand next to it was filled with tapes and discs. Her computer was housed in the family room, though no one else used it.

Once Shelley comes back into my life, I may never see this room—or this house—again, she thought with a jolt. *I may not see Mom and Dad!* That decision would be up to her parents. She couldn't pretend anymore to be somebody she wasn't. She loved her parents dearly, but she knew that if a choice had to be made, Shelley would win.

Her thoughts were interrupted by the return of the telephone voice. "Ms. Wedgeway, Judge Ostcott is too busy to take a personal call right now, but she asked me to advise you that she has no ward named Shelley Brinton."

Dumfounded, Angela murmured, "Thank you," and hung up. Had Shelley lied to her about her guardian? Angela hadn't checked the information out when Shelley first told her about the judge. Kath's story about a judge bringing the folder to Dean Lohman seemed to bear out what Shelley claimed. But if Helen Ostcott really was her guardian, why would she lie about it?

Forestalled from learning anything via that route, Angela didn't know what to try next. Later, when she told Merrill about the call to the judge, her friend listened, then patted her on the back. "Maybe you should try to put Shelley out of your mind, Angie. I'm beginning to believe it's a lost cause. If she really cared as much about you as you care about her, don't you think she would have contacted you before now?"

"I don't know, Merry. The more I picture in my mind the way she was taken away, the more it seems that she was some kind of prisoner."

"You said she didn't even put up a fight."

"She didn't, but she obviously didn't want to go."

"But she went, didn't she?"

Angela couldn't argue against that fact. Of course, Shelley had been taken away on a stretcher, but she'd seemed to accept her removal as inevitable. For the next several days, the redhead mourned the loss of Shelley all over again. Then one morning a courier showed up at the Wedgeway household bearing a small package for her. Angela signed for it, then took it up to her bedroom, curiously turning it over and over in her hands. Nothing was written on the outside except her name and address. She sat at her desk, drew a pair of scissors from the drawer, and cut the package open.

It was a jewel case. Angela opened the case with trembling fingers and gasped when she saw what it contained. Lying on a black velvet background was a gold pendant on a chain. The pendant was a star, intricately carved, with a heart in the center. The letters "A+S" were inscribed inside the heart. There was nothing else with it, but Angela didn't care; she was crying tears of joy. She knew the star was an affirmation, a promise. She knew Shelley would be coming back, and she would wait for her until she did, no matter how long it took.

Fall semester started without any fanfare as the girls prepared for their senior year at Spofford. On the surface nothing
had changed, but each of them felt Shelley's absence keenly,
especially during Angela's protracted silences. The attractive
redhead walked through her days as though she was just putting
in time. She was wise enough not to let her schoolwork suffer,
but she couldn't shake the lost feeling that had settled over her.
Her three friends commiserated, but they knew that only Shelley's return would relieve Angela's misery.

One evening they were chatting in front of the TV at the
Brickhouse. Angela had gone into the kitchenette to get another
soda when suddenly she heard Kath bellow her name. "Angie!
Come here! Quick!"

Startled, she dashed back into the living room to see Kath
pointing to the TV, her finger shaking. She was almost too
excited to talk. Merrill and Marva were looking at her like she
had lost her mind.

"I saw her!" she finally managed to get out. "I just saw
Shelley!"

"Where?" Angela demanded. "What?" She perched on the
edge of the couch between Marva and Kath and looked toward
the TV. The ten o'clock news was on, but she saw only the
anchorwoman talking.

"You missed it. You all missed it," Kath almost whined in
despair. Then her face lit up. "But we can watch the eleven
o'clock news when it comes on. Maybe they'll show her again."

"What was she on for, Kath?" Marva asked.

"I don't know. I wasn't really paying attention. I think it
might have been something to do with that big mob trial that's
been going on for weeks now. There was a film clip of some
interview they were doing, and I glanced up and saw Shelley in
the background. By the time I yelled and you guys looked, the
clip was finished."

"You're sure it was Shelley?" Merrill asked seriously. She
didn't want Angela getting upset over a mistaken identity.

Kath looked at her and raised her eyebrows. "Come on,
Merry, how many tall, slim, black-haired women are as gorgeous
as Shelley? I know it was her."

Merrill patted her calf from her seat on the floor. "Okay,
kiddo, I'm not arguing, just trying to be sure."

The girls set up the VCR to record the news, then sat around for the next hour rehashing the events that had so stirred them all. Angela didn't add much to the conversation, and the others didn't push her, knowing she had to be a nervous wreck. Finally, eleven o'clock came, and they waited anxiously for the news clip to appear. They didn't have long to wait; it was the lead story on the national news front.

The attractive black anchorwoman faced the camera with a serious mien. "In Washington, D.C., as the Gatrone mob trial grinds into its eighth week, it slowly but surely has approached the time for witnesses for the prosecution to begin their testimony. Phil Pasticco has the latest developments."

The clip started and the newsman began his report from the corridor of the courthouse as drawn pictures of the proceedings were flashed on the screen. Just as the pictures ended and the view came back to the newsman, a tall, dark-haired woman moved across the hall some distance behind him. She turned toward the camera for a brief moment as the person behind her took hold of her arm and hurried her forward. There was no doubting that arrogant look. It was Shelley.

Three sets of eyes turned to Angela, who sat stunned. Marva walked over and halted the VCR recording before slumping down next to her friend, her warm brown eyes fixed on Angela's face. When that face crumpled and Angela flung up her hands to cover it, Marva and Merrill each slipped an arm around her, and Kath moved to squeeze her shoulder. Angela's chest heaved several times before she could bring herself under control.

At last, she lowered her hands and swallowed hard. Kath got up and rewound the tape and handed the remote to Angela, who smiled her thanks to her. They sat and watched the clip five times before Angela could trust herself to speak.

"She still looks like a prisoner with those goons grabbing at her, doesn't she?" Angela said hoarsely. She looked at the other three who nodded.

"She's in Washington, D.C. What's the fastest way to get there from here?"

"Plane, I would guess," Merrill answered. "But Washington can't be much more than a three- or four-hour drive from here, don't you think? We can drive down."

Angela swung grateful eyes to Merrill and touched her forehead to her friend's. "Good to go, Merr."

Kath reached onto a bookshelf, pulled down the phone

book, and started riffling through it. "What are you looking for, Kath?" Marva asked.

"I'm going to call the information desk at the library and find out what time the trial starts tomorrow."

Marva grinned. "See, I keep telling you guys she is more than just a pretty face." Her grin broadened to a smile when Kath stuck her tongue out at her.

They waited impatiently while Kath called and spoke to a woman at the library. Kath hung up and turned a frustrated look on them. "She said the trial starts at ten but it's unlikely we can get in unless we have a special pass. It's way too crowded."

"Damn," Angela mumbled. She grabbed a lock of her hair and tugged it.

"If she is a prisoner, they could be concealing her entrance and exit from the courthouse. Even if we camped outside we might never see her," Merrill complained.

"One thing we do know," Marva said and faced three sets of raised eyebrows. "If she's there, she must be going to show up during the trial. We can keep a close watch on the news and in the papers, and eventually they'll report that she's either part of the prosecution or part of the defense."

"But if she's not a big part of either, they might not even mention her," Merrill suggested.

"If I were a courtroom artist, I wouldn't miss a chance to get that face in my drawing no matter how small her part might be," Marva said.

"I think Marva's right," Angela said. "We'll just have to keep watching for her." She took a deep breath and pushed it out. "I can't think of any alternative at the moment, anyhow." She looked around. "Can anyone?" Shaking heads gave their answer.

The trial dragged on and on. The girls met every night to watch the news at ten and to pore over the *Philadelphia Inquirer,* which was reporting closely on the trial. They learned that there were five mobsters on trial, and the preliminary steps were so important that the government was being tediously meticulous in getting its case in order. Finally, the prosecution began calling its witnesses, and time dragged even more. The *Inquirer* claimed that the case didn't look strong enough for the mobsters to get the death penalty sought by the government.

One evening the girls were glued to the set and were astounded when a drawing of Shelley was put up as the newsman on the scene started reporting, "Today the prosecution called its star witness, Ms. Michelle Stella, to the stand. Ms. Stella's testimony sounds like the big break this case has needed. Four years ago, at the age of fourteen, she was an eyewitness to the machine-gunning of mob boss Leo Tarelli at the Golden Tea House Restaurant on Pennsylvania Avenue here in Washington.

"Our sources tell us that Ms. Stella is prepared to identify each of the five defendants as material participants in that murder. Several innocent bystanders were also killed in that barrage, including Ms. Stella's parents. Ms. Stella herself suffered a grievous stomach wound that almost took her life.

"As a key witness, Ms. Stella has been under strict security for the past four years. She has been living under an assumed identity in a government witness protection program. In spite of that, about five months ago an attempt on her life very nearly succeeded, and she has been held under maximum security since then. Her testimony is projected to wrap up in two weeks, and then the defense will offer their side of the case. In another development..."

His voice continued on, but the girls were no longer interested. A bombshell dropped in their midst would not have caused more shock than the news about Shelley had. Each girl had tears in her eyes.

"My God," Angela whispered hoarsely, "she was there when her parents were gunned down—and she was only fourteen." *And she was almost killed too. I saw that scar but didn't give it a second thought. To me it was just a very insignificant flaw on an otherwise perfect body. To her it was a matter of life or death.*

"No wonder she was in an anger management program," Marva said. "She must have been mad at the whole world." The trashed room took on a whole new dimension.

"And she couldn't even live a normal life," Kath offered. "She had to use a fake name and history. I guess that's why she changed schools so many times—to protect her identity."

Merrill looked anguished. "And I didn't trust her! I poisoned your minds against her until Angie very nearly killed her."

Angela put her arm around Merrill. "Come on, Merry, you were only trying to look out for me. I understand that, and so will Shelley." Angela had to smile. "It's just part of your nature to be doggedly persistent. Most of us could use a little more of that ourselves."

She released her best friend and patted her on the back. "Hey, cheer up. That goes for all of us. When this trial is over and these guys get sentenced, Shelley will be free! What do you say we go celebrate for an hour or so?"

It was a bedraggled group that headed for the Steak House that evening, but the girls' hearts were already beginning to lighten as they contemplated Shelley's eventual freedom.

Shelley didn't feel free yet.

After her fracas with Allie, Ted had whisked Shelley off to a remote hospital where he registered her under a different name and set up agents inside and outside her hospital room. Aunt Helen had been allowed just one visit. The operation to remove the bullet had gone smoothly, and as soon as she was comfortable enough to talk, a long line of agents subjected her to a barrage of questions. When that finally ended, she recuperated quickly and was moved to a hotel room with the same strict security measures. It had been quiet, peaceful, and depressingly lonely. Shelley hadn't had contact with anyone except government officials for months, and she was losing what little patience she still had.

Fran Wilkins, the agent stationed in her hotel room, had brought some crossword puzzle books for her own entertainment, and she had shared them with Shelley. Of average height and in excellent physical condition, the older woman treated Shelley with respect, but always with the slightly aloof manner her status as an agent required.

The dark-haired girl had been seated at a table that stood in one corner of the living room. She had just completed running through her fifteenth crossword when the emptiness of her situation finally got to her. She threw the puzzle book across the room, stood up, and flipped the table over, dumping the pencil and several other books onto the carpeted floor.

"I can't stand this any longer," she had raged through clenched teeth as Fran came running into the room from the kitchen. The fair-haired agent came to a distant halt, warily eyeing the taller girl. Shelley had her fists bunched at her side while fire sparked from her eyes, and her body shook with the effort she was making to control herself.

"I need to see Aunt Helen," Shelley barked. "Now!" She really needed to see Angela, but knew there was no hope of that. Maybe Aunt Helen could help her cope with this rotten situation, as she had in the past.

Shelley had been making some real progress under the anger management program. Four years ago, she had suffered near debilitating rage at the loss of her parents and the shattering of her life. Gradually, with a lot of help, she had learned to accept those things, but the rootless life she was forced to lead had generated new fury. Playing softball, attending drama classes, even working in the Steak House had aided her struggle to cope with that.

Finding herself falling in love with Angela had helped the most. Even while under suspicion from all the girls, Shelley had a glimmer of hope that someday, when Angela learned the whole truth, she might have a chance to pursue that love.

Allie's attack on Shelley in the lab had revealed that the coed murders were tied to a search for Shelley, and suddenly a difficult situation became nearly intolerable. With her eyewitness testimony integral to the government's case against the mobsters, Shelley was taken away from Spofford and forced into tight security. Which meant she had no life at all—and no contact with Angela—and it was driving her crazy.

Fran stood just inside the door and nodded. "I'll see what I can do, Shelley. Please stay calm." She pulled out her cell phone, called Jeff Cruz, and identified herself. "Shelley is standing in front of me, and she's very angry. She demands to see her Aunt Helen. I would give this pretty close to emergency status." She listened for a minute, then folded the phone and stuck it back in its holder on her belt.

"He said he would have her here as soon as possible, maybe an hour." Fran looked sympathetically at the beautiful young woman before her. "If you'll clean up that mess, I'll have lunch ready in the kitchen."

Shelley stood there, fighting down her rage, forcing it back into its dark cavern inside her soul. She shook her head and righted the table, then picked up the puzzle books and pencil. Fran could hear her labored breathing and listened with relief as it eventually slowed.

They sat in the kitchen, and Shelley toyed with her lunch, hardly eating. Finally, her ears pricked up as she heard a noise near the outside door. Fran's phone rang, and the outside guard told her that Judge Helen Ostcott had arrived.

Shelley was already at the door, waiting for Fran to open it. Helen Ostcott strode in and enveloped her ward in her motherly arms. They stood clasped together for a long moment as Helen felt the tension in her ward and wished that she could absorb it away from her. Fran retreated to a chair near the door while Helen and Shelley moved further into the living room and sat together on the flowered couch.

As moisture glistened in her eyes, Shelley took Helen's hand and brought it up to her cheek. "God, it's good to see you," she said.

"I feel the same way, darling," Helen answered, "and I know it's harder for you, being confined here." Shelley released her hand, and Helen softly touched her face. "Jeff tells me you're having trouble with your anger again."

Shelley stood up, stuck her hands in her pockets, and started pacing. A pale blue satin shirt over black pants made her eyes even more arresting. "Yeah, I am. You tell Jeff he would be, too, if he were cooped up here all day and all night with nothing to do except watch the boob tube. This just sitting around all the time is driving me up the wall!" She swung around toward Helen with a nasty frown. "Who the hell is the prisoner, here, anyway?" she shouted.

"I wish I had an easy answer for you, Shell, but I don't."

Shelley glared at Helen for a moment before it slowly seeped through her anger that she wasn't her enemy and that she wanted an end to this just as much as Shelley did. She gradually began to calm. "I am getting better at control, Aunt Helen. This time I only threw a book and tipped over a table," she said with a wry smile.

"And you remember doing it," Helen pointed out. "Definitely an improvement. Come here and sit beside me." She patted the cushion next to her.

Shelley sat down and shifted around for a moment, crossing and uncrossing her long legs. "Not a comfortable damn seat in the whole place," she grumbled.

Helen smiled at this remark and made note of it in her mind. "I can tell you that there is one bright spot on the horizon. The trial for these horrible murderers will be underway soon. Your personal purgatory will soon be over."

"Ah, Aunt Helen, that is great news!" Shelley's face lit up in a huge smile. She gave her guardian a hug.

"Soon you'll be able to go back to a normal life."

"Soon you'll be able to go back to a normal life." Those words echoed through Shelley's mind as she sat in her new lounge chair, waiting for Aunt Helen to arrive for another visit. She gave an ironic snort. *Go back?* she thought, her lips twisting into a grimace. *To what? Not my parents, not my home, not my teenage friends—I've grown way past them. There's no way to go back, only forward. But at least I can go forward as myself, Michelle "Shelley" Stella.*

And Angela was waiting for her. Just the thought brought a smile, erasing her brooding expression. Aunt Helen and Angela were the two best things that had happened to her in the last four years, and she was grateful for both of them. An otherwise stormy period had been graced with two bursts of dazzling sunshine.

Her smile increased as she heard Aunt Helen's voice speaking to the guard outside the hotel room door. She hadn't seen her for weeks. The guard radioed in to Fran, who unlocked the door and greeted Helen Ostcott. Shelley swung the lever to move the dark-gray lounge chair upright and jumped up to welcome the judge as she bustled in.

"Grrrrrrr," Shelley growled as she engulfed her guardian in a huge bear hug. "I have missed you so much. How are you?"

"Fine, darling. Let me see how you are." Helen stepped back and looked closely at her child. The chest wound and the constant stress had taken a toll; Shelley looked tired, and the slightly arrogant look that Helen secretly admired was somewhat subdued. Helen made a move to sit in an armchair, and Shelley took her hand.

"No, no, no," she insisted, "you have to try the lounge chair you sent me—it's perfect! Thanks a million for ordering it for me." She led Helen to the chair and watched her settle in. Then Shelley pointed out the lever and pulled it back, opening the chair out as Helen was tilted back in it.

"Oh my, this is heavenly," Helen admitted, closing her eyes. Then they popped back open, and she chuckled as she pulled the lever, bringing the chair upright again. "If I used a chair like this, I would be asleep most of the time. Besides," she said, shaking her head, "there's just something about keeping my feet on the floor that appeals to me." She stood and moved to the armchair, and Shelley's long form flopped with a bounce into the lounge chair.

Shelley's wide smile flashed as she tossed her head to clear unruly bangs. "Doesn't take much to talk me back into it. I feel beat."

Helen sobered. "You look beat, Shell." Security around Shelley was so tight that they had not even been permitted to telephone each other. Helen had been allowed to visit her once in the hospital and once in the hotel, but not since then. Her only information came from the newspapers and TV and an occasional call from Jeff. Now that Shelley had gone on record with most of her testimony, Helen was allowed to see her—after going through several checkpoints. "The court scene getting you down?"

Shelley looked down at her clasped hands, twisting restlessly in her lap. "Yeah," her silken voice reached a deeper register, "it brings back too many...terrible memories."

Just last week, the prosecutor had directed her to identify the killers, asking if she saw them in the courtroom.

"Stand up, Ms. Stella, and point to them if you see them."

The courtroom had become completely silent as the tall dark-haired young woman had stood up. Shelley first looked out at the assemblage gathered to watch the proceedings. Her stately bearing and velvet tones gave a dignity to her words that projected them even more deeply into the hearing of her listeners. "I didn't know the names of the men who murdered my parents, but their faces are stamped in my memory for the rest of my life." She turned toward the five men and pointed to each of them in turn. "You killed them, and you, and you, and you, and you." Then she sat down and the silence grew until the prosecutor cleared his throat and asked the next question.

Helen had been in the courtroom that day. She knew the sacrifices Shelley had made for the last four years, and she recognized the strength of character and soul it had taken for the young girl to stand up against the professional killers.

Now her heart ached as she watched Shelley battle the demons that fought to surface. Tears welled in the girl's crystal-blue eyes, finally spilling over and sliding slowly down her cheeks.

"You're the only one who could make them pay, Shelley, for your parents and all the others they murdered that day."

Shelley nodded and sniffled, still fighting for control. "And for five girls who would be alive today if it weren't for me," she rasped. Shelley's unforgettable eyes came up to meet Helen's shocked expression, despair tingeing them with darkness. She wiped her cheeks with long fingers.

The judge's graying head swiveled slowly back and forth. "No, Shelley, no. Don't take any of that blame on yourself. You didn't send that maniac out; those evil criminals did. They were the ones who killed those girls just as surely as if they had been there. Please...promise me you won't keep blaming yourself for that." *And I promise never to mention that Jeff and I once wondered if the killer could possibly be you. I'll carry my own shame for that.*

Shelley took a deep breath and let it out slowly. "I'll try," she murmured as her eyes dropped away again. *But how do you turn off guilt?* "Did you find out anything about her? About Allie? She really was crazy, you know."

Helen nodded. "I'm not sure the mob realized that when they sent her after you. She's the daughter of Lou Tressia, the one who always sits in the second chair—at least he does in the drawings of the proceedings."

Helen had asked Jeff Cruz to let her know about Allie, and somehow he had managed to get clearance for her to see the woman's papers. "I was allowed to read a copy of her confession. She was in school in Italy and wanted to come home, so she asked for the job of finding you. She wanted to impress her father with how good an assassin she could be. It's unusual for the mob to use a woman assassin, but she sold him on the idea and was given pretty free rein. All they knew was the general area of the college you were in, your description, your age, and that you were an athlete. She thought up the torture method herself. Seems she had an older sister who tortured her with a knife, and no one ever knew. That's probably what warped her mind. The sister disappeared one day and never was found. Allie confessed to her murder, too."

Shelley shivered. "I hope they put her away, and she never gets out."

"Humph," Helen snorted. "These days you just never know. Her trial will come after this one is over, but because she confessed, you won't be cooped up for it like you are now." She stood up. "I have to be getting back, darling."

Shelley rose, too. "You did send that pendant for me, didn't you? To Angela?"

"I certainly did," Helen answered, and was happy to see the change in Shelley's face. "And my spies tell me she's been wearing it every day."

Shelley's face lit up, then clouded a little. "Spies?"

Helen laughed. "Dean Lohman told me. I called yesterday to thank him for helping us. Apparently he heard your friend Kath telling one of the girls in the office about the pendant, and he passed that information along to me." Just as Helen had passed Shelley the information, through Jeff Cruz, that Angela had phoned, looking for her. And Jeff had relayed Shelley's request for the pendant to be made for Angela and sent to her. She had been very specific, even providing her guardian with a drawing of it.

Helen hadn't felt free to talk to Angela the day she called— after all, what could she say that wouldn't endanger Shelley even more? And she hadn't really lied to her; she didn't have a ward named Shelley Brinton. Shelley's last name was Stella. Soon Shelley herself could straighten everything out.

"Thanks, Aunt Helen. Come back when you can, okay?" The two embraced and Helen left.

The news about Angela and the pendant had lightened some of the stress Shelley was under. She had not only the trial to worry her, but also the knowledge that Angela most likely was suffering through a terrible time too. How was she reacting to having shot a friend? How was she handling Shelley's "abandonment" of her? She knew that her concern about Angela's current state of mind wouldn't be put to rest until she could see her face to face.

Chapter
15

Shelley was forced to stay under tight security until the end of the trial. When it was finally over, the five defendants received the death penalty—thanks chiefly to the girl's eyewitness testimony. She hadn't been able to contact Angela prior to the verdict and wouldn't have anyway; she was determined that her life with Angela would be completely divorced from the traumatic distress of the trial.

When she was released, Jeff Cruz took her to Helen's house. He greeted the judge, then took his leave. After a prolonged hug, Helen ushered Shelley to the kitchen table, where she doled out a bowl of homemade vegetable soup accompanied with a fresh loaf of Italian bread.

Helen sat and watched her ward eat, happy to see the heavy responsibilities of the trial lifted from her young shoulders. Four years of waiting for the hammer to fall had exacted sacrifices from both of them, and now it was over. But Shelley looked exhausted; dark circles lay beneath her intense eyes, and her mouth drooped.

"Shelley, I think you should take a long vacation. Why don't you just stay here with me for a month; get yourself rested and relaxed; decide what you want to do? I'll make sure that no one bothers you here." Helen's head tilted questioningly.

Shelley spooned the last of the soup into her mouth and swallowed it before meeting her guardian's eyes. "I've had plenty of time to think about what I want to do, Aunt Helen. I really appreciate what you are suggesting. I am tired and I know I need to rest and relax, but I want to do it with Angela."

"Darling, I don't mean to sound like a cautious mother figure, but just how much can you depend on Angela? You barely had a chance to get to know each other, and you've been separated for months now. Her feelings might have changed. I don't want you to be hurt."

The dark-haired girl leaned away from the table and settled back against the chair with a soft look on her face. Her full lips curved into a gentle smile. "I fought against being attracted to Angela. When I realized I was losing that battle, I was pretty upset, because I thought she already had a girlfriend." Remembrance of the day she found out differently warmed her thoughts. "When I asked her if she did, and she said no, something happened between us, like our hearts just slid together in a perfect fit. I knew then that Angela and I are soul mates. I know she feels that way too."

As tired as she was, an aura of self-confidence that had been missing for a long time radiated from Shelley. Helen became convinced that her ward believed in Angela's love, so she did the only thing she could do. "You can take the Durango," she offered.

Shelley jumped up and pushed her tiredness deeper inside. She threw her arms around Helen and gave her a big kiss. "Thanks, Aunt Helen, you're the greatest!"

The judge laughed and hugged her back. "Go get my pocketbook and I'll give you the keys; time's a-wasting."

Helen handed Shelley four keys and grinned when the tall girl quirked her eyebrow in question. "I went ahead and registered you at Spofford this year. One extra key is for your locker and another for your apartment at Bricker Apartments—the same one. I packed a trunk for you, and your bike's in the back of the Durango."

Shelley just embraced her again, without a word, but her body language said it all.

It was Saturday morning, and the girls had finished softball practice and returned home to shower and enjoy a long brunch. They were just cleaning up—spurred as usual by Merrill and

Angela—when someone knocked on the apartment door.

Angela hung a damp dishcloth beneath the sink and grabbed a towel. "I'll get it."

She sauntered to the apartment door, drying her hands on the towel, when another knock came. "Okay, okay, I'm coming," she grumbled.

She turned the lock, opened the door, and dropped the towel to the floor from suddenly numb fingers. Her heart thudded in her chest as her startled eyes met Shelley's. The taller girl's voice caressed the one word, "Angela," as she watched the play of emotions across her love's face. She walked into the room and closed her eyes with joy as Angela's arms lifted around her neck and they kissed. They stood locked together, drinking in their connection, and when they parted, neither one could speak past her emotion.

The other girls continued cleaning up the kitchen and chatting for a little while before it dawned on them that the redhead hadn't returned. Marva, closest to the living room doorway, looked through and turned back with an ear-to-ear smile. She put her finger to her lips to shush the girls and beckoned them over to the door.

Angela felt Shelley stiffen and turned to follow the path of her eyes to the girls in the kitchen doorway. With her right arm still around her love, and Shelley's left around her, she beckoned them into the living room. "Look who's back," she finally managed to say.

The girls came in slowly, all a little wary of what Shelley's reception of them would be. After all, they had suspected her of being a murderer. The icy stare they were currently being exposed to added to their discomfort.

Angela, puzzled by the reactions of both Shelley and her friends, asked, "What's going on here, guys? Aren't you happy to see each other?"

Merrill stepped forward, her face burning with embarrassment. "Of course we're happy to see you, Shelley. We feel pretty sick about suspecting you of killing those girls." Her curls danced as she shook her head. "Especially me. I was the worst of all. And I apologize."

"But we were all suspicious," Kath interposed. "It's just so many things pointed to you: your past history, the switchblade, the record of the killings you had taped to your closet door..."

Shelley's stony expression hardened to granite. "My past

history?" she echoed, each word grating against the next.

Now it was Kath's turn to blush. "I saw a report about you lying on Dean Lohman's desk. I know I shouldn't have read it, but I did. It told all about the trouble you had with the law when you were fourteen."

Shelley's jaw clenched, the muscles rippling across it. Angela tightened the arm she still had around the taller girl's waist. "And who did you tell about it?"

Angela shivered as she wondered how such a quiet voice could sound so menacing. She put her left hand on the long one lying against her stomach and began stroking it with her fingers.

Kath's hand swiveled on her wrist, indicating the others. "Just us. No one el...else," she answered, her voice wavering.

"It scared us, Shelley," Marva admitted. "We know now we were wrong to be scared, and we're truly sorry we suspected you. But at the time, your guilt really seemed possible to all of us...that is, all except Angie. She never believed you were guilty."

The ice-blue eyes shifted down toward Angela. The redhead squeezed Shelley's waist and slowly, a sad smile crossed her face. "I was fooled in the lab—and even I lost faith in you for a short time. Can you ever forgive us?"

Merrill marched her five-foot-tall body up to Shelley, tilted her head back, and stared up into the frigid pools. "We really are sorry we misjudged you so badly, Shelley. Mostly we were worried for Angie's sake. We knew she was falling for you, and we didn't want her to get hurt. We were all overjoyed to hear you were innocent." She stopped a moment, stretched as tall as she could, and said sternly, "But if you ever harm her, in any way at all, you are going to have to answer to me."

Angela's eyes widened as they looked from Merrill to Shelley and back again. *Oh, God, please don't let her lose her temper. Merry will be toast.* She breathed a quiet sigh of relief when she felt Shelley's stiff body relax, and a quick look up at her face revealed a melting of the icy glare.

A twitch moved one corner of Shelley's sculpted lips before she spoke. "Good for you, Merr. Looks like we're both on the same side." Shelley extended her hand, and Merrill looked at it for a moment before clasping it with both of her own.

"Welcome back, Shelley," she said, pushing her lips together in a slightly embarrassed smile.

The other two girls came forward and shook her hand also,

welcoming her. Shelley saw Merrill stoop down and pick up the dishtowel Angela had dropped. The dark-haired girl's eyes caught Marva's, who shrugged and grinned. "You know they're both neatniks. That'll never change."

Merrill made a face at Marva and took the towel back into the kitchen as Angela led Shelley to the couch. Marva and Kath sat on the floor, and Merrill soon joined them.

Sitting next to her love, Angela slipped an arm behind her waist. "We're dying to hear your side of everything that happened. Do you feel up to telling us now?"

The blue eyes were warming up and had a special glow when they looked at Angela. "Sure," she agreed. She fingered the star pendant hanging from its chain around Angela's neck, and when the redhead lifted her face in a smile, Shelley kissed her.

"You think we'll ever hear this story?" Marva stage-whispered after a long moment. Shelley and Angela started chuckling and broke apart, but Angela immediately rested her head on Shelley's shoulder as long arms slipped tightly around her and lips pressed against the side of her forehead.

"We all want to hear about the 'real' Michelle Stella, the details of the fight, and your recuperation...and the trial. But before you start on that," Angela announced, "I have something to ask you that is really bugging me."

Shelley tilted her head down and looked into Angela's eyes. "And what is that?"

"When we had all those suspicions about you, why didn't you just tell us you were sneaking into the labs? That might have taken some flak off of you."

The dark-haired girl straightened up and rested her head against the wall behind the couch. "Do you know Ernie Fleer, the night watchman at the science building?" The girls shook their heads no. "What with my working, doing drama classes, and playing softball, there just weren't enough daytime hours for me to keep up with my lab work, so I paid him to let me sneak in and catch up on it."

Kath raised her eyebrows. "And he agreed to that?"

Shelley's head bobbed against the wall as she nodded. "He's got a sick wife to support and could use the money. But he was scared that he could lose his job, so I gave him my solemn word I wouldn't tell anyone. I had to beg him for a week, and he finally agreed when I convinced him I would fail otherwise."

The girls looked dubious, and Angela voiced their problem. "That doesn't sound like much of a reason to let yourself be suspected of murder, Shelley."

"Well, your suspicions didn't seem all that serious to me, except for keeping you from trusting me. And I knew that eventually I would be cleared, and your worries would be resolved."

Angela tilted her head back against Shelley's shoulder so she could see her love's face. "But you could have trusted me not to tell on the watchman," she insisted. "It would have saved us both a lot of grief."

"Listen to yourself, sweetheart." Shelley closed her eyes, then reopened them and glanced down at the redhead. "You're promising you would keep your word at the same time you're saying I should have broken mine."

After a moment's hesitation, Angela sighed and nodded. "You're right. But it sure played havoc with my thoughts."

"I'm really sorry about that. It upset me, too, but a promise is a promise," Shelley murmured and kissed the top of Angela's head.

Shelley spent the next hour describing and explaining past events and answering the girls' questions. Kath, in particular, wanted to know more about Ted's involvement.

Shelley knew Kath had really liked Ted, and she made an effort to be kind. "I did get a chance to speak to Ted, Kath, and I asked him about his part in the whole affair. The local police were in charge of the murder investigation, but the FBI became concerned that the murders might be a disguised attempt to kill me. They sent him to Spofford as a student to keep an eye on the investigation and to protect me." *Which didn't work out at all,* she thought, but neglected to say.

"When he revived from the knockout drops and confirmed what they were, he knew the murderer was making a move. The same drugs had been found in the other victims. He called the police and dashed out of the hospital because he was frantic that something might happen to me before he could stop it."

"Why did he let us follow you if he thought there might be trouble?" Merrill asked. "Wasn't that pretty dangerous for us?"

Shelley pursed her lips and nodded. "It did turn out to be pretty dangerous for Angela," she said and glanced down at her love, "but she wasn't supposed to follow me into the building." She grinned at the blush that rose across the redhead's complexion.

"He was trying to cover as many bases as he could. For all he knew, one of you could have been the killer. By keeping you busy and knowing where you were, he had more free time to search out other possibilities. He said he knew I was sneaking into the college, and other than your discovering that, he presumed that nothing was likely to happen there. But when Allie's plans to knock me out were botched, he realized anything was possible, so he was desperate to get there and protect me."

Noticing that Shelley was approaching exhaustion, Angela called a stop. "Okay, guys, time out. Shelley looks like she could use a rest. We can mop up any other questions later." The other girls got up and Merrill went next door with Kath and Marva, leaving Shelley and Angela alone.

They enjoyed a long, lingering kiss, then Shelley yawned and stretched. "I think I need a nap," she said ruefully.

"You can sleep in my bed if you want," Angela offered, and blushed at Shelley's wicked little laugh.

Then the dark-haired girl relented. "Don't worry, sweetheart. I said this courtship would be slow and thorough, and I meant that. We'll go at whatever pace you want. I still have the apartment upstairs; Aunt Helen kept it for me."

"That's good news! About the apartment, I mean...that you still have it." Angela blushed again then laughed at herself. "You know what I mean."

"Yeah, I do," Shelley said and grinned back even as her eyelids drooped.

Angela slipped out of their embrace and stood. "Stay right here, why don't you? I'll get you a pillow and cover."

Shelley lifted her feet onto the couch and slid down, and by the time Angela returned, she was sound asleep. The redhead gently placed the pillow under her head and covered her, then pushed the raven hair back and kissed her forehead. Her heart sang, thudding against the wall of her chest, "Shel...ley, Shel...ley." *My love is back, and I'm content.*

The girls piled out of the car with their softball gear and trekked to the field. The team was in decent shape this year, having lost only two starters and a pitcher to graduation—and, of course, Shelley and Allie. The new outfielders were proving to be excellent in the field, and Angela and the coach had been working on their batting, which was showing progress.

As they approached the field, quite a few of the girls recognized Shelley and called out to her, welcoming her back. She smiled and waved in acknowledgement.

Coach Palmer's attention really perked up when she saw Angela coming toward her with a tall, familiar figure at her side. "Hi, Coach," both girls greeted her.

"Shelley's back!" Angela enthused and the coach's interest turned to ecstatic joy. "Only now her name is Michelle Stella," Angela supplied.

Coach Palmer put out her hand and Shelley took it. "Welcome back, Michelle," she said with a huge grin.

"I'm still Shelley," replied the velvet voice that the coach remembered. "That was my nickname, and I've just kept it as my given name."

"Fine with me. You ready to play first base?"

Shelley glanced down at Angela and raised her eyebrows. The redhead just grinned and nodded.

Coach Palmer looked from one to the other. "Angie didn't tell you? She's our new shortstop. That rifle arm of hers and her remarkable fielding made her a shoo-in for the position when Roz graduated."

Delighted, Shelley hit Angela's arm with her elbow. "You go, girl. I'm sure you're a great shortstop. You like it?"

"I love it," Angela admitted. "I always wanted to play shortstop, but never had the arm for it. Until now." She threw Shelley a grateful look that melted her heart.

"How do the team's chances at first place look this season?" Shelley asked.

"They look darn good, and now that you're back, they look terrific!" Coach Palmer literally beamed. "Let's get to work and get those skills sharpened up."

Shelley and Angela started to move to their respective positions when the coach spoke once more. "Shelley, you know what Stella means, don't you?

Shelley rubbed the back of her neck and could feel the heat rising from her chest and moving up her face. "Yeah, I do," she answered.

Angela watched this exchange curiously. "What does Stella mean?" she asked. Shelley gave Coach Palmer a beseeching look, and the coach just grinned.

"Ask Shelley," Palmer suggested.

Angela let a small chuckle erupt from her body. "I don't think I've ever seen you blush so red before, Shelley. What the heck does it mean?"

"It means 'star,'" Shelley mumbled.

"Star!" Angela shouted so loudly that Shelley jumped then tried to shush her. But Angela showed no mercy. "Hey, guys," she hollered to her teammates, capturing their attention. "Shelley's last name means 'star'!"

Shelley shook her head and gave Angela a withering glance. When she saw that her teammates liked the association, her mood improved, but she knew she would be stuck with the nickname forever.

Angela was enjoying Shelley's discomfort. She moved closer to her and murmured, "What was that you said to me one day? Win some, lose some?"

"Remember, I will get even later," Shelley murmured back, and Angela shivered at the delicious feeling the deepened voice spread through her.

"Yeah, yeah, yeah," she laughed and shoved Shelley's shoulder. "Go play first base, Star, and stop your moaning."

"You nervous?" Shelley glanced over at Angela, then brought her eyes back to the road. The Durango drove beautifully, and she liked the vehicle's high profile; it provided a wider and farther view of both traffic and scenery.

Angela turned her head toward the dark-haired girl, letting her eyes pleasure themselves with her beauty. "Yeah, I am, a little. Your Aunt Helen is special to you, and I don't want her to be disappointed in me."

Shelley reached down and squeezed the hand that rested deliciously on her thigh. "She can't possibly be disappointed in you. I know I'm not."

Angela twisted her hand over and returned the squeeze. "Yeah, but you are biased," she said, grinning.

Shelley let go of Angela and spun the wheel into a driveway. "Well, we'll soon find out. Here we are." She bounced out of the vehicle and hurried to Angela's side as she stepped out.

The judge's home was lovely. Made of smooth, white stucco that had mellowed to ivory, the house sat back two hundred feet from the road on a lot covered with trees. The cozy-looking building was at a slight distance from the similarly stuccoed garage, and at some point a brownstone breezeway had been added. The deep-set windows were framed on either side with dark-brown shutters that matched the roof and the front door, which had a small entryway surrounding it.

Shelley tucked Angela's hand in the corner of her elbow and they walked up to the house. The front door opened before they had a chance to ring the bell, and Aunt Helen beckoned them in. Shelley gave her a big hug, then turned to introduce Angela.

"Angela...at last," Aunt Helen said with a wide smile. She opened her arms and gave Angela a hug too.

"Wow," Angela said, encircled in the welcoming arms, "are you sure you two aren't related? You both give the same great hugs." She and the judge both chuckled as Angela stepped back.

Shelley was relieved to see that the women hit it off right away. Aunt Helen gave Angela a tour of her house, and the red-head fell in love with it, especially the kitchen. "Omigosh, this room is perfect! A cook's dream come true." She glanced at Helen. "Did you design this?"

"No, I did," Shelley joked then squeaked as Aunt Helen pinched her side.

"That would be the day," the judge rolled her eyes. "This room is alien territory to our girl. Never could get her interested in cooking. Yes, I did design it. Maybe you'd like to help me fix supper later on?"

Angela's eyes lit up. "I would love to."

"We have a date, then, about three o'clock. By the way, Shelley, I have something for you." As Shelley lifted an eyebrow, Helen went to a drawer and pulled out the item to which she was referring.

Shelley grinned as she recognized the switchblade. "So you did get it? Super! I wish I could have seen that...idiotic...cop's face when he had to hand it over. What a jerk!"

Angela eyed the knife warily. "You aren't really going to keep carrying that, are you?"

Shelley gazed at her for a long moment then sighed. "No, I guess not. I don't need it anymore. Aunt Helen bought this for me a couple of years ago when we had a scare that someone had discovered who I was."

Helen commented, "It was a false alarm, just some kid who had taken a fancy to Shelley and was following her, but I wanted her to have something for protection." Then she grimaced.

"When she really needed it, she didn't have it."

"Thanks to that stupid cop. I guess you can retire it, Aunt Helen." She handed it back to the judge, who grinned, well aware that Angela had made that decision. *Looks like Shell has a new guardian.*

"I'll put it in the living room on the mantel. If you ever change your mind, it will be there."

"Thanks," Shelley said. "By the way, do you think you could give Angela your recipe for chocolate chip cookies?"

"Of course I will," the judge answered, "and I'm glad you reminded me." She bustled over to the counter and picked up a cookie jar shaped like a roly-poly little girl dressed in a blue dirndl and white blouse, complete with blonde, ceramic pigtails.

Holding it against her ample bosom, she brought it back to the two girls and lifted the lid.

"Ooooohhh," Shelley groaned in anticipation. She reached in, grabbed a cookie, and handed it to Angela. "Take a bite of food for the Gods," she said as she lifted one to her own lips, and Helen took one too.

It struck Shelley that this simple moment was one of the happiest in her life. The two women she loved most in the world were by her side, sharing this tiny moment of joy. "I really am a very lucky girl," she said distinctly, and bent down to get two great hugs at the same time.

Chapter
16

Beyond their time together on the softball field, Shelley courted Angela as thoroughly as she could on a limited budget, taking her to movies or an occasional dinner, but mostly just going on long walks, talking, and getting to know each other. Neither ever questioned their love, which grew deeper day by day.

Angela had been squirreling money away for weeks with the intention of surprising Shelley with a treat. She hadn't decided on what to get her until Marva came in with the news that the amusement park that had been under construction just outside of town was finally opening. "Would you like to go?" Angela asked Shelley.

"Sounds like fun. I haven't been to an amusement park since I was I little kid," Shelley answered. Her expression shifted as the thought triggered memories of her parents.

"Okay then," Angela rushed to say, anxious to replace that shadowed look. "You are invited to accompany me for a day at the park—my treat."

"Angela, you don't have that kind of money. We can share the costs," Shelley countered.

"No, no, I insist. Either I take you, or I don't go. I have money saved up and this sounds like a good way to enjoy spending it. I will love taking you on all the rides." She turned entreating eyes on Shelley, took her arm, and shook it with both hands.

"Let me do this. Please?"

How can I refuse her anything? "All right, but only if you let me buy the food," Shelley acquiesced.

"Ha! You may have gotten the worst of this bargain," Angela said with an impish smile.

The appointed day came, complete with beautiful weather, and all five women went to the park. Spread out over acres and acres of ground, the place offered numerous rides, water adventures, eateries with food from around the world, and nearly a hundred booths hawking everything from souvenirs, to games of skill or chance, to live pets.

With the blessing of the other three, Shelley and Angela wandered off by themselves and spent hours enjoying the various rides and adventures and investigating a multitude of booths and foods.

As the afternoon was winding down, the two scampered down the ramp from the roller coaster, electrified by the ride. "Damn," Shelley said, laughing as she rubbed a palm against her ear, "that first scream of yours just about broke my eardrum. Not to mention the bruises on my arm from your claws."

"Claws, huh?" Angela smirked and jabbed curled fingers at the tanned arm next to her. "I warned you I was dangerous on roller coasters." She clutched the arm and led Shelley to one of the stands. "Come on, let's have some cotton candy."

Shelley's glance slid sideways, enjoying Angela's lively expression and sparkling eyes. "You're dangerous all right, Reds." *Dangerous to my heart,* she thought, when it skipped as Angela's gaze met hers. "You really want to risk having too much sugar make me hyperactive? Luckily for you, I don't care for cotton candy." She shook her head when the man running the stand held a freshly gathered cone out to her. Pulling some money from a pocket, she paid him and pointed a thumb at her companion. She leaned down and whispered into an enticing ear, "On the other hand, the idea of a hyperactive *you* doesn't sound bad at all." Shelley straightened up and tried to change her grin into a leer, but was having too much fun to make it work.

Feigning indifference, Angela accepted the cone of frothed sugar and strolled back into the crowd with Shelley at her side. "I hate to spoil your fantasies, Star, but I am not the hyperactive type." Well aware that Shelley had stopped dead in her tracks, Angela continued to walk, pulling off chunks of pink cotton candy and stuffing them into her mouth.

Since her halting had proved ineffective, Shelley jogged to catch up and then settled into a walk at Angela's side. "Okay, where did 'Star' come from? I didn't expect to hear that from you." A small frown tugged against shapely brows.

"Oh, I thought you were into nicknames now," Angela responded innocently. "I mean, if you are going to call me 'Reds,' I figure you want me to call you 'Star.'" She turned onto a side path labeled "Garden Delights."

Shelley watched in fascination as Angela finished the cotton candy and meticulously licked her fingers. *Good God, woman, you're driving me crazy.* "You don't like to be called 'Reds?'"

The redhead dropped the empty paper cone into one of the ever-present trash receptacles and made a quick right-hand change of direction that took them into an isolated space behind a nearby building. She stopped and turned around so swiftly that Shelley ran into her. Grabbing the taller woman's arms, Angela pushed her against the building and gave her a fierce look. "No, I don't like to be called 'Reds,' and if you do it ever again, I just might have to smack you." As she looked up into startled blue eyes, a tantalizing grin transformed her expression. "Right now, I guess I have to settle for this kind of smack." She slid her arms up around Shelley's neck, leaned against her, and pulled her down into a soft and tender kiss.

As their bodies met, Angela felt heat surge through Shelley, heightening awareness of the long hands that crept beneath her shirt and spread across the skin of her back. Driven by the aggressiveness building in her, Shelley's hands began to move, one sliding to caress a bra-covered breast. Angela jerked their lips apart and shook her head, laying it on Shelley's shoulder. Respecting Angela's retreat, Shelley groaned and removed the roving hand, returning it to Angela's back.

"I'm sorry," her love murmured against her neck. "I honestly am not trying to tease you. It feels so perfect for me to be in your arms and you in mine. I'm... just not ready for more than that right now." *I love you, my darling. Why can't I just let go? What's holding me back? Is it guilt because I almost killed you and feel I don't deserve you?* Angela didn't know and could only hope that her inability to surrender to her love for Shelley would somehow resolve itself. Maybe a word or a touch would unlock her restraint. *I sure hope it's soon. Poor Shelley.*

Shelley's heart was thumping so hard, it was resonating throughout her body. She pulled her love closer and kissed the top of her head. "That's okay, sweetheart, you're giving me great practice in controlling my passions," she said hoarsely. She grinned as she felt Angela's puff of laughter against her neck.

"And you know what?" She tilted her head to meet Angela's questioning glance. Shelley pushed her tongue out and guided it slowly along her own lips, tasting them. "I think I could learn to like second-hand cotton candy."

Angela's laugh was curtailed by a loud voice that jarred their absorption in each other. "Well, if that isn't just too precious." Liz Hurtz stood spraddle-legged, hands on hips, sneering in their direction. Two of the three women with her mirrored her expression.

As Shelley turned to face the intruders, she tried to push Angela behind her, but the redhead wouldn't allow it. She stepped up right next to Shelley and grasped her hand, twining their fingers together. As usual, she tried to defuse the situation. "Hi, guys. Are you enjoying the rides?"

"Actually, things have been pretty dull. But I think we might have just found some entertainment that will liven things up for us. For you, too, for that matter." Hurtz smirked as her followers giggled. She took a step forward, then hesitated at the ominous change that had dropped over Shelley in the flicker of an eyelid.

Angela felt a hard squeeze on her hand just before it was released. She laid the hand against Shelley's arm and felt the tremors that radiated from it as the tall body tensed. The beautiful face hardened into an ugly mask, and her eyes changed to an icy blue. "Don't," Angela pleaded in a voice only Shelley could hear. Shelley didn't move, and Angela turned her attention to Liz Hurtz.

"Look, Liz. There's no need to have a fight here. You already beat up on Shelley once. You got away with it, because she couldn't draw attention to herself at the time. But if you assault her again, I can report it." She looked in turn at each of the women with Hurtz. "You will all get in trouble. We don't have any argument with you, so why don't you just call it quits?"

The three looked at each other, then one shrugged and spoke up. "She's right, Liz. I have no reason to fight. Star risked her life to get rid of some big-time criminals. I respect that. Count me out." She turned and walked away. The other two looked uncomfortable, but they stayed by a glaring Hurtz.

A nasty smile curled Shelley's lips. "I nearly whipped six of you last time when you caught me by surprise. You think three of you can take me down when I'm ready for you?"

Angela's voice had roughened. "When the two of us are ready for you," she corrected.

Another of Hurtz's cronies urged a change of mind. "Come on, Liz, let's cut out of here. We still have time to catch a few rides. We'll get thrown out of the park if we start trouble."

Hurtz seemed to deflate as she backed up a step. "Yeah, maybe you're right. We can finish this little talk another time."

Anxious to halt the confrontation before it went any further, Angela pulled roughly on Shelley's arm. "Come on, let's get out of here." They had to pass Hurtz to get back out onto the trail. Shelley tried to keep facing the troublemaker, but just as she got next to Hurtz, Angela tripped and jerked Shelley's attention to her. Like a snake, Hurtz struck. She slammed a fist into the side of Shelley's face, missing her jaw only because Shelley was moving away from her. Still, Shelley was stunned and only primal instinct caused her to spring back and strike out, catching Hurtz in the belly. As the instigator doubled over, one of her friends threw a punch that hit Shelley's shoulder. Shelley's vision cleared. She blocked the next punch and then smashed her fist into the woman's nose and mouth. With a bubbling screech, the woman ran away, blood streaming through the hands now plastered against her face.

Hurtz had recovered and charged toward her prey. Shelley swiveled on one leg and hit Hurtz in the side of the face with her foot, just hard enough to stagger her. Then Shelley stepped in with her fists and threw a barrage of measured punches at the hapless woman whose efforts to land a few hits were smothered by the onslaught.

Frustrated, Hurtz squatted down and swung her leg in an arc, trying to take Shelley's feet out from under her. Shelley jumped in the air, avoiding the swipe, came down and smashed an elbow into the side of Hurtz's neck. Knocked over, Hurtz rolled back up and shook her head to get rid of the fuzziness the elbow had sent to her brain.

The third woman had grabbed Angela's hair with both hands as the redhead stepped into the fray. With her head being pulled backward, Angela let herself fall to the ground on her backside. She quickly rolled back onto her shoulders and kicked a foot toward her assailant's head. As the woman let go of the hair to save herself, Angela jumped up, grabbed her arm, and flung her to the ground, knocking the wind out of her. Dusting off her hands, Angela turned toward Shelley just as Hurtz, befuddled, made the mistake of charging toward the redhead.

Shelley grabbed a piece of Hurtz's shirt, yanked her around, and shot a left uppercut to her chin. Releasing the shirt, she nearly decked her with a right cross. Hurtz stumbled on weakened knees but still came on, swinging a punch that Shelley easily ducked.

The other woman had recovered and was starting to rise when a well-placed kick from Angela sent her back to the ground, moaning. Angela watched for a moment as Shelley took care of Hurtz. She winced at a couple of punches that hit the woman's face, but when she recalled how Shelley's had looked after the beating she had taken, she felt less sympathetic. Even so, she called a halt, speaking first and then touching Shelley's arm. "Shelley, that's enough. Please."

Shelley stopped as soon as she felt Angela's touch. Hurtz collapsed into a heap on the ground and showed no sign of resuming the fight. Shelley ran her hand through her hair, pushing her locks off of her face. Angela slipped an arm through hers and they walked back out to the garden trail, finding a wrought-iron bench to sit on. "You're not even breathing hard," Angela marveled.

"That wasn't much of a workout," Shelley said with a lopsided grin. "Thanks for the help, by the way."

"You're welcome," Angela said. "But I didn't mean from the effort. I meant from the anger."

Shelley looked surprised. "You're right." She grew thoughtful. "A long time ago, I beat someone up pretty badly. I was being kept in a home for displaced kids, while the court tried to find if I had any relatives to go to. In the play yard one day, a boy about my size kicked a younger kid between the legs so hard it lifted the kid right off the ground. Then the bully stood there laughing while the little kid was caught between screaming and gasping for air. I went berserk, and beat the hell out of him; damn near killed him. Someone had to pull me off. I didn't even remember what I did. Still don't." Shelley turned her head to meet Angela's eyes. "That's what got me sent to court. Luckily, that turned out to be a good thing for me. That's how I met Aunt Helen."

A lopsided twist pulled against her mouth. "That's the only time I ever attacked a human being without being attacked first.

And I would do it again. But this thing with Hurtz—I was angry, but I don't think I even felt any rage. Or vengeance. I just felt that Hurtz had asked for trouble for no good reason, and she needed punished for that." She looked down and patted the hand that rested in the crook of her arm. "Maybe your good influence is rubbing off on me."

The redhead let out a sigh. "I'm glad to know I'm at least some good to you."

"What?" Shelley's jaw dropped. *She really has no clue how important she is to me?* "Angela..." Shelley lifted the hand that still rested on her arm and raised it to her lips. Her velvet voice deepened. "You are everything to me. You've soothed my heart and opened a whole new world of love to me. I want to spend the rest of my life loving you back for that."

Angela blushed. "If I ever give you a chance to."

Shelley's face lit with a sweet smile. She placed the hand back at her elbow and patted it again. "Don't worry about that; when you're ready, it will come. You're worth waiting for."

Angela tugged her arm closer and kissed her shoulder. "So are you. I'm learning that more and more every day." She leaned back, then reached up and touched Shelley's cheek. "You're going to have a mouse under that eye tomorrow, where that louse sucker-punched you."

"A mouse from a louse—don't go getting poetic on me." Shelley grinned at the groan this brought forth. "I'll just tell everyone I got fresh with you and you bopped me."

"How would you like a mouse under the other eye?"

"Uh-oh, I'll behave. You got me scared with that round-house fling of yours."

"I wasn't sure you saw that." Angela chuckled, then rubbed a finger over the back of Shelley's hand. "And I didn't even bruise my knuckles."

"I'll have to remember that," Shelley said ruefully. "That damn Hurtz has a jaw made of stone."

"Well, you sure put a few chips in it. Do you think that's the end of it with her?"

"I think so. She's looked like a loser twice now in front of her friends. I don't think she'll try for a third time."

They sat for a while, arm in arm, relaxing in the garden's serenity. Finally, Shelley broke the silence. "Are you ready now?" She cocked her head toward her companion waiting for the question to arise in the green eyes.

"Ready for what?" came the expected words.

"Ready to give the roller coaster another try." Shelley frowned and tapped her ear as if testing it.

Angela snorted. "You think your ear is up to it?"

"Hey, I can handle it," Shelley bragged. She stood and then pulled Angela up, and they started toward the crowds again. "Only this time you have to sit on my other side." Shelley heard a noise, reached over and tweaked Angela's nose. "And if you keep up that snorting, I'll stop calling you 'Reds' and start calling you 'Piggy.'"

"Yeah? And your name will change from 'Star' to 'Scar.'"

"Oh, I love it when you are so assertive... Was that another snort?" Shelley reached toward Angela's nose, but the redhead ducked, let out a squeal, and took off running.

Shelley eventually caught her in a big hug, marking the day at the amusement park as a great success.

Chapter 17

A delicious aroma filled Shelley's apartment as Angela finished cooking dinner and set the table for two. She lit the candelabra borrowed from her own apartment and turned out the overhead light. When everything was ready, she invited the dark-haired girl to a seat. "It's nothing fancy, now, just spaghetti and sausage with salad and garlic bread. I love to cook but I don't really have enough time to do it justice here at school."

"It smells great. Let's give it a try," Shelley said. She wound the long strands on her fork and took a bite. "Um, this is good, Angela." Then she picked up a small piece of sausage and tried it. "Whew! That's pretty spicy," she remarked, reaching for a piece of garlic bread to offset it.

"I used two kinds of Italian sausage, hot and sweet. The hot ones are the shorter pieces. Try a longer one if that's too hot."

Shelley tried a sweet sausage. "Yeah, these are pretty good, but I think I like the hot better." She speared several short pieces from the serving bowl.

Angela grinned. "Somehow I thought you might prefer the hot. Seems to suit your temperament better."

The seductive sidelong glance she received made every minute she had spent cooking worthwhile. "You think I'm hot?" Shelley's voice curled her toes. Then the corners of Shelley's blue eyes crinkled. "You ain't seen nothing yet."

Shelley's pure beauty caught Angela's breath, and she swallowed hard before she could answer. "Promises, promises," she said, trying to treat it as a joke. Shelley just grinned. She twisted the end of a strand on her fork and put it between her lips, then infinitely...slowly...sucked the rest of the strand into her mouth.

Angela had to look away. *Never knew spaghetti could be so darn exciting.* "Behave yourself. You keep that up and we'll never finish dinner."

Shelley laughed out loud at the double meaning, but she went back to eating properly.

In spite of Angela's disclaimers, the dinner was tasty and they both enjoyed it. They cleaned up afterward and went to sit in the living room.

BANG! Both girls jumped and then flopped onto the green-carpeted floor. Shelley threw herself on top of Angela as they landed. After a moment, they realized the sound must have been a car backfiring.

Shelley sat up against the base of the couch and pulled a shaking Angela up into her arms. "I think we need to talk about this, Angela," she said.

"Ta...talk about what?"

"About your shooting me. That's why you're shaking, isn't it? It still bothers you?"

Angela buried her head against the chest she had put a bullet in. She nodded and shuddered. "I feel so damn guilty. I love you so much and still I shot you. I could have killed you."

"You should have."

Angela's head jerked back, and she looked up at Shelley's somber face. "What are you saying?"

"You thought I was the killer and that I was coming back to finish you off. You were right to shoot me—you should have killed me. How could you know I was innocent? If I really were that maniac, I could have murdered you and gone on to kill a lot of other girls."

Angela grimaced. "I keep telling myself it was a case of mistaken identity, but I still feel guilty. I think I always will, sweetheart. You're the last person I would ever want to hurt." Angela shook her head. "But I wish I had killed Allie," she muttered. "She deserved killing. All those girls..."

"No, Angela, you couldn't kill anyone without regretting it the rest of your life," Shelley said. "That's why I stopped you." Then her expression grew pained. "All those girls died because of me."

Angela looked deeply into her love's anguished blue eyes and saw the torment in them. She reached a hand to Shelley's cheek and cupped it in her palm. "Don't torture yourself with those thoughts, sweetheart. It all goes back four years ago to the murders in the restaurant. That was the real cause, not you."

The dark-haired girl winced, and her voice thickened for a moment. "Like you, I have trouble convincing myself of that. Someday I'll talk to you about that awful time, Angela—about my parents." *Dying as they lay across my body.* "I'm just not ready to yet."

Angela stroked Shelley's cheek with her thumb and felt her leaning into it. "Tell you what, honey. You help me with my guilt, and I'll help you with yours. Deal?"

Shelley smiled sadly and nodded. "Deal."

"Let's talk about something more pleasant. Like us." Angela pulled gently with her cupped hand and lifted her lips to meet Shelley's. She felt like she was drowning in the blue pools that fluttered closed as their mouths joined. She wondered which was more precious—the kiss, or watching those magnificent eyes reopen, hooded with passion, as their lips separated.

"I love you, Angela," Shelley said, her voice rumbling through the warm body she held tightly against her. For someone who had difficulty managing her passions, Shelley had done a remarkable job of reining in her ardor, waiting for Angela to signal her readiness to proceed. Right now she could feel an internal vibration as every fiber in her being wanted to express her love.

"I love you too, Shelley," Angela responded. "I love your voice...and the way you say my name. Everyone else calls me Angie but you call me..."

"Angela," Shelley murmured on cue. "Your name is as beautiful as you are."

"You make me feel beautiful when you say it. Your voice is like warm, thick syrup seeping slowly into every single part of my body, clear down to my toes. I can't begin to describe what effect it has on me." She wriggled closer. "I just know it makes me tingle all over."

"Hmmmm. Maybe I should investigate all these places my voice is traveling to." Shelley's tone dropped as she lifted an eyebrow.

Angela could feel the heat rising in her body, but it wasn't a blush this time, it was desire...the desire that had been so elusive for so long. Somewhere, far off in her mind, she questioned what had finally triggered it. But that question lasted only for a split second as waves of yearning finally filled her. She slipped a hand beneath Shelley's shirt and began to stroke a path across her belly and up her ribs, setting sensitive muscles in motion. "Sounds like a great idea to me," she murmured in urgent tones as their lips met again. Recognizing and thrilling to Angela's long-awaited acceptance, Shelley sent her own eager hands on a thorough exploration of her love's lush curves.

Wrapped in each other's arms, they rolled over onto the carpet. Shelley's deep kiss was the sweetest Angela had ever experienced, except, perhaps, for their first one. This time, however, there was no need to pull away, and Angela delighted in its sweet passion. Her heart was thudding even before Shelley stopped the kiss and knelt up, straddling her. Shelley very gently lifted first Angela's then her own T-shirt off and dropped them onto the floor, followed by two sports bras. She knelt there for a moment, feasting on the sight of her love's body.

A small whimper escaped Angela as she saw the bullet scar in the skin below Shelley's shoulder. She reached a hand to gently touch it and looked up sadly at her love.

"Kiss it," Shelley said hoarsely, her eyes intense. When Angela's eyes widened, she repeated, "Kiss it. Kiss it hello, good-bye, whatever. Then forget about it. I have."

Angela reached for the dark-haired girl's shoulders and slowly pulled her near. She kissed the slightly puckered scar, then outlined it with her tongue and kissed it again. She slid her hands down the muscled back and moved her lips from the scar to Shelley's breast. With a moan, the long body lowered to meet Angela's.

Shelley's lips, tongue, and hands moved across moist, rounded flesh, breathing extra fire into Angela's desire. Quickly, the rest of their clothing was discarded as Angela intensified her caresses to Shelley's silky skin, and the two of them slid together, touching, moving, twisting, and surging against each other until they reached the heights of their passion. The heavens seemed to open to them, drawing them into exquisite pleasure.

It was an exciting, sensuous journey of discovery, and they reveled in it. At last they paused, panting from the exhilaration.

Angela rolled onto her back and threw her arms above her head. The specter of Vicki's humiliation that had haunted her for months had just been banished forever. "Oh, Shelley, my girl, why did I let you wait so long?"

"You're calling me 'girl'? Don't I qualify as a woman yet?" A lopsided smile and devilish eyes raking the length of her form stirred Angela all over again. She rolled back against her lover and began kissing the slippery, salty body that she suddenly couldn't get enough of.

She folded her arms around Shelley's neck and pulled herself up to her ear, breasts sliding against breasts and stomach against stomach. "I think we need a few more tries before I make that judgment," she whispered, then outlined the ear with her tongue and began nibbling its lobe.

Shelley moaned and grabbed Angela's buttocks. And they soared again...and again.

Finally spent, they wandered hand in hand into the bedroom and fell into the large bed. Angela tucked her head against Shelley's shoulder, and their arms twined around each other.

"Good night, sweetheart," Shelley said.

"Good night...woman," Angela answered, and grinned sleepily as she felt Shelley's chuckle bubble through her.

Kath and Marva showed up at their neighbors' apartment the next morning as usual. Silly grins appeared on their faces as they noticed Angela's conspicuous absence. "All right, you guys, no teasing when you see them," Merrill warned, pointing a finger at them.

"Who, me tease?" Marva faked an injured pout. "I'd be scared to tease Shelley, and I'm too damn jealous to tease them anyway."

"Jealous? I thought you and Barb were making some progress," Merrill said, surprised at Marva's answer. Marva and Barb Olanti had been meeting each other for months now. Marva hadn't offered any explanations, but the girls had assumed that they were getting pretty friendly.

"No progress that way," Marva admitted. "We found out we're too much alike. But we enjoy each other's company, so we've been hanging around together, checking out the dating scene. Having company makes it a lot more fun."

Kath looked at her best friend wistfully. "Too bad we weren't either both gay or both straight. We could keep each other company. Life's funny sometimes, isn't it? Like there's somebody out there who occasionally likes to play jokes with people's lives."

Marva threw an arm across Kath's shoulder and gave her a hug. "It's too early to despair, darlin'. There's gotta be a straight Marv and a gay Kath out there somewhere looking for us. Though we're probably way too different to ever make it as lovers," she said with some truth.

The idea made Kath chuckle. Marva always had been able to lift her spirits.

A knock came on the door and Merrill moved to open it. A girl stood outside with a basket of flowers wrapped in gift paper. "These flowers are for 110A and no one answers. Can I leave them here?"

"Sure," Merrill answered, taking them from her while Marva and Kath raised their eyebrows at each other. Merrill looked at the card. "They're for you, Kath," she announced, handing them to her.

"Who the heck is sending me flowers?" Kath mused. Instead of the usual florist's card, a long envelope was attached. Kath removed the envelope, then tore off the gift paper and threw it away. Everyone admired the flowers, and she set the basket on the lamp table. As she opened the letter and read it, her face turned scarlet.

"Well, come on, sweetie, tell us who it's from," begged Marva.

"It's from Ted Hoffman," she said breathlessly. "I'll read it to you." She sat on the couch and began:

> *Dear Kath,*
>
> *I know I have no right to be sending you anything, and I don't blame you if you totally ignore this. But there are a few things I must tell you.*
> *Firstly, I am truly sorry if I hurt you in any way. Dating you was not part of my duties; in fact, I shouldn't have dated you at all. But I was very attracted to you and wasn't strong enough to stay away from you, so I rationalized that dating you was helping my case.*
> *Secondly, I suppose by now that Shelley has told you of my involvement with her problems. If not, let me just say that it was my job to protect her and I very nearly*

failed. I just got lucky that Shelley and Angela's own resourcefulness saved their lives, no thanks to me.

Thirdly, I was afraid that you would feel that I had used you, and I was too cowardly up to now to contact you and tell you differently.

Last, but not least, I find myself thinking of you constantly. You have made an impression on me that no other woman has ever made. I humbly ask that you will let me call you and start our relationship over, on an honest basis this time. If you would be kind enough to give me a second chance, I will be eternally grateful.

Please mark the enclosed postcard with your answer and send it back to me. I am anxiously awaiting your decision.

Your friend, Ted Hoffman.

Kath glanced down at Marva and Merrill, who were sitting on the floor. "What do you think?"

The two girls looked at each other and grinned. Marva started the answer, "Anyone who writes a love letter that has firstly, secondly, thirdly in it..." she stopped and laid her palm out, offering Merrill a chance to continue the sentence.

"...has to be the right guy for you," Merrill finished, her curls bouncing as she and Marva chuckled. "And I bet the postcard has tick boxes on it, right?"

Kath reddened, but she laughed, too, as she turned the stamped postcard around and showed them the boxes. The sentence next to the first box said "Drop dead, I hate you," and the second said, "Call me and let's talk."

"No contest, Kath, you have to let the guy call you. We all liked him from the start, and I definitely approve," Marva said.

"Me, too," Merrill agreed, her cheeks dimpling. "There's a pen in the lamp table drawer," she added.

Kath, her face still red, pulled the pen out and checked the tick box next to "Call me and let's talk."

Merrill got up and kissed Kath's cheek. "Good luck, honey. Let's hope this is the beginning of a long relationship."

A key turned in the lock and Angela and Shelley strolled in, the dark-haired girl already wearing her game uniform. They were slightly embarrassed as everyone grinned at them, but their self-consciousness was eased by Kath's news.

Angela gave her a hug. "That is so cool, Kath," she said, "I really liked Ted."

"Yeah, Kath, me, too," Shelley added.

Merrill looked at her watch. "Almost time to head out for the game. Guess we better get our uniforms on."

Shelley waited on the couch while the others went off to change. When all were ready, they got in the car and headed for the field.

This was the most important game of the season. If the Spofford Jaguars won, they would go to the regional playoffs. If they lost, they would have to play a rubber game against the Scatsboro Pumas to determine the division winner. Coach Palmer was working hard to look cool while her insides churned with excitement.

She strode over to Shelley, who was scheduled to pitch the game and was warming up near the home team dugout. She watched the six-foot-tall girl leap from the practice mound with each windmill pitch, flinging the ball from a shortened distance that made the batter feel like she was jumping down her throat.

"Looking good, Shelley," she praised. "Feel ready for the big one?"

"Just about, Coach. A couple more tosses and I'll be ready to kick butt."

Coach Palmer laughed. "Just what I like to hear." She waved and walked away, studying the other team's lineup from the card she held in her hand.

Marva caught Shelley's next few throws, then walked up to her when she finished. "You know, Shelley," she said in a quiet voice, fighting to keep a straight face, "they say you shouldn't be 'doing it' the night before a big game; it saps your strength."

"Really?" A full smile spread across Shelley's countenance, and she bounced on the balls of her feet. "Just you watch, Marv. I am so damn high on joy right now that win, lose, or draw, I won't come down for a week."

Marva chuckled. "I believe you. You two have sunshine bursting out at your seams. Let's hope it means good luck for the team."

The game started and momentum seesawed back and forth from inning to inning, but neither team was able to score until the top of the fourth. With two out, and 2-2 on the batter, Shelley threw two borderline strikes that were called balls, and the batter walked to first base. The next batter caught a hanging curve and blasted it off the wall in the left centerfield gap, tripling the runner home.

Shelley was fuming, and Marva and Angela both walked up to her and calmed her down a bit. Scatsboro's next batter popped out, leaving the score at 1-0.

Spofford's team came into the dugout, and Shelley threw her glove against the ground. "Damn umpire! That batter was struck out!"

Angela grabbed her arm and started rubbing it, knowing she had the power to help soothe the volatile, complex woman she loved. "We all know she was, but don't worry, Shelley. We'll get it back. I know we will. Remember what the coach always says about keeping the score close and staying in the game. Come on, use that anger to keep getting them out, don't let it burn you out."

Marva was right behind them. "Yeah, what happened to that high you said you were on?" she asked, then winked.

Shelley hesitated, fighting for control, and finally nodded. "You're right. You're both right." She picked her glove back up, dusted it off against her leg, and laid it on the bench. "Let's go get 'em."

Unfortunately, it wasn't that easy. Scatsboro's pitcher was tossing a tough game. But Shelley continued her strong effort, and Spofford came to the bottom of the seventh still trailing by the one run.

Barb Olanti went down on a third strike that she tipped and the catcher caught. Amber Zorno, playing right field and batting third, hit a hard grounder to the first baseman. The girl bobbled the ball, but recovered in time to beat Amber to the bag for the second out. Angela came up next and hit a long double off the wall in left centerfield, but that took the bat out of Shelley's hands. With an eerie sense that the tall girl was the player who could beat her team, the Scatsboro coach decided to intentionally walk her. Although it wasn't a good idea to put the winning run on base, she realized that, statistically, her pitcher had a better chance of getting the next batter out. Shelley had burned her team before, and she knew the girl was quite capable of hitting the ball over the fence.

Marva stepped to the plate with her nerves as tight as strung wire. This was an important game, and she realized the outcome of it might rest squarely on her shoulders. In disbelief she watched as two strikes were called, both borderline pitches. *Why the hell didn't you call those for Shelley, you idiot?* she thought, silently cursing the umpire. She stepped away from the plate and wiped her wristband across her forehead, trying to catch the sweat that was overflowing her headband.

Both teams were startled when Shelley called time out and went trotting in to the plate. She slowed as she approached a wide-eyed Marva and stopped right next to her. Leaning down, she whispered in her ear, "You weren't by any chance 'doing it' last night, were you, Marv?"

Stunned for a moment, Marva hesitated, then almost laughed out loud at the outrageous question. "Hell, no, I'm not as lucky as you are," she answered flippantly.

"Then you've got no excuse—you better slam the damn ball," Shelley whispered fiercely, then flashed her wickedest smile. She turned around and jogged back to first base, leaving a very loose Marva grinning after her.

Marva stepped back in to the plate, saw a rising fast ball coming at her that looked like a cantaloupe, and swung as hard as she could. The ball sailed in a line drive over the infield, bounced once and skidded past the center fielder as it headed for the gap. The fielder hurried to the ball and quickly threw it to the relay player. The shortstop had to turn around to make her throw, but she threw a perfect strike to home plate.

With two out, Angela and Shelley started running at the crack of the bat. Angela charged around third base as fast as she could. Shelley's long legs were eating up ground, and the redhead could hear her closing the gap between them as she headed toward home plate, her heart slamming against her rib cage.

Angela had no sooner crossed the plate when she heard the *whap* as the catcher received the ball, and she turned around as quickly as her momentum would allow. Shelley and the ball arrived at the plate at almost the same moment, and the scene played out in front of Angela in slow motion. The catcher's leg came across the edge of the plate to block it as she came around with her mitt to make the tag.

Shelley launched herself off toward the back side of the plate to avoid the catcher's shin guard block. She slid on her face and belly with her left hand high in the air, and the catcher's tag went under it, just missing her. Before the catcher could recover,

Shelley's long arm came down and touched the plate as her body skidded past it.

The umpire had been right on top of the bang-bang play, and when his arms went out in the "safe" sign, Spofford's bench and fans erupted.

Angela barely had time to help Shelley up and attempt to dust off her scraped face before Marva ran back from first base and the rest of the Jaguars converged on her and Shelley with thumps and shouts of joy. Kath grabbed Coach Palmer's hand and pulled her out onto the field to join the happy chaos. The coach joined in with the rest of them and even took her own pummeling in stride. Two of the girls managed to get her raised on their shoulders, and they carried an ecstatic coach off the field.

Eventually the pandemonium quieted down a bit, and the team members shook hands with the Scatsboro players, then headed back to their dugout to clean up their equipment.

Angela took a good look at her dirt-covered lover and her raw-looking cheek and winced. "Gods, Shelley, you look awful."

Shelley flapped dust from the front of her shirt and pulled against the belt of her shorts, trying to dislodge some of the dirt that had made its way under the fabric. "Gee, thanks, Angela," she answered. "I feel pretty awful too. Or maybe I should say pretty itchy."

Angela chuckled, then her eyes gleamed with pride. "You were absolutely great, scoring that winning run. I thought you were going to run right up my back."

Marva stuck her head up from behind Angela and laid her chin on her shoulder. "Yeah, I thought so, too. Guess Angie was the one whose strength got sapped," she laughed.

"What are you talking about?" Angela pulled her head back to look at her friend.

"Never mind, kiddo. Shelley will explain." Shelley shook a fist at Marva, then quickly hid it behind her back as Angela's gaze came back to her, eyebrows raised.

"Er...ah...later. I'll explain it later," the taller girl said with a toss of her head. Angela reached up and pushed her lover's bangs back from her face.

"By the way, just what did you say to Marv at the plate?" she asked.

"Heh heh." Shelley reddened and tried for an innocent look that didn't quite work. "I'll explain that later too," she promised.

"Aren't we going to the Steak House to celebrate?" Marva asked loudly, coming to Shelley's rescue.

"Yeah!" came a chorus from behind her.

"Well, what are we waiting for? Let's go!"

Angela shook her head as Shelley grinned, grabbed her shoulders, turned her around, and guided her out of the dugout right behind a chuckling Marva.

The celebration went on for several hours, and finally Shelley and Angela talked the other girls into going home. Shelley went up to her apartment with a promise from Angela to come up as soon as she showered and changed.

The hour was late, so Shelley showered and dressed for bed in a navy blue T-shirt over panties. When the knock came on the door, she jumped up from the couch and let Angela in. The door barely closed before they were in each other's arms, their lips melting together. They moved to the couch and kissed several times before pausing. Angela settled down against Shelley's shoulder, and the dark-haired girl kissed the top of her head.

"Ummm, I love that strawberry shampoo you use," she murmured.

Angela chuckled. "Remember last year when you were teaching me to throw? You said my hair smelled like strawberries, and then you plopped down onto the ground and started plucking grass. You looked so forlorn."

"Hey, don't laugh. I worked hard on reeling you in with that 'poor, pathetic, lost-little-girl' look."

"Right." Angela reached back and poked her thumb into Shelley's side.

Shelley jumped, then laughed, and tightened her arms around the redhead, drumming her fingers on her stomach. "Well, it must have worked, 'cause I caught ya."

Angela was wearing only a gray halter and loose shorts, and Shelley's restless hand on the bare skin of her midriff was adding to the excitement for both of them.

Suddenly Angela pulled back and turned toward her. "Did you put anything on your face? You have a pretty nasty scrape there."

"Nah, it'll be all right. Just lost a little skin is all."

Angela got up and headed toward the bathroom. "I'm going to get some ointment for it. Do you have anything?"

Shelley almost forgot to answer the question as she watched the sway of Angela's hips. "Oh, yeah, there should be an antibiotic ointment in the medicine cabinet." Shelley leaned way over the side of the couch, following Angela's progress, knowing what would happen when she walked into the bedroom on her way to the bathroom.

Sure enough, right inside the bedroom door, Angela bent over and picked up Shelley's discarded clothes and put them in the hamper. *Whoooee, what a picture! I think I'll throw my dirty clothes on the floor forever.* Shelley joked to herself about it but she knew that her lifestyle was about to change. Life with a neatnik would take some getting used to. *But Angela's worth it,* her racing heartbeat emphasized.

The redhead brought the ointment back and knelt on the couch next to her lover, facing her. She leaned forward and gently applied the salve to the cheek, which at the moment looked pretty sore. "You know you'll have to learn to take better care of the face I love," Angela scolded. "That must hurt."

Shelley's smile curled up on the "good" side of her face. "I'll try to remember that," she promised. She reached up and touched the star pendant, then hooked a finger in the center of Angela's halter and tugged it away from her. "Right now the view is taking away any soreness. But it sure is messing up my loins."

"Messing up your loins?" Angela repeated with a grin as she set the ointment down and playfully slapped Shelley's hand away. "That doesn't sound too romantic."

"Romantic? You want romantic? Sit back and stay very still, and I'll show you romantic." Shelley grabbed the slapping hand and sucked the redhead's thumb into her mouth, curling her tongue around it. Angela sat back as directed and smilingly watched her lover in action. One at a time, Shelley drew the fingers into her mouth and tasted them while treating them to the feel of her textured tongue. Then she moved to Angela's arm, mouthing, tasting, and nipping it all along the underside of its length as she worked her way up to and across her collarbone and onto her neck.

She continued the seductive assault across Angela's jaw and cheek until she captured her lips and Angela's arms encircled her neck. Her tongue delved deeply into the moist cavern, searching for its companion. She ran the tip of her tongue slowly up and down Angela's and across the roof of her mouth. Then she pulled away with a quick brush of a kiss and moved from Angela's arms.

"Stay still, remember?" she whispered. With a roguish grin at the surprised redhead, she dropped to the floor and fastened a hand around Angela's ankle. Her mouth started a second assault up the leg of sun-tinted skin that was lightly sprinkled with freckles.

Angela moaned as Shelley's mouth passed over her knee and reached the inside of her thigh, slowly but surely moving higher and higher. She couldn't help herself; her hands twined in the raven hair that edged toward her center, but Shelley teasingly skipped past the shorts and moved her lips to Angela's belly. She ringed her navel with her tongue, then reached a hand to pull the tie holding the halter closed. The material came apart and the sight of Angela's full breasts drew a choked cry from Shelley. She gazed in awe for a moment as they rose and fell with Angela's quickened breathing, then both hands came up to hold and caress them, softening the erect nipples with her thumbs. "God, Angela, you are so beautiful," Shelley whispered, her low voice thick with emotion. The hands that were still twisted in her hair urged her closer, and Shelley tasted and suckled, savoring the gift Angela was so freely giving her.

She reluctantly lifted her lips away and with a slightly arrogant tilt to her head, grinned seductively up toward the hazel eyes grown dark with passion. "Have I put you in the mood?" she murmured, her voice erotic enough to accomplish that on its own.

"Oh yeah," Angela said on a soft breath, loving that haughty look. She loosened her hold on the raven hair and opened her arms. "Come closer. I want to touch you."

Shelley quivered with anticipation. She reached behind her head, grabbed the neck of her shirt, and pulled it off with one quick motion, dropping it on the floor. She lowered herself against her lover, and one hand continued stroking as the other curled behind Angela's neck.

As soon as Shelley's body came within reach, Angela's hands carried out their own bold expedition on her slippery skin—exploring, stroking and teasing.

Shelley's mouth touched on her lover's racing pulse point, then she seized the lips that opened to her, drawing her in. Her tongue searched aggressively for an opponent this time, and when the two met, they twisted and turned and battled, mirroring the two heated bodies that now writhed against each other.

Their lips parted as they paused to renew their breath.

"Please," Angela whispered, "let's go to your bed."

Shelley stood and removed the rest of Angela's clothing and her own. She reached under Angela's knees and around her back and effortlessly picked her up, glorying in the ability to sweep her lover into her arms.

"You mean 'our' bed," Shelley corrected in her silken voice, raising a euphoric smile on Angela's face as she laid her gently on the mattress.

"Always," the redhead answered. Their hungry lips and bodies met again, and Angela's arms closed even more tightly around Shelley's neck as one long leg stretched out its toes and pushed the door closed.

Other titles to look for in the coming months from
Quest Books

Blue Holes To Terror By Trish Kocialski

Anne Azel's Murder Mysteries #1 By Anne Azel

Gun Shy By Lori Lake

High Intensity By Belle Reilly

Another Nann Dunne title from
Yellow Rose Books

True Colours: Book One

by Karen King and Nann Dunne

TJ Meridian, crippled in an attack on her and her brother, returns to Meridianville, Texas, a small town that her father all but destroyed ten years ago when he closed his ranch and meatpacking plant. Intending to right the wrongs, TJ, with the help of two friends, proposes to bring prosperity back to the area by restocking the ranch and modernizing the packing plant. When TJ's prized horse becomes ill, a local veterinarian is called to treat the animal. The vet, Dr. Mare Gillespie, has lived in Meridianville for the past ten years and has seen the poverty caused by Thomas Meridian's withdrawal from the area. Like most of the native residents, she harbors a great dislike for the family, yet she and TJ are each intrigued by the other woman and a relationship develops. Together they discover love and friendship that endures through personal misunderstandings, a night attack on the ranch, and an ecological disaster that could destroy the town and surrounding lands. Culminating in a life-threatening accident that requires some hard decisions, *True Colours* is the exploration of hope and love and one woman's struggle to clear her name.

Available through your favorite local or online booksellers.

Coming soon from
Yellow Rose Books

Many Roads to Travel
True Colours: Book Two

by Karen King and Nann Dunne

The sequel to *True Colours: Book 1*, this second book in the lives of Mare and TJ concentrates on the four friends dealing with the aftermath of the accident. TJ needs to work through the consequences of a second operation on her back and learn that her disabilities do not make her a lesser person.

Mare learns that sometimes things can't be fixed and that all she can do is offer support and be understanding. The story also develops her relationship with her newly found father. The girls, Paula and Erin, discover that a second surgery for TJ opens their eyes in the need for them to get away for a while and maybe a place of their own is needed.

Together they work through the trials and tribulations of the operation, the discovery of TJ's half brother and his mother. And overcoming old ghosts and discovering new depths to their relationships.

Available Summer 2001.

Nann lives in southeastern Pennsylvania with her daughter's family in a big, old, rambly, Colonial era home. She holds a position as a consulting publications editor in the Corporate Communications department of a large multinational corporation.

Much of Nann's free time is spent in writing fiction, a passion she discovered only five years ago. "I had done a lot of business-communications-type writing, but had never tried fiction. When I finally did, I got hooked. Something in me connected with creating characters, putting them into a world of my making, then 'discovering' how they could resolve their problems. It's a very satisfying challenge."

Nann played and coached softball for close to 15 years, which suggested the background setting for *Staying in the Game.*

Printed in the United States
1985

9 781930 928602